TRUSTING THE DRAGON

Stonefire Dragons #14

JESSIE DONOVAN

Mythical Lake Press, LLC

Trusting the Dragon

Copyright © 2022 Laura Hoak-Kagey

Mythical Lake Press, LLC

First Print Edition

Cover Art by Laura Hoak-Kagey of Mythical Lake Design

ISBN: 978-1944776282

Books in this series:

Stonefire Dragons

Trusting the Dragon Synopsis

Finally divorced and free of her bastard ex-husband, Sarah MacKintosh Carter looks forward to living with the Scottish dragon clan and attempting a normal life. However, a letter arrives and says she has thirty days to mate a dragon-shifter, or she has to return to a human city. If she leaves, she knows her former in-laws will be determined to take custody of her sons. So the countdown begins on finding a dragonman to mate her. There's just one rule: no falling in love so she can protect her heart.

Hudson Wells hasn't stopped thinking about the female he met by chance two years ago—she's the only one he's wanted in his life and his bed since the loss of his late mate. When the chance comes to claim Sarah as his own, Hudson puts his name forth to be her mate. Now he just needs to convince her to pick him. Despite the fact she's divorced, Hudson soon discovers that Sarah was neglected, so he makes it his job to prove how desirable she really is.

As Hudson does his best to persuade Sarah of how they're combustible together in bed and a good team as parents out of it, her past comes back to haunt her. Not only does it threaten one of her sons, but it could also end up destroying the future she now yearns for with Hudson. Will she find a way to seize a happy ending for once? Or will Sarah end up losing everything she cares about?

The Stonefire and Lochguard series intertwine with one another. (As well as with one Tahoe Dragon Mates book.) Since so many readers ask for the overall reading order, I've included it with this book. (The most up-to-date version is on my website.)

Sacrificed to the Dragon (Stonefire Dragons #1)
Seducing the Dragon (Stonefire Dragons #2)
Revealing the Dragons (Stonefire Dragons #3)
Healed by the Dragon (Stonefire Dragons #4)
Reawakening the Dragon (Stonefire Dragons #5)
The Dragon's Dilemma (Lochguard Highland Dragons #1)
Loved by the Dragon (Stonefire Dragons #6)
The Dragon Guardian (Lochguard Highland Dragons #2)
Surrendering to the Dragon (Stonefire Dragons #7)
The Dragon's Heart (Lochguard Highland Dragons #3)
Cured by the Dragon (Stonefire Dragons #8)
The Dragon Warrior (Lochguard Highland Dragons #4)
Aiding the Dragon (Stonefire Dragons #9)
Finding the Dragon (Stonefire Dragons #10)
Craved by the Dragon (Stonefire Dragons #11)
The Dragon Family (Lochguard Highland Dragons #5)
Winning Skyhunter (Stonefire Dragons Universe #1)

The Dragon's Discovery (Lochguard Highland Dragons #6)

Transforming Snowridge (Stonefire Dragons Universe #2)

The Dragon's Pursuit (Lochguard Highland Dragons #7)

Persuading the Dragon (Stonefire Dragons #12)

Treasured by the Dragon (Stonefire Dragons #13)

The Dragon Collective (Lochguard Highland Dragons #8)

The Dragon's Bidder (Tahoe Dragon Mates #3)

The Dragon's Chance (Lochguard Highland Dragons #9)

Summer at Lochguard (Dragon Clan Gatherings #1)

Trusting the Dragon (Stonefire Dragons #14)

The Dragon's Memory (Lochguard Highland Dragons #10, May 5, 2022)

Taught by the Dragon (Stonefire Dragons #15, 2023)

Short stories that lead up to *Persuading the Dragon* / *Treasured by the Dragon*:

Meeting the Humans (Stonefire Dragons Shorts #1)
The Dragon Camp (Stonefire Dragons Shorts #2)
The Dragon Play (Stonefire Dragons Shorts #3)

Semi-related dragon stories set in the USA, beginning sometime around *The Dragon's Discovery* / *Transforming Snowridge*:

The Dragon's Choice (Tahoe Dragon Mates #1)
The Dragon's Need (Tahoe Dragon Mates #2)
The Dragon's Bidder (Tahoe Dragon Mates #3)
The Dragon's Charge (Tahoe Dragon Mates #4)
The Dragon's Weakness (Tahoe Dragon Mates #5)
The Dragon's Rival (Tahoe Dragon Mates #6, TBD)

Chapter One

Sarah MacKintosh Carter had learned at an early age not to fidget. After all, any sort of movement would've drawn her father's eye and attention, and not in a good way.

The bastard had liked to beat his wife and children as he blamed them for all his troubles. So, aye, she'd learned to be as still and small as possible, something that was ingrained in her to this day.

Even now in her late twenties, as she merely awaited a solicitor who wouldn't care if she fidgeted, she did her best to sit still. Some things were just difficult to forget, especially when her life was turning to shite once more.

Glancing down at the papers in front of her, she wished she could burn them and erase the newest set of troubles to come her way. Or maybe rip the papers to shreds and post them back to her ex-husband's parents, telling them what she thought of their rubbish.

But rationally she knew none of that would work. Her ex-in-laws were using human laws to their advantage, which was something Sarah didn't know very well despite being a human herself.

No, she needed help if she was going to keep custody of her two sons. Which was why she sat inside a conference room, one inside the main security building for Clan Lochguard in the Scottish Highlands, and waited for the bloody solicitor to arrive, the one whom the dragon clan leader had found for her.

Aye, she was grateful for Finn Stewart's assistance. Without him working his magic, Sarah wouldn't have been able to stay with the Scottish dragon clan for roughly the past year, despite the fact she wasn't mated to a dragon-shifter, nor mother to one.

No, it had been because her older brother, Lachlan, had mated a dragonwoman named Cat. That was the leverage Finn had used to garner permission for Sarah and her lads to stay.

However, as she glared at the papers in front of her again, everything was about to come crashing down if she couldn't find a way to fix things.

Because the Department of Dragon Affairs—the DDA—had sent a letter saying if she remained unmated to a dragon-shifter, then she'd have to leave

Lochguard within the next thirty days. And if she refused by the deadline, she'd be arrested and her children taken from her.

Anger churned her stomach at the thought of her sons being swept away to a family who didn't really care about them but rather only wanted her sons so they could lord it over her and mold them into their versions of what little boys should be.

Which would mean strict discipline, little emotion, and unreasonable expectations. In other words, pure hell for any child, let alone her curious and sweet boys.

No, she needed to do whatever it took to keep her lads with her. Especially since her sons, Mark and Joey, were happier on Lochguard than she'd ever seen before in their lives. To be honest, they'd blossomed without the stress, and rows, and tension that had existed in their home before her divorce from her ex-husband. Not only had they formed a closer relationship with their uncle Lachlan, but for the first time, her lads had positive male role models in their lives, ones they adored more than anything.

Which, after years of dealing with their worthless father, was a breath of fresh air.

Not wanting to think of her rash decision to marry her ex—Rob Carter—as a young woman, Sarah took a biscuit from the plate in the middle of the table and nibbled, doing her best to be patient and not panic.

After a few more minutes, a knock sounded on the door before it opened. The blond, fair-skinned form of Lochguard's clan leader, Finn, walked in first, followed closely by a woman with hair already falling out of her long braid, her cardigan not buttoned evenly, and her glasses slightly askew.

First impressions would say the woman was a mess, but Sarah knew not to judge by appearances. After all, everyone had thought her father the perfect husband while he was still alive, since he'd been able to charm everyone outside of the family. No one was the wiser about how it was part of his schtick to do what he wished inside the walls of his home without suspicion.

Standing, Sarah looked to Finn. The dragonman nodded and then gestured toward the woman. "This is Hayley Beckett, the solicitor here to help you. Ms. Beckett, this is Sarah Carter, the human female we told you about."

After briefly shaking hands, they sat. Before Sarah could say anything, Hayley jumped right in, her accent telling Sarah she was from somewhere in the south of England. "I'll get straight to the point. If you want to continue living with a dragon clan, there's only one guaranteed way to do that, and that's if you mate a dragon-shifter. So let me start by asking—is there anyone you fancy on Lochguard?"

Sarah blinked. "Pardon?"

"Is there someone you fancy? That'll solve all your problems, if he'll mate you, that is."

Sarah looked to Finn but saw he was as nonplussed as she was at the blunt opening. Returning her gaze back to Hayley, she said, "No. I've barely received my final divorce papers. Dating was the furthest thing from my mind."

As Hayley frowned, Sarah's stomach dropped. She had a feeling the woman wasn't going to be as much help as Finn had said she would be. Hayley shrugged. "Well, there are a few other options then."

Sarah let out a sigh of relief.

Little did she know, it would be short-lived.

Hayley continued, "We can try to fight this, but it will be a long-drawn-out battle, with little precedent since you're unmated with human children, and the odds aren't in your favor. Which is a bloody shame since your ex-husband was only recently let out of jail and isn't exactly the paragon of fatherhood. Clever for his parents to stir this fuss for him since they don't have any blemishes on their record."

Rob's arrest and short prison sentence was the reason Sarah had won full custody of her lads in the first place.

Sarah opened her mouth, but Hayley carried on without missing a beat. "The other option is to find a dragonman—or woman, if that's your fancy—and have a mating of convenience. Maybe someone who is looking for a friend rather than a lover, and one who'll agree to remain mated for at least two years. I'm sure by then I can either find a way to get you to stay if you divorce, or my colleagues working with the DDA will make it so some individuals can live with a dragon clan, if they so choose, with less uncertainty." Hayley raised her brows. "How does that sound?"

Blinking, Sarah took a second to find her voice. "You want me to find some random bloke to mate me for a few years and then get divorced again? You do understand I have children, and it's hard enough for my lads this time around. If they grow close to whomever I mate, it'll be even worse."

Finn finally spoke up. "I know it's not the best situation, lass, but it has a better ending than fighting the DDA and hoping you can win in the end. Normally, I fight them anytime I can. But it's your very future at stake, Sarah. So it might be best to choose the path with least resistance, aye?"

Over the last year, Sarah had learned a lot about dragon-shifters, especially when it came to them fighting tooth and nail to have the same rights as humans.

Oh, aye, things had improved. But true equality was a long way off.

Fighting the DDA would probably end in failure, especially since it wasn't just her involved, but her sons as well.

Damn the Carters for using Mark and Joey as

toys in their game to see her destroyed for what they saw as Sarah abandoning Rob, no matter that she had spent years trying to get him help for his problems and gambling addiction.

But when he'd been ready to sacrifice the lives of their sons a year ago, just so he could give a double-finger salute to the dragon-shifters, she'd had enough and left him.

Hayley reached across and took Sarah's hand. Her first instinct was to yank out of the other woman's grip, something she'd learned in childhood to protect herself.

However, the woman squeezed her fingers, and somehow Sarah resisted breaking Hayley's hold. "I know it's not exactly a fairy-tale ending. And given all you've been through, you deserve one. However, from everything I could dredge up about your in-laws, they're horrid people. A few years living with a friend to ensure your boys can stay safe amongst a dragon clan might not be so bad. Right?"

Even putting aside the ridiculous nature of the woman's suggestion, there was a huge flaw in Hayley's proposal.

Namely, Sarah didn't have many friends, and almost none of them were men.

And those she would consider friend-like were her brother's in-laws, and they were all too young and brash for her and her lads to live with for a long period of time.

She'd go mad within a month of living with one of the MacAllister lads, no matter how much her sons, especially Mark, would probably enjoy it.

Sarah filed that away as a last resort, in case she couldn't find another way.

As if sensing her thoughts, Finn cleared his throat and said, "Let me start by saying this isn't public knowledge yet, aye? Only Hayley, Bram, and I know about the DDA's letter and demands. But Bram and I suspected it might come to you having to mate someone to stay, so both of us have come up with a list of possible mates for you, Sarah. If you're interested."

Bram was the dragon-shifter leader of Clan Stonefire in the North of England. She'd only seen him a few times in the past without talking to him beyond a greeting. For the dragonman to know her personal life in such detail, Sarah didn't know whether she should be embarrassed or furious.

Finn being Finn, carried on as if he hadn't said anything outrageous or daft. "I know it's almost like you're being offered as a potential sacrifice, but there would be no expectation of you needing to bear a child, lass. Not unless you want one, aye?"

Sarah had learned how some human women, termed sacrifices, agreed to bear a dragon-shifter child in exchange for a vial of dragon's blood with healing properties, which they could either use or sell.

One of the nurses on Lochguard, Holly MacKenzie, had been one such thing.

But if Sarah wasn't to provide a bairn for some dragonman, she wondered what they'd get out of it. So she blurted, "Then why would they agree to mate me in the first place? Or at least be put on this bloody list?"

Not that she wanted to consider the idea.

Even if she'd seen how the dragonmen—and women—who loved their mates adored them, took care of them, and were a true partner in every sense.

Which was the complete opposite of what Sarah had known her entire life. And as a result, made her a wee bit jealous. On occasion.

Such as every day.

It's not for you, Sarah. Men have only ever let you down.

Pushing aside those thoughts, she focused on Finn's reply. "Some of the males have a desire to help. Others have lost mates before and are lonely. And others have children of their own and thought it might be a good experience for dragon and human children to grow up together, even if it's only for a few years." Finn leaned forward. "But all of the males on our lists are good blokes, I promise you that. I know you haven't had the easiest life, but none of these candidates would ever hurt you. No matter if you end up on Stonefire or on Lochguard, you'll always have Bram's and my protection, I vow it."

She eyed Finn, knowing how seriously the dragonman took his vows. After all, he'd kept his promise to take care of Sarah and her sons, ensuring their acceptance on Lochguard. Well, for as long as he could, before the DDA had taken it out of his hands.

And even then, he was trying to find a way for her to stay with the dragon-shifters.

In other words, Finn Stewart was one of the few people she trusted.

Hayley finally spoke up again. "It couldn't hurt to at least meet with the dragonmen, Sarah. I'll keep looking for other avenues, but I can't guarantee I'll find one."

Finn nodded. "Besides, you'll be going to Stonefire in a few days for the children's play, aye? One of the candidates has a son who's also in the play. It'd be a good time to chat a bit and see how it goes."

Only a few weeks ago, Sarah had been sighing in relief over the finalization of her divorce. And now here she was, being almost forced to go looking for a new husband.

Although the thought of leaving Lochguard and heading back to Glasgow, where her in-laws could harass her and make her life hell even if their custody battle failed, wasn't really an option. If she couldn't find a proper job, one that would pay the bills, she could end up losing her sons eventually. After all, it wasn't as if Rob was going to pay anything toward their upkeep, and even with government assistance, her in-laws would no doubt use it to prove she wasn't a good mother.

At least with the dragon-shifters she had references for her work with the children, helping with childcare and the primary-aged classes as a teacher's assistant. Not to mention she'd built a reputation for clothing alterations and custom-made orders. Between the two, she earned enough to take care of her sons without worry.

To keep that life, though, she'd have to find a new husband, whether she wanted one or not.

Someone less cynical might say it was a chance to find a good one.

But Sarah didn't hold out such hope. She had always attracted and picked the wrong sorts of men, probably because they were easily distracted with a smile or tight top. Combined with her constant yearning to be wanted, desired, and loved, she'd also been blind to their major faults in her quest for all those things.

Of course now she was painfully aware of how attraction and desire didn't lead to love or happiness. Rob had taught her that.

Yet as she eyed Finn and Hayley, the more practical side of Sarah reared its head, and she sighed. "I'll meet them, but only in case Hayley can't find any other way for me to stay."

Finn grinned. "Brilliant. I'll set things up with

Bram and Dawn. She's a human mated to a dragon-shifter on Stonefire, one with her own human child and also twin dragon children. Dawn understands your situation better than most and should be a great help."

Sarah frowned. "She also had to mate someone to stay on Stonefire?"

Finn shook his head. "Not exactly. Blake is her true mate. But her ex's family tried to take her human daughter away as well. With Hayley's help, they won the case."

Hayley snorted. "More like Dawn's daughter won the case."

Finn waved a hand in dismissal. "Either way, Dawn won." He stood. "I'm going to ring Bram now and make sure everything is set up for you to meet at least one of the dragonmen. Come see me later, Sarah, and I'll give you a few more details."

Sarah could do nothing but nod. Once Finn was gone, Hayley smiled kindly at her. "It's going to all work out for the best, you'll see."

She did her best to smile, but all Sarah could think about was that she'd met a dragonman from Stonefire roughly two years ago, one with a son. He'd been kind to her when her son had been lost during a holiday to the Lake District, and she'd needed help finding him.

Could it be him?

Then she mentally snorted. Of course it wouldn't

be. That would be too happy of a coincidence for her lot in life.

So after she said her goodbyes to Hayley and walked back toward her cottage, Sarah instead focused on all that needed to be done before the children's play. Aye, she'd focus on the costumes that needed to be finished and not on being offered as some sort of horse at auction to a pack of dragonmen. She'd have plenty of time to deal with that scenario later, provided the men were as good as Finn and Bram purported them to be.

And if not, well, she'd just have to scramble for a different plan. But one thing at a time had become her motto over the last year, and she was sticking to it.

Chapter Two

A few days later, Sarah watched as her two lads were taken with the rest of the Lochguard children to meet with their counterparts on Stonefire. Even though she trusted the Lochguard teachers to watch over her sons, she still wished to follow them.

Partly to ensure they were okay, but also to avoid the meeting she knew awaited her inside Stonefire's main security building.

Sarah had always had trouble getting along with other women, at least in adulthood, and Dawn Chadwick-Whitby was expecting her.

No doubt the woman was lovely. After all, she'd volunteered her time and had even sent Sarah a kind email about what to expect.

And yet, apart from her brother's in-laws, Sarah didn't have any female friends. She'd lost them over the years she'd been married to Rob. Between trying to keep him from gambling their lives away and shielding her lads from their father's faults as much as she could, she just hadn't had the time or energy to be cheery, or teasing, or even muster up the strength to gossip.

But you no longer have to worry about Rob. Just be yourself and it'll be fine, aye?

It was what Cat, her brother's mate, had said to her a few hours ago.

If only it were that simple, and all she had to do was embrace Cat's words and be someone more interesting.

A dragonwoman with black hair and dark brown eyes walked up to her and smiled. Her accent said she was from Stonefire. "Hello, Sarah. My name's Nikki Hartley-Gray, and I've been sent to escort you inside." She lowered her voice. "I'm sure the Lochguard lot have told you tales about us and how we're a bit more serious and less crazy here. But it's not as bad as all that. Not everyone will glower at you, I promise. My mate, perhaps, but he's a bit protective and thinks everyone is out to harm our daughter."

She blinked. "Pardon?"

Nikki laughed, and her voice returned to a normal level. "My mate, Rafe, is human but just as bad as any dragonman when it comes to protectiveness. It doesn't help he was so bloody good at his job in the army, either. It went to his head. " She gestured toward the door. "At any rate, Dawn's waiting for us. The pair of us will take you over to the great hall soon enough to meet your blind date."

"Date?" She was sounding like a daft idiot now, what with her one-word questions, but no one had mentioned a date. No, it was supposed to be a casual chat as the children readied for the play.

Sarah hadn't been on a date in a long, long while. And the last one she'd had, well, that had resulted in her marrying her ex.

Nikki shrugged, cutting through Sarah's beginnings of panic. "Whatever you want to call it. Our head Protector had to give his best glare to keep Hudson from pacing the halls and heading straight here when the Lochguard lot arrived. But we wanted you to have a chance to chat with Dawn first, in case you had any last-minute questions."

Hudson? That had been the name of the dragonman who'd helped her two years ago, the kind one from Stonefire.

But no, it couldn't be. He was too handsome and kind and all-around nice to want to shackle himself to her or to take on Sarah's mountain of problems.

Oh, aye, she'd been sent a message about her potential mate. However, she'd been too nervous to read it and had wanted to meet the dragonman without any sort of preconceptions. The last thing she needed was to build something up in her head and then see the man run the other way after talking with her.

If her heart had been thumping hard before, it now raced. Because if it was that fit dragonman from that time in the Lake District, Sarah wasn't sure what she'd do. After all, her plan was to find some dragon-shifter she could stand and be friends with, not one that drew her eye and made her want more.

Nikki threaded her arm through Sarah's and gently tugged her along. "He's a good male, you'll see. It's about time he tried looking for someone else. Everyone loved his late mate, but no one deserves to live constantly in the past."

She frowned as the dragonwoman guided them down a corridor. Nikki must've had an easy life to say something so casually. Because Sarah struggled every day to try and not be a prisoner to her past.

And most of the time, she failed.

But not wanting to dwell on that, she focused on the bits concerning Hudson. "What do you mean? What happened to his late wife?"

Nikki shook her head. "It's not my story to tell." She stopped in front of a door, knocked, and entered with Sarah in tow.

Inside sat a blonde woman with a small baby in her lap. But at their entrance, the woman smiled and stood. "You must be Sarah. I'm Dawn."

The woman's smile and warm tone made Sarah a wee bit uneasy.

For most of her life, someone being nice had meant they either wanted to catch her off guard, or they wanted something.

Stop it, Sarah. The people of Lochguard had, for the most part, been nice to her without ever hurting her. She should give the people of Stonefire the benefit of the doubt, no matter how much it went against her sense of self-preservation to do so.

Dawn readjusted the hold on the small lad in her arms and came over. "Don't mind Jasper here. He gets rather cross whenever he's not with me. I swear he lives to wind up his father. And for tonight, I wanted as much peace as possible." She sighed. "Especially since my daughter Daisy was put in charge of helping the Lochguard children. The assignment has quite gone to her head. I love my daughter, but she could do with a bit of humility every now and then."

Nikki snorted. "Daisy will rule the world one day. Just wait and see."

For a split second, jealousy flared at how easily the two women talked and joked. At one time, she'd had that with two girls in her youth.

Until Rob had crashed into her life and guilt-tripped her into severing ties.

Dawn spoke up again. "But Daisy is thrilled to meet your boys, Sarah. Not many human children live with dragon clans, and she's determined to start a club, of sorts."

Since she truly had a love of children, Sarah managed to ask, "How old is Daisy?"

"Twelve. Heaven help me when she starts acting like a teenager." Dawn readjusted her hold on her son, who had started to squirm. "Mark and Joey are eight and six, right?" She nodded. "They're close in age to Elliott, Hudson's son. That should work out brilliantly."

At hearing the name Hudson again, Sarah's curiosity finally overcame her shyness. "Is Hudson a common name here?"

Nikki shook her head. "It's a bit unusual, truth be told, especially in England nearly forty years ago. But his parents named him and his brothers after places in New York City. It seemed quite the thing to do back then, find themes and naming children after them. Why, another family named their kids Cassidy and Wyatt after American cowboys."

Nikki snorted, but Sarah barely paid attention. The name Hudson, the mention of a son, and that he lived on Stonefire made Sarah really wonder if the dragonman she'd met two years ago was the same as the one she was about to meet.

The thought of seeing his smile and the determination in his eyes, like she had once before, sent a thrill through Sarah's body. Never in her life had she met a man—a human man, not a dragonman—who truly went out of his way to help a stranger merely because it was the right thing to do and not for some sort of reward.

And yet Hudson had. Only later would she learn that more dragon-shifters would do that. Not all, but more than at least the human men she'd known.

But the biggest question was whether Hudson knew it was her? Or was he merely being gallant once more, offering to help someone in need?

That had to be it—Hudson was being a hero, nothing more. After all, Sarah had been a mess the day Joey had wandered off, and far from nice to him. Oh, aye, she'd thanked him. But worry had turned her voice sharp and her manners nonexistent.

He might very well run the other way once he saw her again after she reminded them of how they'd met before.

Dawn walked toward the door, cutting through her thoughts. "We can chat as we walk, but I don't like leaving my power-drunk daughter on her own too long. Especially since Blake is still struggling to find his place as her stepfather after Daisy's initial angel period after our mating."

The mention of a dragonman being a stepfather to a human child managed to focus Sarah. Her lads were all that mattered, and it was why she even had considered mating a dragonman she didn't know in the first place.

She asked, "Does he mind? That his stepdaughter is human?"

Dawn smiled warmly, in a way that made Sarah relax a fraction.

In that moment, she realized how lovely it would've been to have a mother like Dawn instead of her own.

Thankfully Dawn replied and stopped Sarah's mind from wandering down memory lane. "Blake has always loved working with the children and has the patience of a saint. He loves Daisy and would fight to protect her like he would for his own two sons." She laid a hand on Sarah's bicep, and for once, Sarah barely noticed the gentle touch. "Hudson is the same. He does both IT work and teaches computer science and maths to the older students. If you two hit it off, don't worry about how he'll treat your two boys. Hudson is the type of dragonman who'll give his life to protect a child, any child."

It was hard for Sarah to imagine such a man, despite her year on Lochguard, surrounded by people like Finn Stewart and Grant McFarland. Both of the dragonmen had done much to keep the clan safe, including Sarah and her lads.

But the thought of such a man being interested in her was almost laughable.

She could all but hear Cat's scold. *Stop putting yourself down. Your ex was a bloody selfish bastard. Nothing he said about you was true, I would bet my life on it.*

If only she could wipe it all away so easily. But nearly a decade of verbal abuse wasn't so easy to brush aside, especially when combined with her shitty childhood.

For a split second, Sarah wondered what she was doing here. She was barely divorced, had the worst track record with men, and had more baggage than probably all of Stonefire put together.

Any man who agreed to mate her so quickly would soon come to regret it.

Then Dawn took her hand and squeezed until Sarah met her gaze. The other woman said softly, "I know what it's like to have a rotten ex, to have to sacrifice so much to safeguard your child and to think happiness for yourself is out of reach. But trust me, finding the right partner can make everything better. So for tonight, just be Sarah, the woman who does whatever she needs to do to protect her sons, the woman who is lonelier than she'll ever admit, and the woman who is looking to turn the page of her life and start a new chapter." Dawn squeezed her fingers again. "And as hard as it is, try to find that piece of you that's just a woman, that small bit we keep of ourselves even as we do all that we can for our children. Because that piece is what's needed to grow and bloom so you can bask in the light once more, to show the world who you are, and to maybe even find love."

Her throat closed up at such kindness, and she felt guilty about her earlier misgivings about the woman. Even if she'd only just met Dawn, Sarah wanted more than anything to be the woman's friend.

She nodded. "I'll try."

Nikki finally cleared her throat, garnering their attention. "While I wouldn't mind lingering here all day, we don't have much longer before the play starts. So if you want to meet Hudson now and not wait another few hours, then let's go."

As Dawn and Nikki led Sarah out of the building and down a path toward a large structure in the distance, she took a few deep breaths and willed herself to get her emotions under control. She needed a clear head for her upcoming meeting with a certain dragonman.

And yet she couldn't quite get the memories of Hudson Wells on that day two years ago, when he'd helped her find her son, out of her mind. The only question was whether he'd live up to the memory or not.

Chapter Three

Roughly Two Years Ago
Near Keswick, Lake District, England

Hudson Wells watched as his son rolled down the small hill stretched out like a log, the boy laughing as he came to a stop at the bottom, flinging his arms out to lay sprawled on the grass. His son's antics only made him smile.

And to think Hudson had stopped coming to this spot, not far from the small town of Keswick, afraid of how the memories would overwhelm both him and his son, and not in a good way.

His inner dragon—the second personality inside his head—spoke up. *Staying away only denied us some of the lovely memories we have of Charlie.*

Charlotte—better known as Charlie to everyone who'd loved her—had been Hudson's mate and one of Stonefire's Protectors.

He'd been so proud of his mate for being one of the few females to earn a spot in the clan's security team.

But then she'd been captured by dragon hunters during one of her assignments and killed in one of the worst ways possible for a dragon-shifter—the hunters had slowly drained Charlie of blood in her dragon form until her heart stopped beating, and she finally died.

Even now, months and months later, he still wished he could've been the one to take Charlie's place, to have given his mate the chance to see their son grow up.

His dragon said softly, *Charlie knew what her role entailed, as well as the risks. Since no one can change the past, the best we can do is to ensure Elliott never forgets her.*

Which was why Hudson had finally given in to his son's badgering to come to this lovely spot near Keswick, with its gentle green hills, streams, and some of the best views in the area of the nearby lake and charming town.

He and Charlie had often taken Elliott here during the summer. And more than that, it was a favorite spot of his and Charlie's from when they were younger and where Hudson had finally asked Charlotte Gibbons to be his mate.

In some ways, this particular spot reminded him more of Charlie than just about anything else, except for maybe their son.

Before more memories could overtake him, his nearly seven-year-old son scrambled up the hill, a grin on his face, and Hudson couldn't help but smile again.

Seeing the pure joy on his boy's face, Hudson had definitely stayed away from one of his son's favorite places for far too long.

When Elliott finally reached him, he was slightly out of breath, his eyes flashing between round and slitted as he said, "Your turn, Dad."

He shook his head. "I'd rather watch you go again."

Elliott took his hand and leaned back, trying to tug him forward. "But you go so much faster. Show me how, Daddy. Show me."

Not wanting to see his son's rare show of happiness fade again—only in recent months had Elliott finally stopped crying at night for his mum, all thanks to his inner dragon finally speaking to him and giving his son a much-needed best friend— Hudson nodded. "Okay, but just the one time. Otherwise we won't be able to get scones with clotted cream before heading back to Stonefire."

Elliott's eyes widened. "Mrs. MacGuffin's scones? The best ones ever?"

He grinned. "The very ones. So don't ask for me

to go again after this, okay, or we won't have time to get any today."

Elliott nodded enthusiastically, and Hudson couldn't help but chuckle. Scones and cakes were the best way to bribe his son.

His dragon snorted. *Which you do too often these days.*

Before he could lay on the ground and explain to Elliott the best way to tuck up and roll, a short, pretty female with dark hair and blue eyes dashed from over the hill and stopped at the sight of him for a beat. As she shook her head and rushed over, he could tell she was human from her scent. Hudson quickly whispered to his son, "Keep your dragon quiet, and don't mention we're dragon-shifters, okay?"

Since Elliott knew better than most how dangerous certain humans were, such as dragon hunters, he nodded and slipped his hand into Hudson's. He'd barely squeezed his son's hand when the female stopped in front of him. Her accent told him she was Scottish. "Have you seen a wee lad, about four years old with dark hair come this way?"

He shook his head and the female inhaled quickly, as if she were about to cry. His dragon stirred, not liking to see any female in distress.

Sensing she wasn't a threat to him, he asked, "Who're you looking for?"

"My son. One second he was there, and the next…"

Her voice cracked, and his heart squeezed at her pain. He couldn't imagine if Elliott were lost.

He had no idea if she already had others searching the area or not, but he decided more bodies couldn't hurt. "I can help you look for him if you want."

The female took a deep breath, and her eyes turned guarded. "Why?"

He blinked at her tone. It was almost as if she expected him to take advantage of her.

His dragon flicked his wings inside his mind, but he willed his beast to remain silent. For all he knew, his flashing dragon eyes would send her running for the nearest bobby. "Because I have a son and would be just as frantic as you if he went missing. So tell me who's gone searching in which direction, a quick description of your son, and I'll search in another area. My son can help me search, too, since he's good at spotting details like no other."

She bit her bottom lip, and for a split second, he couldn't help but notice how full it was or wonder how it'd feel pressed against his.

What the fuck? He quickly banished the thought, feeling like the worst sort of cad. Not only because the female was in distress, but it felt like a betrayal to his own late mate.

Thankfully she spoke before his dragon decided to go on about how it was time to start looking at other females again. "It's just me and my older son searching. His father's who the bloody hell knows where." She took a deep breath as if to steady herself and pointed in various directions. "We've searched those ways, but there's still so many places he could be. If he's fallen into the water or even tripped down a steep hill…"

She closed her eyes a second, no doubt trying to pull it together. Every part of him wanted to take her hand, pull her close, and try to comfort her.

And he nearly frowned at that thought. She was married and off-limits. Besides, he wasn't looking for another female anyway.

Focusing back on what was important—finding the lost boy—he said, "My son and I can search this area." He waved to a large portion behind him. "If we find him, where should we go?"

She gave the name of a bed-and-breakfast in Keswick. "We'll be meeting back there, since mobile service is spotty at best here."

Hudson nodded, knowing that fact well, given that he lived not too far from here. "I'll be there in about two hours, no matter what. If we haven't found him by then, I suggest going to the police."

She nodded reluctantly. "Aye, I suppose. Although my husband won't like it."

Some husband he was if he wasn't around to help his wife and children when they needed him most.

Not wanting to waste any more time or thoughts on things that didn't truly concern him, he gave his best reassuring smile and replied, "You'll find him, I promise. Mrs....?"

"Just call me Sarah."

He nodded. "I'm Hudson. And your missing son's name?"

"Joey."

She also gave a quick description and showed him a picture on her phone before Hudson spoke again. "Right. Now, go. The more ground we cover, the better chance we have at finding Joey."

She bobbed her head and ran in a different direction. He turned to survey the area below. "Help me look for the little boy, Elliott, just like if it were a lesson."

His son stood tall. "I'm the best at finding things. I'll help."

All of the dragon children were taught to look for clues in their surroundings at a young age, beginning in primary school. Usually the teachers made it into a game by placing stuffed toys or colorful markers in random locations to help train them.

Elliott was always the first to find them.

And Hudson could use all the help he could get.

His son tugged on his hand and pointed. "I think there's a human there, near the water."

Searching, Hudson spotted the tiny speck of dark hair following after a lost sheep and her lamb.

He was definitely small enough to be four years old, like the female had mentioned, although he couldn't quite make out the details to see if the boy matched the picture he'd seen. "Can you keep up or should I carry you?"

He tried to stand even taller. "I can keep up."

Ever since Elliott's dragon had started talking to him, his boy had began acting more grown-up.

Far too soon for Hudson's liking.

But that didn't matter now. He raced down the hill, glad that Elliott mostly kept up, certainly close enough that Hudson didn't worry about him getting left behind.

As he approached the boy and the sheep, the animals raced off. However, before the boy could do the same, Hudson reached out and grabbed the back of his shirt.

The young boy looked up at him and instantly shrunk in on himself, as if he was afraid of what Hudson would do to him.

A warning chill raced down his spine, but all he could do was try to calm the boy. So keeping his voice soft, he said, "Your mother's looking for you, Joey."

At his name, the boy's wariness faded a fraction. "Who're you?"

"My name's Hudson." Elliott finally reached them and stopped, breathing heavily. "And this is my son, Elliott."

Somehow in the excitement, his son must've forgotten about keeping his dragon quiet—a hard task for the young—and his pupils flashed to slits and back.

Joey's mouth fell open as he stared at Elliott's flashing eyes. "A-are you a dragon?"

Never a shy one, Elliott nodded. "Yes." He took one last deep breath before he added with pride, "I'm a dragon-shifter."

The boy didn't seem afraid, which was good. Although before his son could start trying to impress the human—no doubt by trying to shift a finger into a talon, which was all Elliott could manage so far—Hudson spoke again. "Right, now we all know each other. How about if we go meet your mother, Joey? She's worried and waiting for you."

"Does Dad know?" he whispered.

The fear in the boy's tone rattled both man and beast. Something wasn't right in the lad's family.

And for a split second, all Hudson wanted to do was find a way to help the boy. However, he knew he wouldn't be able to, no matter how much it irked him. All Joey's father had to do was concoct a lie about some supposed crime, and Hudson would be tossed into jail within minutes, no matter if it was untrue. That would leave his son without any parent at all until his clan leader could try to get Hudson released.

His inner beast growled. *Fucking stupid that a human's word means so much more.*

He agreed, but such was the life of a dragon-shifter these days.

No, all he could do was reunite the boy with his mother. At least Sarah seemed to care about her children. That would just have to be good enough.

Even if it fucking wasn't. No child should live in such fear.

A sense of helplessness crashed over him, much as it had first after his mother's death and then later Charlie's. It seemed like Hudson was forever doomed to failure with those who truly needed his help.

His dragon spoke up. *We are helping. His mother will be grateful we found him.*

And that would just have to be enough.

Joey's mouth gaped again, this time at his flashing eyes, and Hudson smiled. "Yes, I'm a dragon-shifter too. But it's a secret, okay?"

The boy merely nodded before Elliott took the younger male's hand. Hudson's son tugged. "Come on. Maybe my dad will get you some scones too. They're the best ever at Mrs. MacGuffin's. Do you like scones?"

Joey nodded and started walking with Elliott, and Hudson could do nothing but follow, hoping the boy's father wouldn't be around when he escorted them into Keswick. Because if the human male tried to harm the boy or his mother, Hudson would probably —no, he most definitely—would do something rash to try and protect them.

However, for Elliott's sake, he had to avoid that sort of conflict at any cost. So he just hoped the bastard stayed away and didn't tempt him.

SARAH WAS BARELY HOLDING it together by a thread.

After nearly two more hours of searching, she still hadn't found Joey. And unless the stranger and his son had found him, she'd have to go to the police.

Which Rob would no doubt fume over and demand a much too harsh punishment for their youngest.

Why she'd thought this mini holiday was what they'd needed as a family, she didn't know. And to think, she'd scrimped and saved for them to come here too.

But if anything, it only reinforced what she'd been thinking for a long time now—her husband Rob was a useless bastard who wasn't worth the trouble. Maybe it was time to think about divorcing him.

However, as she neared the cheap bed-and-breakfast where they were staying, she pushed those thoughts aside. All that mattered for now was finding Joey.

When she rushed into the front room, her heart stilled to find it empty. So much for the proprietor keeping an eye on her eldest, Mark.

But Mark was older and would no doubt be in his room playing games on the old, spare mobile phone she'd given him.

Taking a deep breath, she pushed back her hair from her face and tried to keep her panic from clawing out and clouding her judgment. She needed to go to the police.

Just as she headed for the front door, it opened, and in streamed Mark, Joey, and the stranger with his son.

At the sight of Joey, she rushed over, knelt, and hugged her youngest close. For a second, she merely inhaled his little-boy scent and did her best not to cry. Because as shitty as her husband was, her two boys were her darlings and the light of her world.

And she had her youngest one back.

Joey wiggled. "Mummy, stop."

After one last squeeze, she moved back a little but still kept her hands on his shoulders, almost as if she were afraid he'd disappear again. "Where did you go, Joey?"

"Hudson got us scones."

She darted a quick glance at the man in question, who nodded, but she quickly returned the focus to her son. "No, before that. You wandered away, and you were supposed to stay near me. What happened?"

The stranger's son spoke up. "He followed a stray

sheep and her lamb, that's all. But we found him, and he's safe."

She glanced at the lad and then his father. Hudson bobbed his head. "He was chasing after them near a stream, not far from where you first came across us. And since we had some time before we were to meet here, I decided to get the boys a snack."

Later, she'd realize how unreasonable she was being. But still recovering from the loss of her son and worrying she'd never see him again, she snapped, "You should've stayed here and waited for me. When I came back and saw no one was here, I feared the worst."

The man's gaze turned remorseful. "I'm sorry. I didn't mean to worry you further."

Bloody hell. If anyone should be sorry, it was her. Here she was shouting at the man who'd helped her. "No, I should be thanking you."

He smiled, and the sight did something to her insides. If only she had a husband more like him.

No. She'd played that game of what-ifs inside her head for years, and it only caused more heartache in the long run. For better or worse, her rash decision to marry Rob Carter was hers and hers alone.

Standing, she hugged Joey to her side and kept him in place with a hand on his shoulder. "Aye, well, I'm just glad you were the one to locate him. The dragons don't live far from here, and who knows what they would've done if they'd found him first."

Hudson frowned. But before he could say anything, the man's son spoke up. "But we're dragons and we'd never hurt Joey!"

She would've brushed off the words if the lad's pupils didn't flash to slits right that second, like a dragon-shifter's would.

Her jaw dropped open, but Joey spoke before he could. "Aye, they're dragons, Mum! It's brilliant."

Sarah moved her gaze back to Hudson. He smiled and let his own eyes flash. For some reason, instead of fear, it sent a delightful shiver through her body. Thankfully he spoke again before her cheeks heated at her ridiculous reaction. "It's true. My son and I live on Stonefire, the dragon clan not far from here." He winked. "And don't worry, we've had our monthly quota of human snacks, so you're safe."

Sarah stared as she tried to reconcile the kind, teasing man in front of her with all the stories she'd heard over the years about dragon-shifters—from stealing women in the night, or kidnapping children, or any other number of crimes and horror stories.

Then her mobile phone rang, and she took it out of her pocket and noticed her husband was calling. With a sigh, she let it go to voicemail and looked back at Hudson. "I'm grateful for all you've done, Hudson. Truly. But my husband will probably be back soon, and it's best if you're not here."

Joey nodded. "Dad really, really hates dragons."

Hudson bobbed his head in understanding and put a hand on his son's shoulder. "Then we'll be leaving." He paused to stare at her a beat too long, and she wished she could read his mind. Normally she didn't like being the focus of anyone's attention. However, with this dragonman, it wasn't uncomfortable or threatening. No, it was actually… quite nice. Almost as if he were trying to see into her soul.

But Hudson cleared his throat, breaking the spell, and merely murmured, "Take care, Sarah."

Joey broke her hold and raced over to Hudson. "Will I see you again? I want a dragon friend."

Hudson smiled and looked down toward the boy. "I can't promise anything, Joey. But remember what we talked about, right?"

He nodded. "Look after Mum."

"Right, both you and your brother." He flashed one more smile at Sarah that made her heart skip a beat, and then he quickly guided his son out of the building.

Joey sighed. "I wish they didn't have to go home."

While she didn't voice it aloud, Sarah thought, *Me too, lad. Me too.*

But when her phone rang again, she knew she'd better answer it. Knowing Rob, he was probably hip-deep in some sort of trouble and needed her to sort it out.

And as she tried to listen to her husband's latest excuse about why he was abandoned on the side of the road without any money, she watched the retreating figure of Hudson and his son through the front window, wishing one last time she'd had a better lot in life. One where she might've even had a husband more like the dragonman who'd helped her simply because he'd wanted to.

But she didn't. And so all she could do was look after her lads the best she could.

Chapter Four

Present Day

Hudson Wells kept one eye on his son, Elliott, and the other on the door on the far side of the room being used to prep some of the children for the play.

At any moment, Sarah MacKintosh Carter should walk through the door.

From the moment he'd seen the picture Bram had sent him, he'd known it was *her*, the female he'd helped nearly two years ago.

The one who'd been so sad, and lonely, and angry. Oh, she'd hidden it well enough, doing her best to put her son's welfare first and foremost. But he'd glimpsed the emotions easily, calling to the part of him that yearned to help.

But wanting to help her wasn't the end of it. No, Sarah's long, dark hair and deep blue eyes had stirred something he'd thought long gone—desire.

Not since the death of his late mate, Charlie, had Hudson ever looked twice at a female.

Until Sarah's sad eyes and determined chin had garnered his notice.

And after all this time, he was going to meet her again without a husband to worry about, let alone get in the way of acting how he truly wanted to with the human.

To be able to touch her, or chat with her, or maybe eventually even kiss her, made heat rush through his body, and only a tremendous amount of willpower kept his cock soft. He wasn't about to lose control in front of the children.

It was as if the human female had woven some kind of magic over him and possessed some sort of draw he couldn't push aside. After all, no other female had stirred him even a little in the two years since he'd met Sarah.

His dragon spoke up. *As much as I want you to kiss her and maybe fuck her, remember what Bram said—she's had a hard time of it, and we need to take it slow. We'll never have her if you push too fast.*

Given that Sarah had been frantically searching for her lost child at their first meeting, her husband's whereabouts unknown, and the female on the verge of tears, Hudson had known her life had been difficult.

It'd taken every bit of strength he'd possessed not to hunt down the human male and knock some sense into him. Especially since his dragon had taken a pointed interest in the female as well, and his beast had wanted to gut the human male and be done with it.

If not for his own son needing him, Hudson would've done exactly that. Well, gone after her husband and shaken some sense into him, not the gutting part.

His dragon grunted. *It doesn't matter now. She's free of the bastard and in a new sort of trouble. But we can help her this time around.*

More like we have to convince her to mate us in a relatively short amount of time before we can be of any real help.

Maybe some would think it rash, but as soon as he'd learned she needed his help again, he'd wanted to give it, even if it was merely through the protection of being his mate.

At least at first. Because Hudson wanted more than a platonic, distant mating. No, he wanted to see the female laugh or smile or just sigh in pleasure as he made her come.

Oh, he'd keep his hands to himself unless she wanted it, but something inside him wanted to woo the human and make her his.

His dragon spoke up. *I won't complain. Even if she's not our true mate, I want her.*

True mates were supposedly a dragon-shifter's best chance at happiness. And yet, Charlie had been his, and their happiness had been short-lived.

He wouldn't trade the time he'd had with Charlie for anything in the world, but he was one of the few who doubted the old adage about true mates were all that a dragon should look for, ever. This time it wasn't some instinct that drove him to want to woo Sarah, but just himself.

And that should be enough.

His dragon said softly, *Or it's just because you want to be able to protect someone, to be their hero, like we couldn't do with Charlie.*

The door opened before he could reply to that statement and in rushed some of the children from Lochguard. At the tail end was a boy he hadn't seen for two years, but he still could identify. When Joey spotted him, his mouth dropped open. He rushed over and skidded to a halt in front of Hudson. "It's you."

The corner of his mouth ticked up. "So you remember me?"

Joey nodded enthusiastically. "Oh, aye. You were my first dragon-shifter. Although now I know heaps, you were the first." He lowered his voice. "My friends in Glasgow all wished they'd met a dragon too."

So much for the boy keeping his meeting with Hudson and Elliott a secret.

Speaking of Elliott, he raced up and smiled at Joey. "Hello, Joey. I heard you and your brother were coming. Come on. Mr. MacLeod and Daisy will be back soon, and we need to get you changed first. Otherwise, Daisy will nag and nag and act like she's an adult." Elliott rolled his eyes. "She likes to pretend she's a dragon-shifter and at the top of the dominance scale."

Before Elliott could drag Joey away, Hudson asked, "Where's your mum?"

Joey shrugged. "She had to talk to some Stonefire people but said she'd be here soon. She made some of the costumes, so she'll have to make sure everything's good before the play."

As he watched the boys go toward the side, where a few lingering costumes awaited the Lochguard children, Hudson wondered who was talking with Sarah. To be honest, he'd been surprised that Bram had suggested meeting her right before the play, given how hectic it was with children running about and the parents trying to prevent disasters.

The only thing he could think of was that Bram wanted to give Sarah a quick out if she didn't like him.

Although considering how she'd surely been sent a write-up about him like he'd received about her,

Sarah had to know who he was and that they'd met before.

His dragon spoke up. *She might be embarrassed. After all, she was frantic and emotional that day.*

As if that matters.

Maybe it does to her.

At that moment, one of Stonefire's Protectors—Nikki—poked her head into the room, met his gaze, and motioned for him to come into the hall.

No doubt, it was time to finally meet Sarah again.

Since there were a few other parents in the room, Hudson caught one of their eyes and motioned he was leaving.

As soon as he was in the hall, Nikki spoke. "Come on. Sarah had to go fix one of the costumes that tore under suspicious circumstances. I'm to bring you to her." As they started walking, Nikki added, "Are you sure about this, Hudson? I don't know this female well, but she seems a bit...damaged. And the opposite of Charlie. I worry about if you'll suit."

Since Nikki had worked with Charlie—all but idolized his late mate, to be honest—Hudson tamped down his irritation of the younger female questioning his decision. "As you know, I've met this female before. And I plan to help her if she'll let me."

Nikki looked about ready to say something else but then closed her mouth and shrugged.

His dragon said, *You'd better get used to it. Everyone's going to act this way if Sarah agrees to mate you.*

For years, almost everyone on Stonefire had pitied Hudson and his son. Charlie had given the ultimate sacrifice, but she'd still left behind a family.

While good intentioned, Hudson knew they wouldn't have been as harsh if Charlie had been a male who'd lost his life. Despite all Charlie's hard work to become one of Stonefire's best Protectors, she still suffered discrimination in death because she had been female.

And despite some progress, especially in recent years, quite a few older dragon-shifters still thought of females as breeders and homemakers.

He replied to his beast, *I can handle whatever people say. All that matters is what we think, right?*

His dragon huffed. *And what about Sarah? It sounds like she's been through hell and doesn't need the censure and stress.*

If she's willing to mate a complete stranger to keep living with dragon-shifters, then she's stronger than everyone assumes she is.

And he had a feeling she'd blossom even more, with the right male at her side.

His brothers thought him mad for casting his lot with a female who wasn't at least required to sleep with him and possibly give him a child. But ever since he'd first met Sarah near Keswick, he'd sensed she was more than she appeared.

And even if she initially only wanted a mate to stay, Hudson would use that to try and win her.

As Nikki stopped in front of the door, she glanced at him before opening it and leading him inside.

Scanning the room, he found Sarah at the far side, stitching a hem for Hudson's nephew, Michael. The boy noticed him and smiled. "Uncle Hudson!"

Sarah stilled and then slowly stood and turned toward him.

And as he met her gaze from across the room, he noted she was even prettier than his memory or her picture. Her dark hair was longer, and she looked to have gained a little bit of weight too. However, what he noticed above everything else were her eyes. Not just because they were a dark blue, like a deep lake. No, because the sadness and fear he'd seen in them two years ago were gone, replaced with intelligence and curiosity.

If anything, the lack of sadness made her more than pretty—it made her bloody beautiful.

Some sort of emotion he couldn't name flickered in her eyes before she returned to a neutral expression. Sarah turned to quickly finish up the hem and then finally made her way toward him and Nikki.

And despite being nearly forty, Hudson's heart beat double-time, like a nervous youth on his first date.

Of course, it was more important than that. Because he only had one chance to get this right, convince Sarah to pick him and give him the chance to be the male she should've always had.

SARAH HAD BEEN both grateful and irritated to be called away to fix a hem on one of the costumes since it gave her time to calm her pounding heart while also delaying the inevitable.

Part of her was afraid she'd built up her memory of Hudson over the years, remembering him as nicer, or funnier, or sexier than he truly was.

But when her charge called out, "Uncle Hudson!" she froze a second before looking over her shoulder, and she spotted *him*.

Tall, with dark hair and gray eyes, Hudson was every bit as handsome as she remembered.

But it was the laugh lines around his mouth and eyes that made her heart skip a beat, as was the flash of heat in his gaze.

Oh, aye, it was gone before she could blink, but the quick blaze stirred to life parts of Sarah she'd long thought dead.

No one had looked at her as if they could devour her since before her marriage all those years ago.

But unlike the easily snared men of her youth, the ones looking for a quick fuck and nothing else, Hudson was different. Not just because he was older, but she remembered how easily he'd interacted with not only her sons but his own.

Hudson Wells wasn't a horny lad who didn't think beyond getting into her pants. No, he was a man who didn't avoid his responsibilities.

And for someone like Sarah, whose entire life had been filled with unreliable tossers who thought of their own selfish needs over anyone else's, it attracted her like no other.

Stop it, Sarah. It's just a glance. Besides, she hadn't talked with the dragonman in years. For all she knew, it could be pure awkwardness between them. And she was probably only imagining any sort of heat. Her ex-husband had constantly reminded her of how she was too skinny and small-chested for any man to truly want to fuck her more than once or twice.

Hudson not being attracted to her she could deal with. However, no matter how much she wanted to remain with a dragon clan, she wouldn't commit herself or her children to years of awkward, uncomfortable silences. The whole point of staying with a dragon clan was so her boys would continue to thrive. Being comfortable around a mate of convenience was the least she could do for her children.

Turning back toward the hem, she finished it quickly. Once the young dragon boy raced off, she stood, took a deep breath, and turned back toward Hudson and Nikki.

Hudson's pupils flashed a few times, reminding her that he was more than a man—he was part dragon.

Maybe that would've scared her a year ago. But she'd seen how happy a dragon-shifter had made her brother and how the dragonwoman had changed him for the better. Sarah couldn't think of a more fun, loving person than her sister-in-law, Cat.

It boiled down to how dragon-shifters weren't much different than humans. Oh, aye, they could change into giant beasts, but she'd long ago dismissed the rumors and tall tales about dragon kind. They suffered love, and grief, and humiliation like anyone else.

Like Sarah had.

Although as she finally stood in front of Hudson, looking up and up and up until she met his gaze, her heart pounded. For a split second, she had to truly wonder why such an attractive man would offer to mate her.

But then he smiled, and it did something to settle her nerves.

One look and she was nearly as relaxed as if she'd just had an orgasm.

Oh, Sarah was going crazy, that was for certain.

Thankfully Hudson spoke before she started mentally listing all the ways she was mad. His deep voice rolled over her as he said, "We meet again."

She nodded, her throat growing dry. If only she

could think of some witty reply. But all she could manage was, "Aye."

They stared at each other, and Sarah tried to think of what she could say. After all, there wasn't exactly a handbook on how to talk to a man who was willing to marry a stranger to protect her and her sons.

Maybe she should've read his little write-up ahead of time to get to know him a wee bit better before this face-to-face meeting.

Hudson smiled down at her, raised a finger, and brushed a few stray strands of her hair off her cheek. She barely repressed a shiver at his warm touch. He murmured, "Are there any other costume emergencies, or can we spend a few minutes alone?"

At the word alone, her brain fog lifted. *Bloody hell.* The dragonman's touch had to be some sort of magic. She replied, "I think everything's in order. At this point, I don't really have time to fix much else. The show will just have to go on."

He offered his arm, like a gentleman from days of old, and waited. "Then let's be off before something else comes up. Having this many children in one place, from two clans, is sure to cause at least five more mini-disasters before the curtain goes up."

She glanced behind her with a frown. The play meant quite a bit to her lads. "But if that's the case, I should stay here to offer advice, if needed."

Hudson raised an eyebrow, almost as if he knew she was making an excuse.

Willing herself not to be a coward—after all, the only way to keep Mark and Joey with her and the dragons was to mate one, most likely—she threaded her arm through Hudson's. As he pulled her a little closer, heat rushed through her body, and she met his eyes again.

As his pupils flashed, she should be scared, or at least a wee bit curious.

And yet, it was almost as if she were mesmerized.

When he grinned, Sarah snapped out of it. "What?"

He chuckled. "It's just that if I wasn't watching you so closely, then I'd never have guessed your emotions. " He leaned down. "But since I have been, I can tell that you at least find me sexy."

Her jaw dropped, which only made him laugh and place a finger under her chin, gently closing her mouth. He whispered, "Come. Right now we have at least fifteen pairs of eyes watching us, and some of the things I really want to say wouldn't be fit for their ears."

Yet again, Sarah didn't know how to respond. Never in her life had a man teased her so much so soon.

Or, for that matter, made her so wet from so few touches.

Oh, for crying out loud. Sarah was a grown woman.

She needed to work harder at being a mother of two and not some starstruck teenager.

Standing tall—which didn't help much, given how Hudson towered over her—she cleared her throat and said, "Remember we're here for the children, sir."

He grinned. "There's no need to be so formal. And the children are fine. Just because we're parents doesn't mean we can't sometimes tease and have fun in more, shall we say, adult ways."

As he winked at her, Sarah's cheeks heated. At this rate, she'd let him strip off her clothes and fuck her quickly before the start of the play.

One of the children ran past them, and it reminded Sarah how more was at stake than slaking her lust. If she was going to mate a dragon-shifter, he needed to be good father material, such as being reliable and responsible. Whether his touch was like a match, sending fire between her legs, let alone if he was good in bed or not, didn't factor.

Liar, whispered through her head.

Hudson gently tugged her toward the door, and she followed. Once they were in the hall, which was relatively quiet compared to the rambunctious lot in the room, she blurted, "Why did you offer to mate me?"

"Straight to the point, I see." He eyed her a second and then nodded down the hall. "There's an empty room just ahead. I'd rather discuss this privately."

She bobbed her head and willed her cheeks to cool. Being alone in a room with Hudson Wells and trying to keep her wits about her was going to be difficult.

Hell, she'd all but purred at him in front of a group of children.

He opened a door and let her enter first. She'd barely noted the table and chairs before the door clicked shut, and she turned back around.

Hudson leaned against the wall, his arms crossed over his chest, which only highlighted the intricate tattoo on his upper arm. The one she wouldn't mind tracing with her tongue.

Stop it, Sarah. Seriously, at this rate, she should just have that phrase tattooed on her arm as a constant reminder.

Thankfully Hudson spoke, garnering her attention. "You asked why I put my name forth." She nodded, and he continued, "For a number of reasons, really. I wanted to help you more than I was allowed two years ago, but couldn't, unlike now." He uncrossed his arms and took a step toward her. "My son would love to have a stepmother and stepbrothers as well." Another step closer. "It would also give me the chance to help someone in need, which has always been a weakness of mine."

He stopped right in front of her, silence falling on

the room. She finally asked, "That's it? Those are all of your reasons?"

Shaking his head, he raised a hand and traced her jaw. The light touches made her shiver. "There are more selfish reasons as well. Do you want to hear them?"

Unable to take her gaze from his flashing dragon eyes, she bobbed her head. He smiled. "You're the first female I've wanted to kiss since my late mate." He leaned closer, his hot breath dancing across her lips as he murmured, "I can tell you feel this intense attraction as much as me, both from your cheeks and your scent. So before we go any further, will you let me kiss you, Sarah? I think it'll go a long way toward convincing you to pick me."

There were a million reasons why she should push Hudson away and tell him no. Her choice was supposed to be rational, one made out of a last-ditch effort to keep her sons away from her in-laws.

And yet, as Hudson's breath continued to brush against her skin, combined with the musky scent that was uniquely him, she didn't have the strength to say no.

He cupped her cheek and asked, "Can I kiss you, Sarah?"

She barely managed a whisper. "Aye."

He lowered his lips, but right before he could make contact, there was a pounding on the door.

Sarah jumped back at the same time Hudson

cursed. He strode to the door, opened it, and barked, "What?"

On the other side of the door stood Dawn Chadwick-Whitby, and to her credit, the human didn't so much as blink at his tone. She looked past him to Sarah. "One of the costumes, shall we say, caught fire. Don't worry, no one was wearing it at the time, but we're trying to hurry and think of a quick replacement and need your help."

Doing her best to will her cheeks to cool, Sarah took a deep breath and walked closer to the door. "No worries."

She chanced a glance at Hudson, and he raised his brows. "Will you meet with me again later?"

Since everyone from Lochguard was spending the night and most of the next day on Lochguard, Sarah knew what he was really asking—did she want to talk with him again?

Talk, and aye, well, maybe more.

Not that the "more" should happen. But she did want to ask more questions, so she suggested, "Maybe we can have breakfast, if I can find someone to watch my boys."

Dawn spoke up. "Don't worry, I can do that. Daisy will be ecstatic to host some human children for a few hours and give them some pointers, whether they want it or not."

"Thank you," she murmured.

Hudson covertly reached out and brushed his

fingers down the back of her hand. Her eyes shot to his, and he winked. "Until tomorrow, if I don't see you before."

Sarah left then, although fled might be a more apt description. And as she tried to replace the destroyed costume, her heartbeat returned to normal, as did some of her sense.

Attraction and charm were all well and good, but that had been how Rob had deceived her at first.

It was only later, with his constant reminders of how lucky she'd been to have him despite how thin and plain she was—with a nose big enough to be seen from space to boot—that she'd learned how his charm had been a front.

And that ultimately his marrying her had been to win a bet and gain a monthly inheritance from his parents.

Of course she'd been pregnant right away and trapped, with no family to help since her brother had been a struggling, recovering drunk at that point in his life. And her parents, well, they'd been useless, like they had been her entire life.

However, this time was different from when she'd married and regretted Rob. Aye, this time around, she had a few options and some freedom to pick from them.

And to that end, charm and attraction were her enemy. By morning, Sarah would have better built up her defenses against it to approach her meeting with

Hudson in a rational manner, one that focused solely on her sons' futures.

Above all else, she was determined to avoid a repeat of her past by not letting her heart and hormones blind her to any sort of consequence.

Chapter Five

Between the play, getting his son settled afterward, and taking extra care with getting ready in the morning, Hudson had been able to distract himself from thoughts of Sarah.

Mostly.

He'd dreamt of her, of actually taking her lips and pulling her close. Of stripping her clothes and licking every inch of her body. Of driving home between her thighs, making them both forget about everything but the pleasure that crashed over them.

Hudson had woken up harder than he'd been in years and had taken himself in hand to try to calm the fuck down.

Not that it had done much. He had no idea why Sarah affected him so, especially as his dragon assured him repeatedly that she wasn't their true mate.

And yet he couldn't help asking his beast again, *Are you sure?*

His dragon sighed. *Yes. As I've said before, she's pretty and calls to your protective nature. Why not just accept that? I'm as eager as you to lick her sweet pussy, so hurry up and convince her to mate us.*

Not that mating him guaranteed such a thing since it was supposed to only be one of convenience. *I'm working on it.*

Elliott came racing down the stairs, and Hudson focused on his son. Elliott was always chatty and immediately blurted, "Is it true? Are you thinking of mating again?"

Hudson blinked. He, Bram, and the Protectors had agreed it was best not to tell Elliott of Hudson's offer until he was certain it would happen so as to not get his son's hopes up. "Where did you hear that?"

He shrugged. "Jayden told me. His dad told him. So, is it true?"

Jayden was one of Hudson's nephews, and the boy's father, Brooklyn, was a massive gossip.

Still, Hudson had hoped his brother would've kept his mouth shut for something this important.

With a sigh, he answered, "I'm considering it, but nothing is final, Elliott. Which is why I didn't say anything yet."

His son frowned. "Will I have to call her my mum?"

Hudson laid a hand on his son's shoulder. "If, and

that's a big if, I do take a mate, that will be up to you. No one will force you to do it, son. I promise."

Elliott nodded and fell unusually quiet. The boy only had bits and pieces of memories of his mother, and Hudson knew he held on to them dearly.

He squatted down until he was at Elliott's eye level. "All of this is putting the cart before the horse, though. I promise that if I intend to mate someone, I will talk to you about it before making any sort of final decision. Okay?" Elliott nodded, and Hudson squeezed his boy's shoulder. "Right. Then let's hurry and get you some breakfast before I take you over to your uncle's house."

"Are you meeting the female you might mate today?"

He smiled. "You're just as clever as your mother, even at nearly nine."

Elliott beamed, and as if to reinforce the point, repeated, "Are you?"

"Yes. But nothing is certain like I said. So no sneaking out of your uncle's house to spy on me, okay?"

Elliott sighed dramatically. "Fine. Although Jayden's been teaching me how to be more…what is it? Stealthy. That's it. Like a cat."

His nephew Jayden was now a teenager, which didn't bode well if he was trying to teach Elliott some of his tricks. He'd have to speak to his brother later about talking with Jayden.

But not now. He ruffled Elliott's hair. "I don't care what you do in the garden or around the house, but no sneaking out. Promise?"

After a beat, Elliott finally nodded.

Hudson guided them both to the fridge in the kitchen. "Now, it's going to have to be a quick breakfast, which means you're going to have to help."

And as Hudson and his son made eggs on toast with cheese, it helped to calm Hudson down a bit. This was his routine, feeding and chatting with his son in the morning, one he'd done for years.

Although he was more than willing to change it slightly for a certain blue-eyed human female. But rather than wonder what it would be like to have her and her two sons in the same kitchen, he spent the time focused on his son. No matter what happened, he would have to prioritize Elliott over his own wants.

And while he didn't think his son would have a problem with gaining a new instant family, he never, ever wanted Elliott to feel slighted or neglected. He would always have to make time for his son, just as he always had.

SARAH PACED the small room inside Stonefire's security building and clenched and unclenched her fingers, unsure if she wanted Hudson to show up or cancel.

She wasn't worried about Dawn watching her lads. They seemed to feel at ease around her, which didn't surprise Sarah since even she, the most skittish person she knew, had started to trust the other woman already.

No, her main nervousness stemmed from Hayley Beckett's email earlier in the morning, which had revealed no progress on another alternative to mating a dragon-shifter. While there was still a little bit of time until the DDA's deadline to leave Lochguard, it wasn't much.

And if she didn't select Hudson, then she would have to pick someone else.

Not that she wanted to, but it could be easier to select a dragonman who didn't invade her dreams, or make her stomach twist in nerves, or stir the maelstrom of emotions inside her like Hudson did.

Dawn had tried to say emotions weren't necessarily a bad thing. Sarah had merely smiled and brushed the comments off. True, Dawn had also fallen in love with someone who had eventually abandoned her, but Sarah didn't think the woman had suffered years of verbal abuse, of being made to feel incompetent, unattractive, and useless.

And before she could stop, those kind of words rushed up from her memories:

Can't you even cook a decent meal? What's the point of you, if all you'll do is poison me?

I can't get hard because you're skinny and boy-like. I should've married someone with more meat and bigger tits.

It's your fault the rent is late. You're supposed to handle the bills. I gave you the money, remember? You lost it because you're a daft, thick bitch.

Although the worst of it was that by the end of her marriage, Sarah had even doubted if she'd been a good mother.

Joey got lost today because of you. You obviously don't love him, or you'd have watched him better. Maybe I should give the lads over to my parents. They would do a better job.

Taking a deep breath, she tried to erase the memories. A year away from Rob and his toxic words had helped, but her self-doubts still lingered.

And thinking of her ex only reinforced how horrible her instincts were with men.

With human men, perhaps. But maybe it would be different with a dragonman. Of course that could just be an excuse, one that would let her pussy make the decision but later only lead her back down the path to suffering.

Someone knocked, and she jumped at the sound. Doing her best to calm her whirring mind, she managed, "Come in."

Hudson walked in, took one look at her with flashing pupils, shut the door, and asked softly, "What's wrong?"

Her eyes unexpectedly heated with tears at the heartfelt concern in his voice. While her brother was better these days, their relationship was still strained and trying to find its footing. And not since she'd been a wee girl had anyone asked her what was wrong and showed true concern instead of the question being used to guilt-trip and make her hide her troubles quickly, like her ex always had.

And on Lochguard, she'd always done her best to show a strong front so that they wouldn't see her as a liability to their clan.

Hudson continued to stare at her with those soft, questioning eyes, and she felt herself teeter.

No. She shouldn't show weakness. She needed to get a grip on herself.

However, as Sarah tried her best to blink back tears, she must've failed because Hudson was instantly in front of her. He gently brushed away the wetness on her cheeks so tenderly that it only made her choke back a sob.

Hudson gingerly reached out and pulled her against his chest. At his warm, solid presence, her facade cracked, and she did what she hadn't done in the year, since leaving her own personal hell—she cried.

More like sobbed uncontrollably. All the years of hate and contempt, of feeling small and unwanted, of trying to hide the worst of her husband from her children to spare them, came rushing out in tears, and cries, and sounds she couldn't even name.

One rash decision at a young age had changed her life from merely hellish to full-on suffering, one of her own making.

And while she was free of the bastard who'd done so much to extinguish what light she'd had left after her father's abuse and mother's neglect, she faced yet another choice that could change her life, her future uncertain no matter which way she went.

Although as Hudson rubbed her back and murmured soothing words, each pass of his hand wiped away a little of her sadness and fear and even lessened the rotten, lingering effects of her memories. As the minutes went by, she started to calm down.

There was something about the dragonman that soothed her soul with little more than a touch.

And yet, she didn't trust her instincts. She needed to do what was best for Mark and Joey, to prove she was the right caretaker to look after them.

Little by little, her tears slowed, and her cries retreated until she was standing silent and worn out, needing to leave Hudson's arms and yet afraid she might stumble from her emotional exhaustion if she did.

For a few minutes, they stood in silence, with Hudson continuing to stroke her back and hold her close. When Sarah finally found the strength to push gently against his chest, he released her, no questions asked.

She quickly sat in the chair before she found her voice, careful to stare at her hands in her lap and not into Hudson's eyes. The last thing she needed was to see pity, or panic, or anything else that told her he was ready to run as far away as possible. "I'm sorry."

For a beat, he said nothing. But then Hudson squatted down until he could meet her gaze. His pupils flashed a few times before he replied, "Don't apologize. I'd much rather hear what's wrong. Is it your boys? The DDA?" He reached up and tentatively placed a hand over her clenched ones. "Tell me."

There was zero reason she should. For all his kindness, Hudson Wells was still a stranger.

And yet the words spilled from her lips before she could stop it, almost as if she couldn't keep it from him if she tried. "I-I didn't have a good marriage." He nodded and waited. Sarah finally continued, "And whilst waiting for you, memories overtook me, ones that make me think that no one would want me." His eyes flashed, but she hurried on before he spoke. "But it was your true concern and a simple question that undid me." Her voice fell to a whisper. "No one has really cared about me in a long, long time."

He frowned. "But weren't you staying on Lochguard because of your brother?"

She shrugged and looked back down at her lap. "Lachlan was an alcoholic for years, and toward the end, before he got help, our close relationship shattered. True, he's better now, and we talk more. But it's still...delicate. We both act as if truly speaking our minds or relating our past will drive us apart again." She tried to twist her hands, but Hudson's grip only tightened a fraction. The action gave her the courage to also say, "And his new in-laws are kind, but they're all just so...happy. I never wanted to burden them with my darkness. They don't deserve that."

When Hudson remained quiet, she looked up. She couldn't read his expression, although his eyes were focused solely on her, as if trying to figure out the puzzle that was Sarah MacKintosh Carter.

Just as she was about to squirm from his scrutiny, he gently squeezed her hands again. "I would easily care for you, Sarah, and your sons. We barely know each other, and you have every reason to think the worst of me, given your experiences in life so far. But know that I would always have concern for you and your well-being if you mated me. I vow it."

Searching his gaze, she wanted to believe him. Oh, how she wanted to.

However, as stupid as it was to not immediately jump at what he was offering, she wanted to ensure Hudson wouldn't instantly regret taking care of her.

He was a kind, gentle, attractive man. He should be more than a hero, should expect more from a mate.

So even though it made her cheeks burn and she suffered a crash of memories of Rob criticizing her body as nothing a man would ever want, she blurted, "I'll only consider it after you kiss me."

He raised an eyebrow. "Are you sure? I don't want to take advantage of you, Sarah. I offer my protection without any strings."

She bit her lip a beat before moving one of her hands from under his and to his chest, doing her best to focus on her words and not the firm muscle under her fingertips. "Your kiss will tell me your true answer. If you don't want to, if you're having second thoughts after my outburst, I understand. I'm more than aware I'm damaged and not the prettiest woman alive."

Sarah moved to retract her hand, but Hudson caught it and gently brought it to his mouth. As his warm, firm lips brushed her palm, a spark of heat rushed through her body, ending between her thighs. After kissing her skin again, his voice was a wee bit deeper as he murmured, "You're fucking beautiful, and I spent the night dreaming of more than kissing you, Sarah. Trust me, second thoughts are the farthest thing from my mind right now."

His eyes sizzled with heat, and she wished she could believe it was only for her. That he truly found her attractive, wanted her in a way no man had really ever done, to the point he would fuck her against a wall because he couldn't wait long enough to get her to a bed.

The fantasy of Hudson doing exactly that, as he pounded into her and dominated her mouth, made even more wetness rush between her thighs.

Then she pushed it all aside. If she mated him, it wouldn't be because of some great passion. Sex with her wasn't a requirement, after all.

Doubts began to creep in again, but she caught herself. *Stop it, Sarah.* She was dismissing him without even giving the dragonman a chance.

Silly as it might seem to others, just knowing he wanted to protect her and could possibly desire her was more than she'd ever had with any man in her life before.

And she wanted it desperately to be true. But she'd never find out what could be, or even what he truly thought of her, if she wasn't brave right here, right now, in this pivotal moment.

Taking a deep breath, she leaned forward a little. "Then kiss me, dragonman. And let's see if we'll suit."

HUDSON BARELY CONTAINED himself as first Sarah asked him to kiss her, and then his senses filled with the scent of her arousal.

All he wanted to do was strip her down and show her how much he loved her slight curves, her short frame, and her long, thick hair that begged for him to lightly tug it as he took her from behind.

And even if she hadn't agreed to mate him yet, he still itched to find the bastard who'd made her doubt herself, her beauty, her sense of worth, and teach him a lesson.

His dragon growled. *I say we find him, but later. Right now, she wants us to kiss her.*

And when Sarah leaned forward and said it clearly, to see if they suited, his restraint shattered. Hudson leaned forward and pressed his lips to hers. Gently at first, but at the contact, Sarah gasped, and he took advantage, plunging his tongue into her mouth. In the next instant, she lightly kissed him back by stroking her tongue against his. Hudson growled as he deepened the kiss, licking, and exploring, and sucking her tongue.

But the kiss wasn't nearly enough. He stood, hauling her body against his and lifting her leg to his hip. He'd been hard since her first mention of kissing, so he ground against her, loving the moan in her throat, and soon she moved too, as if she needed what he could give her.

Cupping her arse, he rocked her, wanting her to feel his cock, needing her to take what she wanted and find her release. She deserved the pleasure, and the fact he would cause it made him growl and take the kiss even deeper.

His free hand went to her hair, threaded it through, and adjusted the angle of her head to let him taste her even more.

He had no idea how long they kissed, and ground against each other, and clung to one another as if this was a reawakening to life for the both of them, to a future neither had thought would include passion or such pleasure.

Sarah finally cried out as her orgasm crashed over her, breaking their kiss, and Hudson took advantage of the moment to nibble where her neck met her shoulder, biting lightly, needing to mark her in some way even without a mate-claim frenzy.

He was close, so close, to coming. But then Sarah collapsed against him, breathing heavily, and his entire focus switched to her.

Because after that kiss, after the brief glimpse of what could be, he wanted her. Desperately.

And so he needed to woo her, convince her, and show how he should be her mate, her male, the only one to touch, and fondle, and caress her until she came apart in his arms.

Not wanting her to spook, he lightly rubbed her lower back for a few beats before asking, "So what's the verdict? What did my kiss tell you?"

She leaned against him, her hand clutching his

shirt a few beats before she finally replied, "I-I think you find me at least a wee bit attractive."

He bit his lip to keep from laughing at the "wee bit" part of her words—he'd been seconds away from coming in his trousers—sensing it would break the moment. He raised his hand to brush a few strands of hair off her cheek. "If you need further convincing of how attracted I am to you, then all you have to do is ask." He pressed her lower back to push her flush against his front, and he barely resisted a hiss at her soft belly against his dick. "Even now, you can still feel how fucking hard I am for you, Sarah. That's all for you."

She glanced up at him, her look unsure, and cautious, and wary.

That look went right to his soul. It suddenly became imperative that he be the one to banish those demons, to the point they rarely surfaced and were replaced with happiness, and joy, and a dozen other positive emotions.

Her voice was so low that if he wasn't a dragon-shifter with exceptional hearing, he would've missed it, "How would you prove it further? Tell me, please. Just with words."

A spark of mischief flared inside him. Could it be possible his little human liked dirty talk?

His beast spoke up. *Or it might just be that she's afraid of anything more physical right now.*

That could be true. If her bastard of an ex had

convinced her she wasn't pretty, or attractive, or desirable, then their recent encounter could be overwhelming.

Either way, he was more than happy to oblige as he rather liked stoking desire with nothing more than words. Hudson caressed her jaw, lowered his mouth closer to her ear, and murmured, "First, I'd need to strip off your clothes. Slowly, so each inch the material drags over your stomach, your breasts, your shoulder, it makes you aware of each and every sensation against your skin. Then I'd take it off and use the shirt to rub back and forth against your nipples, to make you mad for more before my fingers even touch you. Only once you started to squirm would I finally toss it aside."

Again, her voice was low, as if she didn't think she should ask but somehow dared. "And then?"

He nuzzled her cheek before he continued, "Then I'd caress what skin I could see, running my fingers over your sides, your back, your arms, until I could draw the strap of your bra down. Slowly, oh so slowly, until you all but shivered in anticipation, your pussy already drenched and waiting for my fingers."

She swallowed, but the scent of her arousal grew even stronger, if that were possible.

And Hudson wished he could rip off her jeans, her underwear, and part her already swollen lips to lap and lick her pussy until she screamed his name.

But he was getting ahead of himself. He asked, "Do you want me to stop?"

Sarah took her time to answer, but then she leaned more against his chest, as if she was afraid he would disappear if she didn't touch him, and shook her head. "No."

He smiled. "Good, because next I'd extend a talon, slice off your bra, and gently run the back of my talon over your nipple until it bunched and hardened into a sweet little peak. Only then would I lick it, and suck it, and bite it until you squirmed. I'd do the same to the other one, to see if I could make you come with only my hands and mouth."

Her breathing quickened, as did her heart rate.

Hudson had deliberately incorporated part of his dragon self, his talon, into the fantasy to see if it'd scare her.

However, if anything, she'd been turned on more, which please both man and beast. After all, his dragon sometimes took over his human form and liked to claim, and would want the same with Sarah.

His dragon spoke up. *I'd bloody well better get a chance to do it.*

Hush, I'm still trying to convince her to pick us.

Then try harder.

Sarah's question brought Hudson's attention back to her. "Is that even possible? I-I don't have large breasts. They wouldn't hold your interest for very long."

A blast of anger at her ex raged through his body. Someday, he wanted her to tell him more of what the fucking bastard had put her through, all he said so that Hudson could show how each and every word was a bloody lie.

But at the moment, he was more determined to convince her that she was sexy and beautiful and more than female enough for him.

He moved his hand to her ribcage, running his fingers up and down, close to the edge of her tit, but never quite touching it. "They're perfect." She opened her mouth to protest, but he beat her to it. "Just a slight handful, enough for me to take you into my mouth and suck you hard. And given how your nipples poked into my chest, I'm more than eager to see what they look like. Are they rosy pink? Or a deeper red? More pointed and ruched? Or more rounded, like a pearl?" He lightly worried her earlobe, and Sarah let out a sigh. He released her flesh and continued, "If you think we suit, if you agree to be my mate and desire it, I will take my time showing you just how much your tits please me, Sarah. You can still feel how much I want you with my hard cock pressing against your belly. If anything, all this talk of your breasts has made me ache more for you."

It wasn't the most romantic thing on the planet, and nothing a poet would wax on about, but the words suited the moment, the female, their situation.

She didn't believe herself desirable, and as long as that was the case, he'd continue to whisper dirty words and fantasies.

And more, of course. After today, this meeting, he wanted to see Sarah smile, or laugh, or simply enjoy herself without sadness, worry, or doubt clouding her eyes or voice.

But first, before any of that, Sarah needed to say yes.

SARAH PLAYED with Hudson's top, rubbing the fabric between her fingers, and debated what to do.

Hudson's kiss, and words, and mere presence made her want him naked and above her, showing her what she hadn't had in so many years—hard, slightly rough sex that made both parties lose their minds as they came.

But that fantasy was for her and not for those she needed to protect—her sons.

However, after Hudson had made her come with her clothes still on, Sarah didn't want safe and platonic with a future mate, as had been her first goal.

No, she wanted a decent man who would not only be a good stepfather but who also wanted her naked and in his bed.

To do that, she needed to find out a few more

things about this dragonman. So she said, "I want to say yes, but I think we need to get all of the lads together and see how it goes. What I personally want doesn't matter if my sons are miserable."

She finally looked up at Hudson, his pupils flashing, and waited. If he was upset at her wanting the best for her children, then he would most definitely not be the male she wanted, let alone needed. After all, her ex-husband had barely acknowledged his own sons, and she would never expose her lads to that sort of neglect ever again, with them forever reaching for male attention and affection and never getting it.

Hudson grunted before nodding. "We'll do that later today. I'm sure you can delay your return to Lochguard for a day or two, so we can let the boys mingle."

Her first instinct was to look at the ground and say she should go back to Lochguard first. It would give her distance from Hudson's magnetic presence, allow her to clear her mind, and think about it rationally.

But the idea of leaving, running away, made her think of all the years she hadn't seen the truth of her ex-husband, let alone been able to break free of his abuse and face the scary path of being a single parent on her own.

No, if she was truly determined to live her life, to work on being the woman she wanted to be, she needed to stop running, stop hiding, stop letting her ex's words and actions rule her life.

It wouldn't be an easy thing to do, but this would be a good first step.

Maintaining eye contact—that was one of the things she was determined to work on—she answered, "I'll talk to Bram and see if it's okay, right after I check on my lads at Dawn's."

He gently squeezed her waist and smiled at her. The brief flash of approval and happiness in Hudson's eyes made her heart skip a beat.

She almost believed he truly wanted to spend more time with her.

He kissed her forehead and then stepped back but still kept one of her hands in his. Sarah nearly mewled in protest, almost as if she wanted his heat and strong arms around her always, but managed to contain herself as Hudson said, "Then let's do that now. I'll drop you off at Dawn's, and then I'll speak with Bram myself. The sooner Bram confirms it with Finn, the sooner I can plan a great day of adventure for you and the boys, especially with the later summer weather cooperating."

She nodded, a sudden shyness creeping over her. As if sensing it, Hudson squeezed her hand and asked, "As we walk, why don't you tell me a bit more about your boys? It'll help me figure out what they'd like to do today."

And as Sarah dove into the safe topic, telling him

about Mark's love of football and sports, as well as Joey's interest in birds and animals—or anything to do with nature, really—the walk to Dawn's cottage passed quickly.

Almost too quickly. To the point when Hudson escorted her to Dawn's house to check on her sons and said goodbye, she nearly clamped onto him, afraid he'd never come back.

She had no idea if it showed in her face or not, but Hudson cupped her cheek and whispered, "I'll see you in a few hours, right? You have no reason to believe me, but I'm quite the reliable chap." He leaned closer to say into her ear, "It hides my dirty mouth and sex fantasies quite well, but you know about them now, don't you?" She shivered, and he chuckled. "I'll be by in a few hours."

He kissed her cheek, waved, and walked down the path toward Bram's cottage.

Taking a deep breath, she knocked and willed her cheeks to cool.

Although as soon as Dawn opened the door, the other woman smiled widely. "The boys are in the back but come with me. Let's tidy you up and hide how something must've happened between you and Hudson. Tell me the details, or don't, but I truly hope you'll spill."

She could do nothing but blink as Dawn led her upstairs and slowly managed to wheedle out some of what had happened to her.

Saying the words almost made it all the more real.

But all too soon, she was back into her role as a mother, corralling her lads out the door and telling them about how they'd extend their stay since a text message had come, letting her know Finn had approved the longer visit to Stonefire. Mark was a bit put out to miss his football practice, but he'd live.

And despite herself, Sarah counted down the minutes until she'd see Hudson again, wondering if the same magic would be there after a few hours apart. Given her track record and luck, it wouldn't. However, she wasn't going to set herself up for failure without cause. It was yet another thing she hoped to work on.

Chapter Six

Since Bram had easily dismissed the challenges of allowing Sarah and her sons to stay, saying Finn would agree without hesitation, Hudson had quickly set things in motion for the outing.

He knew it was going to be hard to see Sarah again and not want to touch her, or kiss her, or more. So he devised a picnic lunch and some outdoor activities to keep all of them occupied for a few hours.

Elliott had been more than happy at the news—Hudson suspected his son already had his hopes up of having some kind of mother again—and had found a football and helped pack a lunch for them all.

It wasn't long before he stood at the door of Sarah's temporary house, knocked, and waited. He itched to shuffle his feet in impatience but managed to tamp it down.

His dragon laughed. *You'd best work on that. Despite what happened earlier today, Sarah will take a lot of patience to woo.*

Of course I know that. But it's easier if she's present, so I can work on it. Right now, I'm just standing here, doing nothing.

Before his beast could tease him, Sarah slowly opened the door with a hesitant smile. "You're here."

He didn't like the disbelief in her tone and wondered at just how many people had broken their word to her before. "Of course I'm here. If I say I'll be somewhere, you can guarantee I'll show up, provided some sort of disaster hasn't happened."

Sarah studied him a minute, as if trying to judge if he were spouting shite or not, but Elliott jumped in, oblivious to any sort of tension between them. "Are you lot ready to go?" He held up the football. "I'm ready to play with Mark. I've seen him at a few games before, when my team played Lochguard."

Sarah's face softened as she smiled down at Elliott. "Aye, I'm sure he'll like that. Just a moment, I'll go fetch my lads."

She left the door open and went down the hall. Thanks to his keen hearing, Hudson heard one of Sarah's boys sigh loudly and say, "But I don't want to go. I want to play football back home, with Coach Jamie."

Sarah replied, "Mark, I already told you we're staying here at least a day longer. Whinging won't make me instantly change my mind. Besides, you spend your life practicing and playing football with the same people on Lochguard. Facing a new player should be a good test, aye?"

Mark muttered, "Not if he's rubbish."

Sarah sighed, but then she must've given a look or gesture because soon she marched her two sons down the hall toward the front door.

The instant her gaze met his again, he winked at her as if saying he understood how little boys could be a trial at times. She smiled cautiously at him, but he'd take whatever she'd give him. At least for now.

But all too soon, her sons moved to stand in front of him, staring up with curious eyes—and a little suspicion from the elder—and Hudson focused his attention on them. "Hello, boys. Ready for the outing?"

Mark spoke before anyone else. "Why are we going out with you? Mum said it was important, but why?"

While Hudson usually loved his son's forward manner, Elliott decided to blurt, "Because they might mate. We need to see if we get along."

Mark frowned. "Mate? As in marry?"

Hudson looked to Sarah, not wanting to overstep his bounds.

Sarah cleared her throat. "Aye, although nothing is settled yet."

Mark shook his head. "But Mum doesn't want a husband. She said so. That's why we don't live with Dad."

Sarah gently turned Mark toward her. "If we want to stay with the dragons, I have to marry one. Otherwise we'll have to move to some human city or town and may rarely see them again."

Mark pointed at Hudson. "But he lives on Stonefire, not Lochguard. I like our life on Lochguard."

Sarah said softly, "Give Hudson a chance, Mark. One outing, that's all I ask for now."

The boy looked about ready to argue, but Hudson decided it was best to jump in and try to focus on the moment instead of an argument that would go on in circles. He'd had his fair share of those with his own son over the years. "I have loads planned for today, so we should probably get going. Especially since it's still warm enough to play by the lake we're going to. While there, I can show you my dragon form, if you like."

Sarah's younger son, Joey, looked up at him with wide eyes. "I want to see your dragon." He turned and tugged on Mark's shirt. "Please, Mark. Let's go. I can add him to my collection."

Hudson raised his brows. "Collection?"

Sarah smiled and explained, "He likes to keep a

journal of each dragon he sees. He tries to draw them and add a few characteristics. One of his teachers thought it'd be good for him to not only understand dragon-shifters better but also build up his vocabulary since his reading level is a few years higher than the rest of his class. At the moment I think he's recorded forty-five dragons so far."

"Forty-six, Mum," Joey huffed.

Hudson bit back a smile. He could at least win over one of Sarah's sons easily enough. "I'd be honored to be number forty-seven." He switched his gaze to Mark. "And Elliott is a little older than you, and as a result, has played football longer. He might have a thing or two to teach you, Mark."

Elliott nodded. "Our Stonefire team plays against Coach Jamie's team sometimes. Coach Jamie is good, but so is ours." He leaned over and whispered dramatically, "We could share some plays and not tell anyone. It'd be our secret and make us both better."

Mark frowned and said nothing. Sarah gently nudged his shoulder, and Mark sighed. "Fine. I'll go, but I won't like it."

Sarah shook her head but quickly recovered. "Then let's head out, aye? The weather isn't as changeable as Scotland, but it's still England. Let's go before the clouds come."

Joey raced down the hall and shouted, "Just a second! I need my journal."

Sarah added the clarification, "So he can record your dragon form."

A beat later, Joey returned, notebook and pen in hand. As they all finally departed the house—Sarah's sons had fetched and also carried a few things for their outing—Elliott fell into step with Joey since Mark dragged his feet. Sarah and Hudson brought up the rear. He whispered for her ears only, "It'll be fine, Sarah. Elliott's quite good at sport and should have a thing or two to teach Mark."

"I know. Mark is definitely the moodier of my sons and takes after me. His temper, unfortunately, is from his father. It was hard for him when he felt as if I pushed his father away from us a year ago, especially with me keeping the worst of Rob's actions from my lads. Mark's coach and team on Lochguard truly saved him, I think. I'm just worried that another change will only make him act out more, and not necessarily in a good way."

Hudson lightly brushed the back of her hand with a finger. "I know everyone will say it just takes time for kids to adjust, which is frustrating as hell. But it's true. Elliott struggled after his mum passed. Even if it's not the same with his mum being taken by force instead of being abandoned by choice, I still think time and a stable situation will help. You're trying to give him that, so remember not to be too hard on yourself."

She smiled slightly up at him. "Aye, I know. But I still worry."

He wished he could cup her cheek, or caress it, or offer greater support with his touch. But Mark kept turning and glaring at Hudson, and he wasn't about to anger the boy so early on.

Sarah spoke again, interrupting his thoughts of how to comfort her best without laying a finger on her. "Er, how did she die? Your mate?" He frowned, and she added quickly, "I didn't read the write-up that was sent to me, wanting to determine who you are for myself. And there wasn't enough time after getting back to Dawn's cottage and then my own to do it before the outing."

He hesitated, and his dragon said softly, *She deserves to know; otherwise, it will forever be a distance between you. Especially since you know so much about her.*

Checking ahead to ensure Elliott, Mark, and Joey were all together, with Elliott acting as a guide, but far enough away they wouldn't hear, he finally replied, "She was murdered by dragon hunters."

"I'm so sorry, Hudson."

He nodded, doing his best to fight against the scenarios he'd imagined over the years, of how much pain Charlie must've been in until she'd finally breathed her last. His voice was rough to his own ears as he said, "She was a Protector, one of the first female ones for Stonefire in a long time, if ever. I'd known Charlie since we were children and had been one of the few males who was proud of her accomplishments. Many dragonmen were—and sadly, still are—stuck in the old ways, thinking females should only bear children and stay home.

"But from a young age, Charlie wanted more. She liked protecting people, not to mention she was extremely athletic and clever when it came to strategy. Against her parents' wishes, she joined the British Army as soon as she qualified to get the training she needed to become a Protector. Throughout it all, we kept in touch. Once she finally came back and earned her place, I debated whether she'd want a mate or not, given how much her career choice meant to her."

Sarah smiled. "But obviously she did."

He nodded. "I'd always wanted to kiss her, but when she returned, we were both over twenty, and I could tell she was my true mate—male dragon-shifters can tell after their twentieth birthday, but not females. So I approached Charlie and told her point-blank, knowing she preferred the truth."

Sarah nodded. "Aye, my brother would've liked a warning that Cat was his true mate, but frustratingly for Cat, her dragon couldn't tell before they kissed."

"It's definitely a risk when it's a female dragon-shifter and a human male. The same thing happened to Nikki, although it worked out for her and Rafe in the end."

"So what happened next with Charlie?"

He moved his gaze from the trio of boys to Sarah for a second. There was no jealousy or irritation in her eyes from him discussing his late mate, only curiosity.

And it was yet another thing he liked about her. Because a life never talking about Charlie, never giving Elliott the memories he desperately wanted to hear about, would tear Hudson in two.

His dragon spoke up. *Yes, yes, that's all well and good. Just talk with her. It brings us one step closer to claiming her as our mate and taking her to bed.*

Hudson resisted rolling his eyes at his dragon. After all, most inner beasts had a one-track mind when it came to sex.

Moving his gaze back to the boys to keep an eye on them as they walked toward their final destination, he continued, "Charlie said she'd always wanted to kiss me too. However, before it could happen, she wanted to lay down some conditions. Because even though she knew I supported her, she was still afraid that I'd demand she give up her job as a Protector once our child was born. All mate-claim frenzies result in pregnancy, so it wasn't her being paranoid or anything, but rather being quite practical about it all." He chuckled. "I know it doesn't sound all that romantic, but her method of handling it all charmed me in its own way."

Sarah murmured, "Realizing the importance of

being honest is something I wished I'd learned long before I married."

His curiosity piqued at her statement, but as her face shuttered and she put up whatever walls Sarah used to protect herself, Hudson decided that was a conversation for another day.

Instead, he finished his story about Charlie. Strangely, the more he told Sarah, the less painful it had become, and the more he enjoyed reliving the happier times he'd had with his mate. "Charlie and I mated. Nine months later we had Elliott, and life was good for almost six years total. My deepest regret was twofold. The first being how I didn't enjoy every day I had with her when I had the chance."

He paused, his years of wishing he would've done so bubbling up to the surface again. How he should've said he loved her more, found ways to make her laugh more, treasured her body in the way he should've always done instead of getting comfortable and taking it for granted.

Loss had caused the greatest heartbreak of his life, but it'd also taught him one of his most important lessons—don't always assume tomorrow will be there.

Sarah's voice brought him back as she asked, "And the other?"

Clearing this throat, he answered, "That Elliott didn't truly get to know his mum as he should have. He was five when she died, and his memory of her is hazy at best. Charlie didn't have any siblings, either, and her parents are gone too. So Elliott can't even make a connection to his late mum via her family. I think I'm afraid he'll forget her, and Charlie deserves so much better than that."

"I can't claim to know what it's like to lose someone so dear, but if I had, I think someone talking about them would keep them alive, aye? Do you do that with your son?"

He nodded. "I try to do that more now than in the first year or so of mourning. It was simply too hard for me and for him back then."

Hudson had done what needed to be done to see his son through it. And talking about Charlie in the first few months would've broken him, most likely.

His dragon tried to soothe him, but it was Sarah's small hand brushing and then wrapping around his fingers that helped ease the memories about his early days of grief.

Strange how a female he barely knew could do that to him, but then again, they'd always had some sort of unusual connection from the beginning.

Sarah said softly, "Keep doing that, telling Elliott memories of his mum, and he'll appreciate it. And through the two of you, Charlie will live on."

He dared a glance at Sarah, and despite all of her trials in life, he saw how she was trying to comfort him, trying to empathize.

If he'd wanted to claim her before, he wanted to do it tenfold now.

Afraid he might do something rash, like kiss the female trying to understand his past burdens—it'd been a long time since he'd had any sort of partner to do that—Hudson released her hand and focused back on the boys ahead. "Elliott will be fine, I know that. It's his nature to keep moving forward, no matter what. Although given the way Mark is still glaring at me, I'm a bit worried about him."

Sarah sighed. "It's odd since neither lad was close to their father—Rob always had better things to do than spend time with his children, unless he was shouting at them—but Mark has created some sort of rosy picture of how life used to be and clings to that. I try to talk to him and his teachers to find out if there's anything I can do. But Mark doesn't like change, has held out hope I'll marry his football coach, and will act impulsively if he's in a temper. He's a huge part of why I tried to find another way to stay on Lochguard at first."

Even though he had no intention of giving up on Sarah or her sons, he still asked, "The solicitor still hasn't found another way for you to keep living with the dragon-shifters?"

She shook her head. "No. Hayley really thinks that the law will have to change before humans can live with a dragon clan, willy-nilly. It's quite different for someone like, say, Kaylee MacDonald, who is a single human woman on Lochguard. At least there's a chance she could mate a dragon-shifter, not to mention she doesn't have children, human or otherwise. But human children are a different thing entirely, especially from a PR perspective, according to Hayley. Whilst things are better, quite a few people will remember the rumors of how dragons would steal children and keep them as slaves, or whatever shite people have come up with over the years."

Elliott ran the last few feet to the lake ahead, and he waved back at them. Hudson returned the gesture and added, "I really do hope it will change one day." He switched his gaze to Sarah. "But for now, I still want you as my mate, Sarah. So don't give up hope about staying with a dragon clan for as long as you like."

Before she could create an excuse, he grabbed her hand and picked up their pace until they joined the three boys in setting up their picnic and then enjoying the sunshine, and food, and water nearby.

Chapter Seven

A short time later, Sarah sat with Joey on the ground, keeping an eye on Mark playing football with Elliott, and waited for Hudson to come back in his dragon form.

Despite the year they'd spent on Lochguard, Sarah was still a wee bit uneasy about casual nudity. It came more from her own insecurities than anything else, but Hudson hadn't blinked an eye when she'd suggested it would be best for him to shift just beyond the hill and come back to the lake in his dragon form.

The more she learned about him, the more Hudson seemed to be such a decent man. Well, dragonman.

But despite the fact he could shift into a large beast and could easily crush her with his talons, or jaw, or even drop her from some great height to her death, she felt far more comfortable around him than she ever had with her ex-husband.

For most people, that would be a positive. But such comfort and feeling of ease only made her that much warier.

Because she still couldn't believe such a good, sexy, and kind man would want to shackle himself to her.

Before she could reinforce her mantra of "Stop it, Sarah," Joey laid his notebook on her lap, garnering her attention. She noted the words *Hudson Wells* written at the top of the page, but apart from a few usual markers of "dragon color, markings, clan, and personality," the rest of it remained blank. Joey tapped the empty page on the opposite side, "Should I add a page for Elliott too?"

She glanced at her youngest. "I'm not sure he can fully shift yet, and if so, you can't really add much information, aye?"

Joey shook his head. "Elliott said he can't change completely. But he's still a dragon-shifter and should have a page."

Sarah saw this as an opportunity to talk semi-privately with Joey about Hudson and Elliott, so she asked casually, "Do you like Elliott?"

Joey nodded. "He's nice. And he shares heaps about dragons."

"Like what?"

"Well, like how he talks to his. And how it's like

having a best friend in your head all the time. I asked if Stonefire was different and I could get a dragon for me, but he said no. Still, he didn't laugh at me. Instead he said he'd let me talk to his, once he's better at it."

Of her two lads, Joey was the one who had embraced the dragon-shifters with everything he had. "That's good of him." She paused a beat and blurted, "And what about Hudson?"

Joey looked around as if wishing the dragon would show up. "I think he's nice. Is he your new friend?"

Friend. Is that all she wanted of Hudson? Friendship?

A resounding no screamed through her head.

But it wasn't as if she would embrace her desires or hopes of more in front of her son. So Sarah cleared her throat and replied, "He's my friend, but he wants to be my mate. You know, marry me."

"If you did, I could see his dragon all the time, right? Because that would be brilliant. I'd like that."

She bit back a smile. Joey was easily won over, which she was grateful for. It was Mark who would be the harder one to convince.

But before she could do much more than glance at her older son and see him kicking the ball to Elliott, a dark shadow came over them, and in the next instant, a dragon slowly descended to the grass not far away, his wings causing a gust to blow over them.

Once on the ground, the large, black dragon folded its wings against its back and lowered to all four limbs.

Elliott waved and shouted, "Do the trick, Dad!"

As the sun glinted off Hudson's scales, Sarah's breath hitched. Not out of fear, but at how gorgeous he was in his dragon form. He was tall and well-formed with slightly shiny scales, a long snout, and eyes that, despite being so much bigger, held the same kindness as when Hudson was in his human form.

Joey jumped up. "I want to see the trick, Hudson!"

Sarah stood, and Hudson stared at her a beat, gently nodded at her, and then jumped back into the air. The rush of wind whipped around her, but only for a second.

She and Joey watched as Hudson flapped his wings to raise a little higher and then plunged down toward the deepest part of the lake. His body broke the surface with a giant splash, and then nothing.

She searched the surface, unsure of how long a dragon could stay underwater. That hadn't exactly been part of her dragon-shifter education thus far.

But then Hudson's large black form sprung from the water, somersaulted once, and then dove back down again.

Joey laughed as Hudson did it a few more times before he finally jumped into the air and rose back into the sky. After a few circles in the air, he slowly maneuvered to the grassy patch again and landed. When he lowered his head, Elliott said, "That means you should approach him."

Joey didn't hesitate and ran toward the giant dragon faintly glinting in the sun, revealing a hint of iridescence to the black scales. Mark held back a beat, but Elliott said something, and he also headed toward Hudson.

Sarah followed, although as Hudson stared at her, she suddenly felt shy and awkward. Not only was the dragonman fit and kind in his human form, but he could also transform into such a beautiful beast.

Why would he want her?

Hudson grunted and motioned with a forelimb for her to come closer. Taking a deep breath, Sarah did her best to push aside her negativity and took one step and then another until she finally stood near Hudson's head.

She gingerly raised a hand, wanting to feel his scales, and Hudson moved his snout until it gently made contact with her fingers.

While her brother's in-laws had tried their best to get her to touch their dragon forms and even do silly things like slide down their sides, she'd always held back, apart from a quick touch to Cat's scales a few months ago. As much as she wanted to trust the

MacAllisters, they were Lachlan's new family, not hers.

But with Hudson, touching his smooth, warm scales was more a need than a curiosity. This was a huge part of him, of the man who had kissed her like she was beautiful. A man who had lost love and found a way to do his best for his son.

A man she desperately wanted to trust wholeheartedly.

Not that her briefly held hopes lasted long before Mark crossed his arms and kicked a rock on the ground. "Coach Jamie's a better dragon. He's a brilliant blue and not a dull black."

Sarah had been—and still was—glad that Mark had a positive male role model in his life. But her son's constant attempts to force a match between her and a dragonman nearly a decade her junior was a wee bit irritating.

Still, Sarah took a deep breath and moved closer to Mark before saying, "Aye, Jamie is a fine dragon, but so is Hudson. He's a bit taller and broader through the shoulders. And his hide is more than pure black, if you look close enough."

Mark didn't bother to look as he dug the tip of his shoe into the ground. "It's just black and dull."

Thankfully Joey had finished his walk around Hudson and stood near them again. "He's not just black. There's a gray spot on his tail."

They all looked over, and sure enough, there was a wee spot of gray at the very tip of Hudson's tail.

Elliott had heard and jumped in. "That's from an old injury. It's why we have to be careful with our tails. They're hard to control sometimes, so my dad says, and if it gets burned too badly, the color can change a little after it heals."

Sarah frowned. "Your dad was burned badly?"

She glanced at Hudson's eyes, and he nodded. But since dragons couldn't speak in their dragon forms, Elliott picked up the explanation. "Him and his mates were trying to help with a local fire. Sometimes dragons will carry water and dump it, especially when the fire brigade is really far away. He was young but wanted to help." Elliott shrugged. "He got too close and was burned really badly. That's why I had to promise not to fly too close to a fire before the teachers say it's okay."

While Sarah had known that dragon-shifter parents had a great many things to worry about that humans never thought twice on, it was slowly becoming apparent what being a stepmother to a dragon-shifter boy would entail.

Or, if she mated Hudson and they did have a child, parent to a dragon-shifter.

Not that she was going to think of more children. Bloody hell, she couldn't even get her eldest son to be nice to Hudson. A new child would throw him off even more.

Hudson flapped a wing to get his son's attention, and after some sort of nonverbal exchange, Elliott turned back to them. "Let's go back to the blanket. Dad's going to shift back and join us."

Unable to resist, Sarah put out a hand and gently stroked his hide once more. She wanted to see him a bit longer in his dragon form and maybe touch his tail, or wings, or all the places she'd never really had the chance to stroke before.

But as Mark stomped off, she drew back her hand, gave Hudson one last glance, and herded the lads back to the blanket.

The distance helped, especially as she tried to soothe Mark's ruffled feathers a bit.

Because every time she was near Hudson, it became harder to walk away.

And that scared her to death.

Chapter Eight

Hudson had wanted to stay longer near the lake, trying his best to get to know Sarah's sons, but he and Sarah had an appointment with Bram that couldn't be postponed.

They'd both barely had time to get their kids back, talk to them briefly, and each make their way to Bram's house, separately, as the clan leader had asked them to do.

But as Hudson knocked on Bram's front door, he wondered why they'd been kept apart.

His dragon spoke up quickly. *Probably so Bram or Evie can talk to each of us in turn.*

But Sarah and I haven't even had a chance to talk privately since the outing with all the kids.

Yes, but I'm sure Bram's interested to hear all about it.

The door opened, revealing Bram's mate, Evie Marshall, holding their youngest son in her arms.

She smiled at Hudson. "Hello, you're a little early, but come on in."

He'd barely stepped inside, the door shutting behind him when Bram and Evie's eldest son, Murray, ran past.

Evie sighed. "Murray, what did we say about running in the hall?"

The boy skid to a halt, turned and grinned.

Hudson did his best to bite back a smile. The entire clan knew the boy was a charmer, even if he wasn't yet old enough to go to school.

Murray said, "I dash, not run."

Evie rolled her eyes. "Dashing is running. Who taught you that word?"

"Daisy said dashing is okay."

Evie quickly glanced at Hudson. "Can you take Gideon and wait in the living room? I need to have a quick chat with my son, one that addresses loopholes. Well, the best I can with someone his age, at any rate."

Hudson took the sleeping infant carefully so as to not wake up the baby. He kept his voice soft as he said to Gideon, "Let's give your mum a break."

Hudson smiled at Evie and then watched as she gently took Murray's hand and guided him upstairs.

He finally snorted and went to the empty living room. Gideon stirred a bit, and Hudson swayed gently until he settled.

It'd been a long time since he'd held a baby. His

brothers' children were long past that age and were all older than five now.

Studying the small baby, he noticed how Gideon's hair was reddish compared to Elliott's dark hair. But he still reminded Hudson so much of his son—both were good-tempered babies who didn't really care who held them, as long as someone did.

And for a split second, he wondered what it would be like to have another child. He and Charlie had been talking of trying again right before she was killed.

But then that chance had been ripped away before they could even start it.

Not for the first time, Hudson wished he could have a bit more time alone with Sarah. Even if she didn't want more children, he'd still mate her. But it would be nice to ask some more questions, get to know her, and most definitely kiss her again.

His dragon spoke up. *Yes, yes, we need to kiss her again before she gives an answer. Maybe we can get her alone and make her come on our tongue.*

Before Hudson's mind could linger too long on that fantasy—wondering if Sarah would be even more responsive with her clothes off and pussy exposed to his touch than with her clothes on—Bram walked into the room and smiled at Gideon in Hudson's arms. "I sometimes think it's good our third child is the easiest to handle, given how headstrong the other two are turning out to be. I can take him if you want."

Hudson shook his head. "It's fine. He's asleep, and I don't want to risk waking him."

Bram nodded. "Aye, I suppose you're right. But we need to talk in private, so let's head to my office."

Everyone on Stonefire knew the way to Bram's office. Not because they'd all done something worth a scold, but rather Bram tried to talk to each of his clan members in turn, when he could fit in the visits.

Hudson had been by more than most, though, because of offering his name to be Sarah's mate as well as for some top secret IT projects he'd worked on with the clan's cyber security experts, Nate and Lucien.

Once they were in Bram's office, the door closed. After they'd both sat down on either side of the large desk, Bram leaned back in his chair and raised his brows. "You know what I'm going to ask, so let's get to it—how are things with Sarah?"

Gideon stirred, and Hudson readjusted his hold before answering, "If it were up to me? I'd mate her today. But her eldest son seems bent on living on Lochguard and doesn't want anything to do with me."

Bram tapped his fingers on his desk. "But the youngest is fine?"

"It seems so. He actually keeps a journal of dragon-shifter sketches and notes. I think he'd be happy with any dragon clan. And before you ask, Elliott likes them all. It's no secret he's wanted siblings and a mum for years. I could mate an eighty-year-old grandma, and he'd probably find the positive in it."

Bram snorted. "Maybe so, although I doubt she'd be as nice in your bed as the human female."

A growl rose in Hudson's throat. "Don't think about Sarah naked in bed."

As soon as the words came out, Hudson mentally cursed. He knew Bram was happily mated, would never look at another female besides Evie, and yet he hadn't liked another male thinking such things.

His dragon spoke up. *Because she should be ours. Naked in our bed, crying out our name, digging her nails into our back as we pound into her hot pussy.*

Hudson barely prevented a mental image of just that, not wanting to give away even more of his quickly growing possessiveness of Sarah to Bram.

His clan leader finally cleared his throat and spoke again. "I can see you want a true mating. But if Sarah doesn't want it, that could be a very long, lonely, and frustrating existence, Hudson. And given what you went through with Charlie, you deserve better than that."

With most people, he hated when people brought up Charlie in that tone of voice—like they were trying to be gentle, afraid he'd break.

But with Bram, he knew it was more than that.

No, his clan leader just wanted the best for him and didn't want Hudson to suffer further with the wrong mate.

Hudson finally replied, "You can talk to Sarah yourself, of course, and determine what you will. Although I'd like another few days to try and woo her properly. I think she wants at least the physical aspect of a mating as well but tries to deny it."

Hudson had his own ideas as to why she held back, given some of her past comments, but he didn't want to raise them with Bram when he hadn't even discussed them in-depth with Sarah yet.

Bram stared at him with eyes that could always see more than most, before he finally stood, walked over, and reached for his son. Once Hudson had transferred Gideon, he also stood just as Bram replied, "Aye, of course I'll talk to Sarah. But I won't have an answer for you about if I think it's a good idea for you two to mate or not until after I do."

He didn't hesitate to ask, "Is there a way I could have a little bit of time alone with Sarah before you talk to her?"

Bram raised his brows. "Will it help at all?"

"With what I have in mind, it could, I think."

It just might make Sarah realize a few things she kept denying. Not to mention he could ensure she knew how desirable she was. A fact she seemed not to agree with after so many years with the bastard ex.

Bram studied him a beat and shrugged. "I don't

see why not. Although if your mind works like mine, don't do that in my house. She should be waiting in the living room. Take her to the empty guest cottage a few houses down. It should be unlocked."

He nodded. "Thank you."

He turned toward the door, but Bram's voice stopped him from leaving. "And Hudson?" He turned and met Bram's gaze again. "Be careful with her. If you push too far too quickly, my guess is that she'll run."

He bobbed his head and managed to hold his tongue.

Of course he knew Sarah had gone through hell, better than most, he'd guess, given what she'd told him so far.

But as he approached the doorway to the living room, he stopped, took a deep breath, and willed any lingering irritation away. He wouldn't always hide such things from her, but his irritation was at Bram, not Sarah, and he didn't want to spook her.

Especially not before he tried to convince her of how much he wanted her.

So with a smile, he entered the room. Sarah sat on the sofa, plucking the hem of her top. "Evie said you were already here. Is it my turn then?"

He put out a hand to hers. "Not quite yet. Bram gave us some time alone before that. Will you come with me, Sarah?"

She stared at his outstretched hand, and he

waited. Pushing, or begging, or coaxing wouldn't work. He had a sense that for too long, Sarah hadn't had much control over her life.

But in this, he could give it.

Even if his dragon snarled and paced inside his head, wanting him to toss Sarah over their shoulder and cart her away like a marauder with his spoils, Hudson kept control over his beast and waited.

SARAH HAD SAT in Bram and Evie's living room, trying to sort out her thoughts to what she knew Bram would ask when Hudson appeared in the doorway.

Every argument she'd made about how Mark wanted to live on Lochguard, how she could stomach mating a dragonman she didn't feel attracted to or connected with so that Mark could stay with the clan he loved, fled her mind.

Because just the sight of Hudson's tall, fit form made her jaw drop a fraction. The sight of his broad chest made her wonder if he had any hair there.

And what would it feel like to have his strong arms around her or his muscled stomach under her as she rode him.

What it would be like to wake up next to him, his steady presence never in doubt, nor his desire to take care of not only his son but hers as well.

Maybe if she hadn't been fooled into believing she cared for someone so quickly with her ex—a façade that had cracked within weeks of her marriage—she would've explored it more.

However, as she dredged up the courage to stand and go talk with Bram, Hudson said he wanted to spend time alone. When he asked her point-blank to go with him, she didn't instantly place her hand in his. She couldn't risk being foolish with her sons to think of. So she cleared her throat and asked, "Why?"

Hudson kept his hand outstretched. "Because I saw how torn you were over Mark earlier, how patient you were with him, as if soothing him was all that mattered. And whilst it does matter a great deal, I think you keep forgetting a very important part when it comes to mating a dragon-shifter so you can protect your sons."

His intense gaze made her squirm in her seat. "Which is?"

He lowered his hand but leaned over, closer to her, as he whispered, "That your needs are important too. And I can keep working on Mark to gain his trust. But only if you will acknowledge what you want is just as vital a consideration too." He lightly ran the back of his knuckles down her cheek, and she drew in a breath as heat shot through her body. "Come with me, Sarah, and let me remind you of how what you want, what you need, are important factors in your decision. And if given the chance, I can be the protection you need, the stepfather your boys deserve, and the male you should share your bed with."

As Hudson's pupils flashed, she shivered at both the desire in his eyes and what he'd just said.

She'd long ago thought she'd never find a worthy bloke, one who not only cared about her children but also wanted her for her. Not to gain an inheritance, or to win a bet, or even just to have a body conveniently on hand to fuck when needed.

Her first instinct was to call Hudson out on his bullshit. That he couldn't want her as much as he said, that there had to be some ulterior motive to his pursuit.

Yet as his gaze bore into hers, his pupils flashing faster, she wondered if maybe, just maybe, he did find her attractive. That he wanted her for more than to be a mother to his son.

That maybe, if she could find a way to convince Mark to give Hudson a chance, she could have something closer to what her brother had.

Oh, not a true mate pairing, as she'd kissed Hudson without a mate-claim frenzy. But a closeness she'd always yearned for, a best friend, a man who made her wet with a simple glance, one she wanted to jump and devour, one who got hard for her without trying to explain away how it was her fault he couldn't.

One who could love her.

The last thought made her wince, and she quickly pushed it aside. Wanting love only made her do stupid things that indubitably brought her pain later on. She knew better. After all, she'd learned a hard lesson with Rob, who had professed to love her, but later laughed about how easily she'd eaten up his every word.

Hudson stroked her cheek again, and she met his gaze once more, and all thoughts of her ex vanished. He murmured, "Come with me, Sarah. Even if it's only to tell me what made you wince, that's fine. I won't press you to do anything you don't want to do. But I think we could both do with some adult time, free of children and clan leader interrogations."

If only Hudson wasn't being so bloody nice to her, she'd think of another excuse.

And yet, she was tired of doing just that, of fighting the pull she couldn't seem to push away when it came to this dragonman.

After all, a little time with him shouldn't be so bad. It wasn't as if he was leading her on a walk to her execution, or doom, or some other ridiculous notion.

So she finally sighed and nodded. "Aye, let's go. Although I-I don't know if we'll do more than talk."

He stood, reached for her hand, and then he smiled broadly when she didn't jerk it away.

She was overly aware of his strong, firm fingers wrapped around hers. How they made her feel safe instead of worried about how much taller and stronger he was than her.

Hudson gently tugged her toward the door as he stated, "As I said, I won't force you to do anything you don't want to do." He leaned over and murmured for her ears only. "But I'm not above giving a nudge to see if you want the same as me."

Since they were now outside, she swallowed and grew a wee bit bolder. "And what do you want to do?"

He didn't miss a beat. His intense flashing eyes focused on her. "Devour you slowly until you come on my tongue and then lap at your orgasm, memorizing your taste, before kissing you to remind you of what I'd just done."

She shivered, in a good way, as wetness rushed between her thighs. Never before in her life had she'd been so turned on by a man.

And a hushed what-if raced through her mind, making her wonder how different her life would've been if she'd met someone like Hudson instead of Rob.

Stop it, Sarah. The past couldn't be changed. But this time, with her future on the line, she wanted to be more, so much more. Bolder, more confident, more forward—all those things she'd learned to hide first in childhood to avoid her father's notice and later to avoid Rob's poisonous words.

Taking a deep breath, she somehow found the

strength to retort, "You seem fairly confident that you can do all that. Unless dragon-shifters have some kind of magic saliva, it's not so easy to make a woman come."

He smiled slowly, in the smug way men did sometimes when it came to sex. "Seeing as you came with your clothes on, I can only imagine how much you'll squirm for me when they're off. I don't have magic saliva, but my tongue has a magic of its own."

Her nipples ached at his words, wanting his mouth, his teeth, his tongue to torture her slowly, to make her come hard and scream his name.

Which, of course, made her squirm as her pussy throbbed in anticipation.

Seriously, Hudson made her as randy as a girl with her first lover.

So absorbed in their wordplay, Sarah had barely noticed how they stopped in front of a door. "Who lives here?"

His pupils flashed. "No one. It's just for us."

Before she could open her mouth, Hudson tugged her inside, shut and locked the door, and pierced her with his gray-eyed gaze, pupils flashing to remind her that this wasn't just a man but a dragonman.

That fact didn't scare her. If anything, over the last two days, it'd only made her more curious.

He murmured, "Come. We have much to discuss."

Sarah expected him to lean in, kiss her, or maybe push her against the door as he caressed her breast.

But he merely smiled, turned, and walked down the hallway.

Disappointment coursed through her, but then she remembered how she'd said she only wanted to talk. So talk they would.

Although as she made her way down the hall and followed Hudson into the sparsely furnished living room, her heart rate kicked up, and a battle raged inside her.

Because as he sat on the sofa and stared up at her with heat in his eyes, she wanted to do more than talk.

And yet, she couldn't just give in to that. She had her sons, her future, everything on the line.

Of course, there was one in-between option. She was merely horny, that was all. Maybe if she embraced that and had a quick fuck, then she could get him out of her system.

Aye, that might be the best option. It'd been a long time since she'd had sex, even longer since it was with a man who didn't berate her for her body, her lack of skill, or a million other faults Rob had pointed out on a regular basis.

She could fuck Hudson once, clear her head, and tell Bram that she would go back to Lochguard to find someone there so her sons wouldn't be uprooted yet again.

Plan formed, Sarah walked over to Hudson and sat next to him, close enough that her leg touched his.

But her sudden confidence faded. She didn't know how to do this, how to seduce someone.

And for a split second, it felt wrong somehow to try and take advantage of the dragonman.

However, Hudson reached for her, dragged her into his lap, and said, "Tell me what you want, Sarah. Just ask, and it's yours."

As she searched his gaze, some of her confidence returned at the desire burning there. Maybe she could do this.

Pushing aside her lingering doubts about being able to have sex once with this man and walk away, she gingerly laid a hand on his chest. He sucked in a breath, and the sound finally gave her the courage to say, "Kiss me, Hudson. Just kiss me and see where it goes from there."

And so he cupped her cheek, brought her face to his, and did exactly that.

Chapter Nine

Hudson watched Sarah's internal struggle. The more time he spent with her, the easier it became to read her tells and expressions.

She tended to bite her lip when she was nervous about something. She also plucked some part of her clothing when unsure of herself.

But when she finally looked at him and straightened her shoulders a bit, he knew she'd made a decision. The hard part was not ripping off her clothes, tossing her on the sofa, and having his way with her too quickly.

His dragon sighed. *This is all so fucking annoying. Her arousal scents the air, her nipples are hard, and she keeps glancing at our mouth. She wants us, so take her.*

She's human, not dragon-shifter. She needs a bit more finesse.

His beast growled. *Then do it already, for fuck's sake.*

His human finally sat down next to him and pressed her leg to his. Hudson had fully planned on sitting here and talking about whatever she wanted, to ease her fears, calm her, coax her to trust him.

But the urge—no, need—to touch overrode his caution, and he hauled her into his lap, blurting out his question about what she wanted. The second she placed her hand on his chest, blood rushed straight to his cock, and all he could think about was her delicate hands on his body, caressing his skin, stroking his dick.

And when she said, "Kiss me, Hudson. Just kiss me and see where it goes from there," his control snapped, and he dragged her face to his, crushing his lips against hers.

At the contact, fire flashed through his body. He wanted more and probed her lips, growling when she parted to let him in.

Pushing inside her mouth, he groaned at her heat, her taste, at the hesitant way she kissed him back.

For all her years of marriage and two children, this female almost seemed innocent when it came to true passion.

Not wanting to ruin it with growls and snarls about her useless ex, he threaded his hand through her hair and changed the angle of her head, giving him greater access to plunder, and explore, and coax out the soft moans that made his dick harder by the second.

And the second she wrapped her arms around his neck, pressing closer against him, he needed to feel some of her skin.

Never breaking the kiss, he moved his free hand to the hem of her top and slowly ran his fingers across her lower back. For a second, Sarah stilled. But then she arched into his touch, and Hudson ran his fingers up her spine, caressing her warm skin, until he reached the clasp of her bra. Breaking the kiss, he murmured, "Let me feel more of you, Sarah." He lightly traced the band of her bra. "Tell me I can remove this."

She lightly dug her nails into the fabric of his shirt and moved her head back a fraction. At first, he thought she might bolt.

But then she nodded. "Aye."

His dragon roared, wanting to see her pert nipples and torture them slowly.

However, Hudson knew he needed to move a bit slower to not spook her. So he flicked the clasps and let it fall open, stroking the exposed skin of her spine in slow circles, loving how Sarah sucked in a breath, the scent of her arousal growing stronger.

She whispered, "How can a few touches make me so hot?"

He smiled and continued to stroke her back. "It's all part of the anticipation, Sarah. Sometimes hard,

and quick, and fast is fantastic. And other times..."
His voice trailed off as he moved his hand slowly
around her ribcage, until he traced the bottom edge
of her bra cup, only teasing the soft skin underneath.
"Drawing it out makes it more powerful, prolongs the
need, and makes you come harder at the end of it."

She bit her bottom lip, and he imagined his teeth
doing the same. However, he wanted to draw this
out, make Sarah squirm, and show her how good
they could be together.

Daring to pull one of her bra cups down, he
circled her nipple but never touched the hard point.
Sarah's breathing grew even more labored, and when
he finally tweaked her taut nipple with his thumb and
forefinger, she cried out.

He was just about to do the same to her other
breast when she asked softly, "But why would you do
all this? I can feel your hard cock under my arse.
Why not fuck me quickly and chase your orgasm?"

The tone of her voice said this wasn't a type of
talk to get him further hot and bothered. She was
truly puzzled, as if no male had ever thought her
coming was important.

Not wanting to beat around the bush, he asked,
"Didn't your ex-husband ever make you come before
he did?"

She glanced away and shrugged.

Anger coursed through his body, his dragon
roaring at Sarah's answer. His beast hissed, *The*

arsehole. Now we definitely need to make her come. Several times. Until she realizes how she deserves it as much as any male does.

I agree, but let me do this my way.

His dragon acquiesced, probably because even his beast could sense how sexually neglected Sarah had been in her marriage. Hell, probably for her entire life.

Dragon-shifters prided themselves on sharing pleasure. After all, watching a female come apart in his arms, screaming his name, only made Hudson's own orgasm that much stronger.

He was going to have to teach her that too.

But first, he needed to ensure she didn't spook or put distance between them again. Because this seemed to be a pivotal moment, almost as if Sarah could realize how Hudson wouldn't neglect her, that her happiness and enjoyment were just as important as the well-being of her sons, and only then she might finally agree to mate him.

Lightly running his fingernail over her firm nipple, he asked, "Will you let me undress you and show you what I mean about how drawing it out can be more powerful in the end?"

She finally met his gaze again, searching, as if trying to decide whether she could bare herself to him in such a way.

He gently brushed hair off her face and said, "I want to see you cry out under my fingers and my tongue. It will be all about you, and only you, this time to prove how much I enjoy it even without plunging my cock into your pussy. Will you give me the chance, Sarah?"

After what seemed like hours but was merely a few seconds, she nodded, and both man and beast mentally roared in delight.

And without waiting another second, he changed their position so that Sarah sat on the sofa and he kneeled before her.

"Ready?"

She said so softly he barely heard it. "Aye."

"Then let's get started."

SARAH'S HEART thundered in her chest as she still tried to come to terms with what she'd agreed to.

On the surface, letting Hudson kiss her, and suck her, and probably lick between her thighs wasn't a huge deal. She'd lost her virginity at seventeen and had been married for nearly a decade.

But Rob had never cared if she were wet, let alone if she ever came. If he could even get hard for her, he kept a bottle of lube so he could do the deed, flop on his back, and fall asleep. She'd been better than some sex toy or his hand, as he'd always said. And as much as she'd hated it, she's soon learned that it was easier to just lie there and let him fuck her than to argue or ask for more.

Ridiculously it had been much like days of old, when women had lain there and thought of England to do their duty.

Oh, she knew it could be better. She'd had a few passion-filled times before Rob. And even the first couple months with her ex had been okay.

But none of those men had ever looked at Sarah like Hudson did, as if she were the greatest treat he could ever want, one he desperately wanted to devour. A woman he wanted to caress, push to her limits, and make sure orgasmed before he found his own.

She'd heard a few things about dragon-shifters, especially from the humans on Lochguard, about how they treasured their mates in all ways. But never in a million years had Sarah thought she'd be on the receiving end of such focus, especially with a dragonman who wasn't her true mate.

Yet as Hudson kneeled in front of her, his pupils flashing rapidly, his palms caressing her upper thighs over her jeans, everything but the dark-haired dragonman faded from her mind.

His hands moved to the bottom of her top, and he slowly lifted, kissing her belly as he exposed the flesh, and continued trailing his lips upward until he reached her collarbone and tugged the material over her head. With the shirt gone, her bra easily came off next, and Hudson stared at her tits for a few beats.

It took everything she had not to cover them. She was small, and not even pregnancy had done much for them. She'd never thought much about her chest when she was younger, but it had been Rob's favorite thing to sneer at, degrade, and had done his best to convince her she wasn't feminine enough for any man.

And yet, Hudson's gaze was heated as he stared. He pressed his palm to her nipple and rubbed in slow circles, banishing her worries. Gone were thoughts of how lacking she was, replaced by pleasure that shot straight to her pussy.

When Hudson removed his hand, she nearly drew it back. But after a quick glance to her eyes and licking his lips, he moved down and nuzzled the soft skin of her breast. She moaned at his late-day whiskers and how they tickled in just the right way.

Nuzzling wasn't enough, and Hudson kissed around one tit and then the other, but never touching her nipples. Each warm, wet flick of his tongue against her skin kicked up the temperature in the room, made her nipples ache, her pussy throb, and she eventually squirmed.

He nuzzled one of her taut peaks with his nose as he murmured, "Dusky pink and ruched points. Now I know what they look like, but what about the taste?"

Never breaking eye contact, he sucked her nipple

into his mouth. Hard. And Sarah raised a hand to his hair as she cried out, the sensation making her arch, wanting more than just his mouth on her breast. She wanted his cock inside her while he did it.

Before she could even debate if she could ask such a thing, Hudson nibbled lightly before releasing her hard bud and blowing on it. She murmured, "Fuck," and he chuckled.

Hudson purred, "Time to give the other the same attention."

As he sucked, and nibbled, and drove her crazy, Sarah closed her eyes and reveled in the pleasure, the heat, the sensation surging through her body, culminating in her clit pulsing for attention.

Never before had she felt on edge without ever rubbing between her thighs.

Then she felt fingers pressing against the seam of her jeans, right over her clit, and Sarah opened her eyes as she moaned. Hudson stopped torturing her breasts long enough to say, "Let's make sure your pussy is nice and wet for me before I eat you, hm?"

His mouth crashed down against her, and his fingers stroked, and rubbed, and brought her oh so close. Needing to feel more of his skin, she grabbed his arms, digging her nails and moving her hips against his caresses.

His free hand gently tugged her hair as his other hand pressed harder against her clit, and Sarah screamed, pleasure rushing through her body as an orgasm crashed over her. Wave after wave of intense feeling coursed through her, relaxing her, making her feel as if she were floating somewhere high in the clouds.

She had no idea how long she floated, but when her cunt finally stopped pulsing, she slumped back against the sofa, her eyes trained on Hudson's face. He grinned slowly as he leaned forward to kiss her.

This time it was slow and gentle, almost like a tender caress.

Before she could panic about how much she wanted that sort of kiss every day, his hands moved to the waistband of her jeans. "I want to taste you, Sarah. Tell me I can fuck your pussy with my tongue and then taste your orgasm as you come again."

Even though she'd just experienced the most powerful orgasm of her life, her lower lips throbbed, wanting more than a touch through clothing.

And to have his tongue and lips on her already sensitive clitoris? Oh, aye, she wanted that as well.

Besides, the point of this encounter was to get Hudson Wells out of her system. One orgasm wasn't nearly enough to do that. And, technically, she hadn't fucked him yet.

She brushed some of the hair off his forehead as she replied, "Aye, do it."

His pupils flashed as he growled and he had her jeans off in record time. Her underwear soon followed, until he pushed her thighs wide and merely took a second to stare at her fully exposed flesh.

When he said nothing, all the years of insults and insecurities came back. She wasn't some perfectly waxed porn star who'd had surgery to make everything tight and tidy.

But then Hudson growled again and said, "You're so bloody beautiful," and leaned down to lick her from her slit all the way to her clit, and she forgot about everything but his touch.

WATCHING Sarah arch against his fingers had been fantastic, but at his first lick, Hudson groaned and delved his tongue deeper into her pussy, wanting more of her taste, more of her sweetness coating him.

Just as he'd thought, she was even more responsive with nothing between him and her cunt. She arched, and cried out, and tugged his head closer, almost as if she were afraid he'd leave her before she could come again.

His dragon spoke. *Hurry and make her come. I want to fuck her too, slap her arse as I pound in from behind, and later have her mark our skin as we drive her crazy yet again.*

Soon enough, dragon. Now, shut it.

His beast complied as Hudson better tilted Sarah's hips to open her more to his attentions.

Fuck, as he lapped, and licked, and thrust, he couldn't drink enough of her honey. Her taste alone made him hard as a rock, to the point he might come in his trousers.

But he willed his balls to settle and moved his lips to her clit. A quick swipe with his tongue told him she was still sensitive from before, which meant it wouldn't take much to push her over the edge again.

Suckling her clit between his lips, Sarah went wild beneath him, digging her nails into his scalp, and moved her hips as if she needed him to suck harder, to nibble, to drive her wild.

He'd more than drawn this out, so he did just that, carefully adding two fingers inside her pussy. As he fucked her with his fingers and lightly nibbled her clit, she finally came apart with a cry. And as her cunt milked him, he continued to slowly torture her clit with licks and suckles, drawing out her orgasm to the point that had to hover between pain and pleasure.

Sarah finally relaxed back into the cushions, her fingers loosening in his hair and her voice husky as she said, "That was unbelievable."

Both man and beast took pride in her words, but Hudson wasn't quite done yet.

Removing his fingers, he maintained eye contact with Sarah as he sucked them clean, groaning at her sweet, earthy musk against his tongue.

Her pupils dilated again, and he decided to make good on his words earlier.

So he once again lapped her pussy, moaning at the taste of her orgasm on his tongue, and finally pulled back.

Without a word, he took her lips in a crushing kiss, loving how her tongue stroked against his without question, taking what she wanted and hugging him close against her.

When he finally broke the kiss and laid his forehead against hers, he smiled and asked, "Do you believe me now that I can enjoy making you orgasm and watch you fall apart, all without needing to fuck you with my cock?"

"I-I think so. But…"

As her words trailed off, he cupped her cheek and lightly stroked her slightly damp skin. "But what?" She bit her lip, and he decided to push a little. "You can tell me anything, Sarah."

She gingerly placed a hand on his chest and ran her fingers along his top. She glanced down as she finally answered, "I want to see you naked, too. And…and I want to feel your cock inside me."

His dragon roared. *Yes, yes, it's more than time to fuck her and fuck her hard.*

Ignoring his beast, he focused on Sarah. "Are you sure? I'm more than willing to make this all about you this time. Pleasing you turns me on like nothing else. I could do it all night and never get enough."

Some of the walls that had fallen instantly rose back up in her gaze. Before he could ask what had happened, she wiggled back and away from him, as much as she could on the sofa. "I've been lied to most of my life, Hudson." Her voice went soft. "I thought, or rather hoped, you would be different. But that's almost exactly what *he* told me once."

She managed to scoot and stand and then proceeded to gather her clothes. Hudson stood and reached out a hand to lightly grab her wrist. "What are you talking about?"

Sarah avoided his eyes and stared off to the side. "No man wants to give and give without some sort of plan behind it. What will you get out of this mating? Has my brother offered to pay you to do it? I can't think of who else would."

Hudson blinked. "What are you talking about?"

She tugged her arm, but Hudson didn't release her. This moment, and her panic, were too important to let her run away, not if he wanted any sort of chance with her.

When her gaze met his again, horror crashed through him as tears rolled down Sarah's cheeks. And for a few beats, that sense of helplessness crashed over him again.

However, he quickly pushed it aside. He might not have been able to stop his late mate's murder, what had happened to his mother, or even have been able to help Sarah with her bastard ex-husband two years ago. But right here, right now, he could find out what was going on and maybe finally be able to do something about it.

Taking a step toward her, Hudson kept his voice soft as he asked, "Why would you think someone would pay me to mate you, Sarah? Tell me."

She bit her bottom lip and looked away for a few beats. Sensing she needed the moment, he remained silent. He was rewarded when she whispered, "The only reason Rob married me was to get his monthly inheritance payments from his parents."

Chapter Ten

The moment after Sarah said the words, she wished she could take them back.

She'd never told anyone about what she'd discovered in the weeks after her hasty marriage to Rob, not even to her brother over the last year, when they'd been trying to reforge their relationship.

It was embarrassing, to say the least. Not to mention how it made her look stupid to not have seen through Rob's carefully constructed persona when he'd dated her.

Even if she had been young, it didn't lessen the shame at falling for flattering words and a few hot nights of sex.

And how those few weeks had changed her life and put her in hell as soon as the marriage was legal.

Hudson's voice broke through her whirring mind. "Sarah?"

Her name said in that gentle, deep way of his finally snapped her back to the present. Still keeping her gaze averted, she whispered, "Just forget what I said and let me go, Hudson."

"I'm going to let you go in a second, and if you want to walk away, then feel free to do so. But first, I want you to know that no one is bloody paying me anything, or offering favors, or any other sort of quid pro quo if I mate you. I want you because of the connection we've felt, of how easy it is to talk to you, of how Elliott does everything he can to try to impress you, with hopes of having some sort of female attention. We both want you simply because of who you are. Not to mention how I love children and would love to give your sons a home and stepfather they could rely on." He gently squeezed her wrist. "I would give almost whatever it would take to mate you as soon as tomorrow. That's how much I want a chance with you, Sarah."

She swallowed, wanting to believe his pretty words. But she'd been there before, and she wasn't going to fall for it again. "I wish I could believe you."

After a second of silence, Hudson said softly, "Look at me, Sarah."

Something about his voice made it impossible to ignore. And the moment she met his gaze, she sucked in a breath at the anger there.

Her first instinct was to make herself as small as

possible, like when she was a wee girl, and her father had been in one of his moods.

Hudson instantly released her, took a step back, and put his hands up as if to calm her. "I won't hurt you, Sarah. I don't know what you've gone through, but I would stab myself through the heart before I laid a hand on you in pain or anger."

She expected her cynicism to rear its ugly head. And yet, something about his gaze and his tone made her desperately want to believe him.

However, given her past, trusting her gut when it came to men wasn't a good idea.

She quickly tugged on her clothes, and it gave her time to compose herself. "I wish I could believe you, but I don't know you. And maybe I never will."

She stole a glance from the corner of her eye and noticed his flashing pupils. It was on the tip of her tongue to ask what his dragon said, but she resisted. Asking him that was merely prolonging the fantasy she dreamed of, where Hudson truly wanted her and would be the partner she'd always longed for. One who didn't lie, or berate, or use her as a tool to boost his own ego.

Someone who might, just might, be able to actually love her.

As soon as his pupils remained round, he finally replied, "Then give me a chance to show you who I am. And I can see that me saying something isn't convincing enough. So how about this: you and your sons can come over for dinner tomorrow and meet my brothers and their families. Maybe some people can have a whole family of liars, but that's not mine." He smiled slightly. "Besides, I'm sure my teenage niece and nephew will be brutally honest without even trying."

The thought of being in a house full of strangers made her heart race. "I don't know."

He studied her a beat and then added, "You can bring as many others with you to my house as you want. If having Dawn and her family, and even Bram and his, will ease your anxiety, then bring them. Hell, if any of your in-laws want to fly down and join in, then do that too." He took a step toward her, but Sarah maintained her ground, unable to look away from the kindness in Hudson's eyes. "I wish I could change the past or even murder the bastard who hurt you so, but I can't do either. Just give me one more chance to try and convince you of who I am, Sarah. Please."

It was the "please" part of his words that took her by surprise. In her experience, men demanded or took. Aye, her brother had been different growing up, but she'd always thought that was because of their shared fear of their father, nothing else.

Despite every reason she should refuse, she wanted to say yes. It was almost too good to be true that a sexy, kind, gentle man like Hudson would want her, but she almost believed he did.

And dinner would create enough of a buffer between him and her that she could leave if she wanted.

However, as every doubt and memory of how she'd been tricked raced through her mind, Sarah struggled to say yes.

IT TOOK everything Hudson had to keep his rage in check.

Even if he didn't know all the details of her ex-husband's abuse and scheme to use her for money, he'd heard more than enough.

His dragon growled but managed to keep silent. They'd already argued about the bastard and how killing him wasn't possible.

Although, as he invited Sarah over to meet his family, he watched her continue to hesitate. It twisted and gripped his heart painfully. Someday she would need to unburden quite a bit more than what she'd shared tonight, but now wasn't the time.

Convincing Sarah was a long game and one he was determined to win. Not simply because of the thrill of the chase or to stroke his own ego. No, the more she revealed to him, the more he wanted to hold her, and stroke her, and make her forget about everyone other male but him as he claimed her repeatedly.

He would protect her and be the one to show her not everyone had an ulterior motive or was out to beat her down and treat her like a thing instead of a person.

Although his goal wasn't entirely selfless—Hudson needed this, needed to finally be able to help someone and not have to accept what was or stand by with his hands tied behind his back.

When Sarah shifted her feet, he pushed all his scattered thoughts aside and focused solely on her. He wasn't sure what else he could say, but he'd try.

The human sighed and finally murmured, "I'll go to the dinner."

A thrill of relief rushed through him, but he was careful to keep it from his face. He cleared his throat. "Good. Then bring whoever you want with you and drop by around six tomorrow? That way there's some time to mingle."

She bobbed her head. "Aye, we'll be there. Now I should tidy up and go talk to Bram." She paused a beat and then added, "You should leave first."

His dragon half wanted to roar and say they'd walk her, protect her, ensure no one hurt her. But his human half understood that Sarah needed some space, especially considering how he didn't think she liked mixing with large groups of strangers so would need to fortify herself for the next day. "Until tomorrow, then."

For a beat, they stared at each other, and Hudson was tempted to kiss her goodbye.

However, he somehow found the strength to nod at her and walked toward the door. As he stepped into the cooler evening air, he took in a deep breath.

His beast spoke up. *I still say we should find and kill the bastard.*

He sighed. *It's not possible, and you know it. We'd be put in jail, and then what would happen to Elliott? Although I'm sure we can ask Nikki to track him down and watch his whereabouts. He'll set foot on Stonefire over my dead body.*

His dragon sniffed. *I'd rather walk over his.*

Hudson couldn't resist chuckling at his dragon's petulant tone. *Let's forget about the arsehole and focus on getting things ready for tomorrow.*

You can. I don't care about parties or human dinner activities. I'm taking a nap instead.

As his dragon curled up into a ball, Hudson smiled. At least with his dragon asleep, it would make talking to his brothers easier.

Of course, even as he went about visiting them and setting things up for the next day, he still worried over what Sarah would say to Bram. She had to be talking with him right now.

However, he couldn't control that situation, and it had been a long, hard road learning to work on what he could control, after what had happened to Charlie.

So he put his everything into the planning, hoping it would be enough for Sarah to continue giving him a chance.

Chapter Eleven

The next evening, as Sarah walked a little behind Dawn's family and herded her lads toward Hudson's place, she debated turning right back around for the hundredth time.

She'd barely slept the night before, thanks to Bram's words during their brief meeting: *"What do you want to do, Sarah? That is all that matters. So think on it, lass. Because I can't say anything more about Hudson than I already have."*

Every time she thought of the answer, she wanted to scream how she'd like to stay. Then Hudson's words, which had mirrored Rob's so closely, made her hesitate.

She bloody hated how she always doubted herself and her instincts.

Before she could go back down the road of how much she regretted Rob and how he'd destroyed any trust or self-worth she'd had left after her childhood, Joey reached up and took her hand. As her youngest squeezed her fingers, some of her worries faded. Despite all the shite Rob had put her through, he'd at least given her Mark and Joey.

Joey asked, "Do you think more dragons will let me draw them?"

Mark rolled his eyes on her other side and pointed toward the Whitby family, clearly tired of hearing his brother's favorite topic of dragon-shifters, and raced off toward them.

She resisted shaking her head at her eldest and instead smiled at her youngest. "Not tonight, love. As your auntie Cat and uncle Connor always say, you shouldn't walk up to a stranger and ask to see their dragon. It's a wee bit rude."

Joey frowned. "Why? Dragons are brilliant. They should want to show off, aye?"

To Sarah's surprise, Blake—Dawn's mate—walked back toward them and smiled kindly, first at Sarah and then at Joey. He replied, "I couldn't help but overhear your question. And I'll tell you the honest answer if you want to hear it?" Joey nodded enthusiastically, and Blake added in a loud whisper, "All dragons are taught as kids to be careful. We don't want to shift in front of a bad person and get captured."

Joey's eyes widened. "Captured?"

Part of Sarah wanted to protect Joey from any

sort of harsh truth. And yet, she'd spent so many years trying to hide their father's true nature from her lads, which had ended up backfiring when it came to her eldest son.

As she debated which way was best in this case— protection or honesty—Blake looked to her for permission to continue, and she instantly liked the dragonman a wee bit more. He wasn't as bold or forward as many of the others, and it was almost comforting, in a way.

At that moment, she knew Blake wouldn't reveal enough to scar her wee lad for life. So she finally nodded permission for him to continue, and Blake focused back on Joey. "You know how dragon's blood can heal many illnesses, right?" Joey bobbed his head. "Well, if a dragon hunter or someone working with them captures us, they might kill us to get our 'magic' blood. So we only shift in front of those we think won't harm us."

Joey blurted, "But I wouldn't hurt any dragon! Never, ever."

Blake gently squeezed Joey's shoulder and released it. "I know that, Joey. But still, it's why it's rude to ask straightaway to see someone's dragon form. Just try to know them a bit, and if you mention your journal and sketches, maybe they'll offer. And if they do, that means they like you and know you won't hurt them. Does that make sense?"

Her youngest nodded slowly. "Aye, I think so."

Blake smiled a bit more. "Good. And if you need any help being introduced to all the Wells' cousins, just ask Daisy. She knows everyone."

Joey scrunched up his nose. "Daisy's bossy."

Blake chuckled. "No, she's just a naturally born leader and is struggling to find her way."

Sarah could tell Joey didn't really understand the statement, but he dismissed it and looked up at her. "Can I go walk with Daisy? I want her to help me get to know everyone. And then I can add them to my journal."

She smiled at the determined looked on her son's face. "As long as you stay near her and Dawn until we arrive, then go ahead."

Joey nodded, released her hand, and dashed forward until he caught up with Dawn, Daisy, and Mark. Once he did, Blake asked, "He reminds me a bit of Daisy when she first came here."

Sarah's smile grew wider as she watched the blonde girl lean down to Joey and whisper something. "Which is why you're so good at answering his questions."

Blake shrugged. "For the most part, dragon-shifters treasure children." He paused, eyed her a second, and added, "I hope you've noticed that. You have nothing to fear from Hudson on that score."

"I-I think I know that." If she'd been back with her brother's in-laws, someone would've pushed, as they couldn't help being a tad nosey. But Blake just walked next to her, saying nothing. The silence compelled her to blurt, "Why did Hudson never take another mate in all the years after his first mate's death?"

Blake kept his gaze up ahead, on his family, and shrugged. "He never showed any interest in a female, until now. Everyone has to face their demons and heal their hurts in their own way, in their own time. Only then can they move on and find happiness."

Something about Blake's tone made her study the dragonman a beat. She knew he'd been reclusive before Dawn and still was somewhat shy. But for the first time, she wondered what he'd had to deal with in the past.

However, before she could say anything, Blake looked at her again and smiled warmly. "But tonight is just meant for us to have some fun. One of Hudson's brothers, Brooklyn, loves to talk. So, really, if you want to know anything, ask him, and he'll probably tell you. Maybe it'll help you with whatever struggles you have."

She frowned, wondering if her doubts and questions were so obvious to everyone. However, Dawn, Daisy, Mark, and Joey stopped a few feet away from Hudson's cottage and waited for them, and she pushed the question aside as they reached the group. She instead had to focus on Mark and tried to convince him to at least not glare and frown all the time.

And as Hudson opened the door to greet them, she did her best to avoid his gaze. She was being a coward, she knew it, but she needed a little time to gather up the courage to talk to Hudson again. She'd basically ordered him away rather rudely yesterday. Even if she had her doubts about him, it was a wee bit embarrassing.

So she herded her boys inside and instead concentrated on meeting some new people on Stonefire.

IT DIDN'T TAKE LONG for Hudson to notice how Sarah kept avoiding him. From the moment he opened the door, she averted her gaze.

However, he knew patience was key to the human. And he'd rather let his brothers and their families talk with her, answer some of her questions, and maybe, just maybe, she'd start to believe he wasn't anything like her ex-arsehole.

As he watched his brother Brooklyn and his mate, Letitia, approach her, his dragon spoke up. *I hate this human caution stuff. Kiss her, and she'll forget everything else.*

Kissing might work temporarily, but not for long. We're doing this my way.

His dragon finally huffed and fell silent. It was only then he noticed his eldest brother, Bronx, at his side. It showed just how deeply Hudson had been lost in his thoughts since Bronx had lost part of his leg fighting a fire on Lochguard a little over a year ago, and the prosthetic caused a limp, which made his approach noticeable.

He glanced at his brother, and Bronx said softly, "Her caution reminds me of Edith."

Hudson refused to allow pity to show on his face. After all, Edith was Bronx's late mate, a human who'd been running away from a stalker ex when Bronx had met her and slowly wooed her. Then she'd died in childbirth, like many humans had before recent discoveries had improved their survival rates for bearing dragon-shifter children. "A little. But her wariness runs much, much deeper."

Bronx gripped Hudson's shoulder a moment before releasing it. "If she's what you truly want, then I'll do whatever I can to help your case."

"Just tell her the truth, nothing more. She doesn't need more lies in her life."

Bronx looked at him strangely, but then his brother sighed as his only child, Violet, approached Sarah. "I'd better go, or Violet is going to scare that poor human. I know she likes to learn whatever she can from any human female who shows up on Stonefire, in an effort to better know her mother, but it can be overwhelming to a stranger."

Hudson smiled at Violet's determined stride. "Maybe, but she's also charming. Of everyone here, she and Jayden are the two I think can win Sarah over the easiest." They both looked at thirteen-year-old Jayden as he whispered with Daisy and Elliott. "Speaking of our nephew, let me go ensure they're not planning something dangerous. Elliott's talk of learning how to be stealthy from Jayden is a bit worrying."

Bronx laughed, and they both went in their separate directions. If nothing else, his nephew gave him the perfect distraction to let Sarah be for a bit. He only hoped that the more his family talked about him, the more she'd believe he was far more honorable than her ex-husband.

SARAH HAD BARELY LEARNED the names of Brooklyn, his mate, and their three sons before someone poked her in the arm. Turning, she noticed a teenage girl a wee bit taller than her, with brown hair and brown eyes. Even though she didn't have a tattoo on her bicep yet, her flashing pupils told Sarah she was a dragon-shifter.

She suspected it was another of Hudson's relatives, but she didn't ponder more than that before the lass said, "Hello, I'm Violet Wells. My mum was human, even if I never got to meet her. She died when I was born, you see. So can I ask you some human-related questions?"

Brooklyn's mate Letitia cried out, "Violet!"

Sarah blinked a second. But as the teenager stared at her with an expectant look, as if Sarah would somehow be able to give her a tenable link to her long-dead mother, she found her words again. "No, it's all right, Letitia." She smiled. "What would you like to know, Violet?"

Violet's eyes widened, and she blurted, "Have you ever been to Birmingham? My mum was from there, but I've never been. Dad won't let me visit, although I'd like to know more than what I can find on the internet. Pictures or even videos aren't quite the same thing as walking the high street or strolling through the park my mum might've done when she was little."

Even though Sarah had never had a truly loving relationship with her own mother, her boys had taught her how important such a link could be. Pity rushed through her at how this sweet girl yearned for one, but Sarah managed to focus on the lass and shook her head. "No, I'm afraid I haven't been to Birmingham. I'm from Glasgow, and this is the furthest south I've ever been." Violet's face fell, but Sarah quickly added, "Although my brother has visited the city for his job in the past. Maybe the next time I talk to him, I could ask him about it if you want."

Violet's face lit up. "Oh, that'd be brilliant. Most people from Stonefire only ever go to Manchester or the smaller cities and towns, and never as far south as Birmingham. I'd love to hear what you brother saw."

She nodded and smiled. "Then I'll ask him, aye?"

The young dragonwoman opened her mouth as if to say more but shut it as she looked over Sarah's shoulder. Turning, Sarah noticed a tall dragonman with a slight limp approaching. He looked more like Hudson than Brooklyn did, with the same dark hair and gray eyes, which meant he had to be the oldest Wells brother, Bronx. He also wore a slight frown.

He stopped next to Violet and frowned deeper down at her before looking at Sarah. "My daughter hasn't been bothering you, has she?"

Violet sighed. "Dad, I never bother anyone. I was just chatting."

He snorted but smiled down at his daughter with love in his eyes.

She'd been here for half an hour, and already she could tell how close the entire Wells family was. Not quite in the mayhem-inducing way of her brother's in-laws, but in their own fashion.

Truth be told, she preferred the Wells family's quieter displays of affection to the MacAllisters' antics.

Not wanting to think too closely on that realization, Sarah spoke up. "Your daughter is lovely. She was just asking me about some cities and if I'd visited."

Bronx eyed his daughter a beat. "You're not still asking people to take you to Birmingham, are you? You know it's not safe there for dragon-shifters."

Violet sighed. "I know, I know, you've said that a million times, Dad. No, I was just asking Sarah if she'd been there before. She hasn't, but her brother has. So he might be able to give me some new information for my files."

"Files?" Sarah echoed.

She expected one of the adults to answer, but they all looked at Violet, and some sort of unknown communication passed between them all.

A lump formed in Sarah's throat, wishing her family had been closer, to the point they could speak without words like this one could.

Violet finally answered, "I keep a file of everything I know and learn about my mum. It's the only way I can get to know her, really."

Sarah's heart squeezed at the girl's obvious pain and loss. Just because Violet hadn't ever met her mother didn't mean she couldn't long for her.

She reached out a hand and gently took Violet's. "Then I'll help you, lass, in whatever way I can."

Violet beamed at her and any lingering anxiety she had about the evening vanished. Hudson's family consisted of some truly lovely people.

The teenager then blurted, "Are you really going to mate my uncle Hudson? Then you'd be family, and as much as I love Auntie Letitia, she's a dragon-shifter and not human like you. There's so much I could learn from you if you lived on Stonefire, much more than the other humans. They're always so busy, but if you're family, you'd have to make time for me."

Sarah blinked, some of her uneasiness crashing back down around her at Violet's words.

Then she felt a warm presence at her back, one she wanted to lean into and knew Hudson stood behind her. His voice confirmed it as he said, "I think I heard the timer go off, meaning dinner should be done. Why don't you help your uncles get everything ready, Violet? I'm sure they could use an extra set of hands."

Violet opened her mouth, but one look from her father made her shut it. She grunted. "Fine, I'll go. Come on, Dad. We can't let it overcook like last time."

As Brooklyn, Bronx, and Violet left the room, Letitia smiled at Sarah. "Me, Dawn, and Blake can round up all the children so you can have a moment alone with Hudson."

Before she could say that wasn't necessary, Letitia had gone across the room and started giving instructions. In less than a minute, everyone was gone except for her and Hudson.

Hudson still didn't speak, or force her to turn around, or do anything but remain behind her, his breath lightly brushing her cheek as he did so.

He was giving her time to face him. And at that moment, Sarah decided she was done being a coward, at least for tonight.

Taking a deep breath, she turned around and met his gaze. His pupils flashed, but his eyes were full of concern and kindness.

She didn't want to keep comparing him to Rob. And yet, she was afraid she'd keep doing it.

If only she could find a way to convince her heart to believe what her brain was trying to tell her. After all the experiences she'd had with the dragonman, of all the facts and stories she'd heard, they all said he was a good man. Why was it so hard to make herself fully believe and embrace that?

Hudson raised an eyebrow. "Care to tell me what's on your mind?"

And even now, he wasn't demanding, or angry, or pushing her. He left the question open, giving her the chance to say no.

Deciding to place a wee bit of faith in him, she replied, "You have a lovely family."

The corner of his mouth ticked up. "Most of the time. But if you get to know them better, you'll find out how much of a gossip Brooklyn can be, or how determined Violet and Jayden are."

If, he'd said. If.

She'd need to make a decision soon, of course. But not until the end of the night.

Which meant she had to make the most of it. "I didn't really get to talk with Jayden, but Violet seems sweet. Determined, yes, but it's understandable."

Hudson's gaze softened, and it did things to

Sarah's insides that she didn't want to think about. "Bronx hasn't had an easy time of it, but Violet is what keeps him going. I think Elliott did the same for me, and I suspect your boys for you."

She nodded, and between his gaze and honesty, she couldn't stop one of her secrets from rushing out. "Especially since I lost my first baby. It made me appreciate Mark and Joey all the more when they were born."

Hudson's gaze softened even more. "I'm so sorry, Sarah."

Not wanting to cry, she did her best to shrug and pretend it wasn't as big of a deal as it had been. Hiding emotions was how she'd survived as many years married to Rob as she had done. "I-I know it happens to others. And none of their losses are any less. But what made it the absolute worst for me was that my husband didn't care, brushed it aside as if I'd merely stubbed my toe, and far too soon demanded we try again. When I resisted, he guilt-tripped me into agreeing, like he did with most things." She swallowed, not wanting to reveal even more of how awful Rob had been, but it was as if part of a dam had broken and the rest needed to come out. "Only after Mark was born did I find out that his parents would increase his monthly allowance for each child he had. To him, it was only about the money. And his parents knew it was a way to get what they wanted— grandchildren to carry on their name."

Hudson growled, and his anger flowed off him. However, Sarah didn't flinch or retreat. The anger wasn't directed at her.

Strange to realize she knew that, even without him saying anything.

Hudson finally grunted. "And these are the fuckers who say they'd be better guardians of your sons?"

She shrugged one shoulder. "The only people who knew about the arrangement, of Rob receiving money as long as he remained wed with an increase after each child, were them, me, and a solicitor who's a family friend. Ultimately it would be my word against theirs, and Rob's parents have friends in high places."

Something her in-laws had reminded her of constantly, even to the end, to try and keep Sarah from divorcing their son.

Hudson's voice snapped her back to the present. "But did they never think about you? About all the shite you had to endure?"

Maybe the anger in his tone would scare some, but in this instance, it actually made Sarah want to trust him more. "They never told me why they created the scheme for Rob, of course, but I've had years to think about it. And my theory is that they knew their only child had issues since he constantly fucked up. And if they let him be, he'd probably end up dead in a ditch somewhere after failing to pay a massive gambling debt. So they dangled the money to try and make him behave, to create a fantasy they'd always dreamed of, even if all it did was allow him to continue his unpredictable behavior. As for me? To them, I was little more than a pawn toward reaching their goals, merely a vessel to birth the grandchildren they wanted. They were just as manipulative as Rob, truth be told."

Hudson's pupils flashed faster, and he growled loudly. "And to think I wanted to kill your bastard ex before. Now death is almost too good for the fucker. And his parents are even worse, enabling him to such an extent they didn't care how you were treated."

His anger all but radiated off him in waves. And yet, she knew deep down that he wouldn't strike her because of it or turn his frustrations toward her to let off a little steam with verbal abuse.

This was Hudson Wells—father, widower, and loving brother and uncle. And if that wasn't enough, he wanted to stand up for her, which no one had done since she and Lachlan had moved out of their parents' house.

And if she took a leap of faith, he would never let someone harm her, if he could help it. Both her heart and her head finally understood that.

It just meant doing something she didn't have a good track record with—trusting her gut when it came to a man.

Stop it, Sarah. She was making excuses. And the

thought of going back to Lochguard tomorrow to find some nice, platonic mate to live with didn't seem as rosy as it had a couple days before. Hell, even a few hours before.

If she wanted more time with Hudson—and she did—then she'd just have to roll the dice and hope this time she'd win the gamble.

Taking a step toward him, she laid a hand on his chest. She felt his muscles relax a fraction at her touch, which gave her the courage to meet his gaze dead-on and say, "Murdering Rob or his parents will only land you in jail and probably end with an execution. And if you do that, then what would happen to Elliott? And…"

As her voice trailed off, Hudson traced her cheek with a finger. The warmth of his touch rushed through her body, making her lean more toward him. He asked, "And what?"

Searching his gaze, all she saw was curiosity, kindness, and a wee bit of hope.

It was the last emotion that gave her the courage to say, "And then I'd have to find someone else to mate me, wouldn't I?"

He froze, and for a beat, Sarah wondered if she'd misread the situation. For all she knew, the more he'd learned about her past and baggage, the less he wanted to truly offer for her.

She tried to take a step back as her cheeks heated with humiliation, but Hudson gently wrapped his arms around her waist and pulled her back against his hard, warm body. "So you want to mate me, is that right?"

Her voice wasn't more than a whisper as she replied, "Only if you still want to."

With a soft growl, he lowered his lips to hers, and she instantly opened. His tongue delved inside, stroking, licking, claiming her with a strength she hadn't felt before.

But it didn't frighten her. If anything, it sent even more heat rushing through her body, and she pressed closer against him, needing to feel his warm, solid muscles against her, to convince her this was real and not some sort of dream.

His hands roamed her back, her arse, her sides, and she moaned at his gentle, possessive touch. For whatever reason, this dragonman wanted her. And she was tired of fighting it.

Just as she looped her arms around his neck and started to grind against him, a feminine "Oh!" interrupted the moment.

Sarah's first reaction was to jump away. However, Hudson broke the kiss but kept a hold of her. He said, "Yes, Dawn?"

Not quite ready to face her friend, Sarah leaned her forehead against Hudson's chest as Dawn replied, "Dinner's ready, but no rush. Come when you're finished."

Silence fell, and Sarah finally peeked over her

shoulder to see that Dawn had left them alone again.

Hudson chuckled as he stroked her lower back in slow circles. "There's no need to be embarrassed. Dawn's stumbled upon far worse, I'm sure of it."

She met his gaze and frowned. "What are you talking about?"

He grinned. "Dragons aren't as prudish about sex. It's sometimes fun to go someplace where there's a risk of being caught."

Her first impulse was to tsk at such behavior. And yet, the thought of Hudson taking her outside, behind a tree, where someone could catch them in the act made her pussy throb.

As if sensing her thoughts, he nuzzled her cheek. "All in good time, Sarah. Just know that with me, you can ask for whatever you want. There's no shame in living out your desires and fantasies with someone willing, and I am most assuredly willing."

Her cheeks and upper chest were on fire at this point. And as much as she didn't want to ever think of Rob and his words about how a woman's place was to do what the man wanted and quietly without fuss, they came rushing back regardless. Even early in their marriage, anything she'd asked him to try, he'd made a point of never doing.

Hudson kissed her cheek, and she came back to the moment. He murmured, "For now, our mating is the most important thing, and we can sort everything else out later. So I'm going to ask clearly: Will you be my mate, Sarah?"

As she stared into his flashing eyes, she didn't even hesitate, "Aye."

He smiled a second before he kissed her gently, this time as if they had all the time in the world. And even though it was less intense than the others, it moved her more. It was almost as if Hudson cared about her.

She pushed that thought aside. If she could have a friend and some decent sex, that would have to be good enough. She'd certainly done nothing to deserve love.

After he pulled back, he searched her gaze a moment, as if he could sense her thoughts. However, his pupils flashed once, and he merely nodded. "Good, although I'm almost disappointed I didn't get to strip you naked and convince you some other way."

He waggled his eyebrows, and she smiled. He was teasing her.

And before Hudson, it'd been so bloody long since anyone had done that with her.

He continued before she could say anything. "We'll have to let Finn and Bram know about our decision as soon as possible, of course. But if you're like me, you'll want to tell your boys first."

Sarah bit her lip, thinking of Mark's reaction. Even if she wasn't looking forward to it, she'd deal with it the best she could. "Mark will be the most difficult, so aye, I need to talk to my lads in private. I'll do it tonight."

He brushed a few strands of hair off her face. "Then we'll meet with Bram tomorrow morning and probably be mated within the next week."

The quick timeline brought back some of her doubts of truly knowing Hudson. But then he cupped her cheek, and they faded. He said softly, "Even if the mating ceremony is rushed, we can take all the time in the world to better know each other before I claim you." He paused a beat, searching her eyes, before asking, "You do want that, right, Sarah?"

Even if it would be far less complicated to avoid a physical relationship, Sarah no longer wanted that. No, she wanted everything the dragonman had promised.

More than she had ever realized. "Aye, I do."

"Good." He kissed her again, taking his time to caress her mouth as if it were the most precious thing in the world.

As if *she* were the most precious thing in the world.

When he finally pulled back, she nearly cried out at the loss. However, she fought the reaction and tried to be practical. She cleared her throat. "Everyone is probably waiting for us."

"Sadly, yes." He put a hand on her lower back. Even that slight touch sent a shiver of desire through her body. "The hard part will be keeping the news from my face. Brooklyn is going to poke and prod, so ready yourself."

She walked as he put gentle pressure on her back. "W-will they accept me as your mate?"

Hudson frowned down at her. "Of course they will. If anything, Violet will soon become the best friend you never wanted."

She chuckled at the thought of Violet showing up repeatedly to ask a million questions. "I can handle her. I never had a daughter, so it'll be nice to spend some time with a young lass."

Hudson stopped in the hall, leaned down, and whispered for her ears only, "If you ever want to try for one, all you have to do is ask."

Before she could do more than blink, he winked and led them into the dining room.

As everyone settled down for the meal and chatted about anything and everything, Sarah kept glancing at Hudson and hoped she'd made the right decision listening to her gut this time around.

Chapter Twelve

The next day flew by in a whirlwind as Hudson told Elliott of his plans to mate Sarah. She did the same with her kids, and they told Bram about their decisions.

Everything moved so quickly that he barely had a moment alone with Sarah until the next evening, when they'd decided to have dinner with all three boys. It would be the last one before they all moved in together, since they were to mate the next day.

And as much as Hudson wanted to hurry the meal along and get Sarah alone, he tamped down his desires for the female and focused on finishing the preparations with Elliott. His son seemed genuinely happy to soon gain a stepmother, but Hudson still wanted to keep a close eye on him to ensure Elliott didn't suddenly feel out of place or neglected.

All too soon, the doorbell rang, and Hudson went

to answer it. Sarah stood with a hand on the shoulder of each of her sons. He noticed the worry in her eyes, which stoked a protective need to pull her close, but knew he wouldn't be able to ask her what was wrong until they were alone.

So he looked down at her sons. Joey grinned up at him and then rushed him, hugging his middle. "I can't wait to have a dragon stepdad. It's going to be brilliant. And Mum says we'll be a family from tomorrow."

Hudson barely blinked at the unexpected welcome before Mark crossed his arms over his chest and glared up at Hudson. "You're not my father."

Sarah opened her mouth, but he beat her to it, knowing that he and Mark would have to work on sorting things out on their own if there was to ever be a relationship between them. Hudson had hopes that Mark was merely trying to come to terms with some of the truths of his father, ones Sarah had probably tried to keep away from her boys in the past. "No, I'm not your father. But we'll soon be a family of sorts, Mark. I hope you'll give it a try."

Mark looked away and remained silent. However, Joey released Hudson and spoke up. "Mark's just grumpy because he likes Lochguard and will miss Coach Jamie. But Stonefire is brilliant too. I can't wait to live here and get a new brother."

Mark shook his head. "I don't want any more brothers. You're annoying enough."

Sarah sighed. "Enough, Mark. You promised to behave tonight."

"Only because you threatened to take away my video games for a week," he muttered.

While Hudson's son was a bit more easygoing, Elliott had had his fair share of grumpy moods, especially after the death of his mother. Hudson glanced at Sarah and tried to convey that it would be okay and that the boy just needed time.

He didn't know if she understood the message or not because Elliott raced up and skidded to a halt. "You're all here! Fantastic. Dinner's just about ready. Come on, Mark and Joey. Dad said that after we're done eating, we can play video games in the living room. So the quicker we eat, the sooner we can play."

Joey moved to Elliott's side. "What games do you have?"

"Oh, loads. Come, I can tell you as we finish setting the table."

Joey and Elliott walked down the hall and disappeared into the kitchen. Sarah gently touched Mark's shoulder. "Don't you want to learn which games he has?"

Mark grunted. "Fine, I'll go. But I won't like it."

As he stomped down the hallway, Hudson frowned after the boy. He didn't expect Sarah's sons to instantly accept him, but Hudson had no idea why the lad was so vitriolic and hoped it was merely all the changes in his life that had caused it and not an actual hatred of Hudson. It was yet another thing he added to the list of what he still needed to learn about his new mate and stepsons.

Sarah moved to stand beside him and laid a hand on his arm. He looked down at her, and some of his irritation faded at seeing her face. She squeezed his arm and said, "Mark's going to take some time to adjust. But underneath that grumpy exterior is a protective, clever, kind lad. I'm sure you'll win him over. I mean, if you can convince me to mate you in such a short time, given my past, you must have some sort of human-whisperer ability."

He smiled at Sarah's teasing. While a small thing, it really showed just how far they'd come from the first time they'd met. "I think it only works with a certain female, and maybe one of her sons."

Her smile widened, reaching her eyes, and Hudson stopped breathing. Sarah had always been beautiful to him, but when she smiled, it was as if a ray of sunshine broke through the dark clouds, spreading light throughout his body.

She patted his arm. "Well, aye, at least it's a start." She hesitated a moment, but she continued before he could coax out the words. "My brother and his mate confirmed they'll be here tomorrow."

He stroked her cheek with a finger. "Why does that make you nervous?"

She bit her bottom lip a beat. "Lachlan and I

have a complicated relationship, aye? So don't judge him too harshly in the beginning. He's done his best to mend fences, so please don't hold his past too much against him."

His dragon growled. *Like how he abandoned her when she needed him most and how he let her marry that bastard.*

Hush, dragon. If her brother is important to her, then we need to remember that.

His beast huffed. *You can try to pretend everything is fine. I'm going to keep a close eye on him, though.*

He sighed and could see Sarah's confusion. He explained, "I'll do my best with your brother. My dragon, however, isn't as keen to be nice to him."

"He does have a rather possessive dragonwoman as a mate, and her family will swoop in at a moment's notice if there's a threat. So your beast needs to be a wee bit cautious. I'd rather keep you in one piece if I can help it."

He leaned his head down closer to hers. "And why is that, Sarah?"

Her cheeks turned a fetching pink, and he wondered if she'd ever lose that pseudo-innocence with him, as if she'd never felt desirous before.

His dragon spoke up. *I look forward to trying to break her of it.*

Ignoring his beast, he watched and waited until Sarah whispered, "Because now that I've decided to mate you, I'm eager to, to…"

"To what, my little human?"

She looked off to the side. "To explore those fantasies you said we could do. I've never done that before, aye?"

As he imagined Sarah naked in his bed, asking him to fuck her from behind as he smacked her arse and lightly tugged her hair, blood instantly rushed to his cock.

"Hudson?"

The uncertainty in her voice cut him right to the bone. He took her cheeks in his hands and waited for her to meet his gaze. "Anything and everything you want, Sarah. So take the time between now and whenever you're ready for me to claim you and think of what you want. I want our first time together to be all about you."

She frowned. "All about me?"

"Yes. Oh, I hope it ultimately involves me fucking you and feeling you come around my cock more than once. But however we get there will be up to you."

Her lips parted, and she sucked in a breath. Between that and her dilated pupils, he had a feeling she was already thinking of some sort of scenario.

His dragon hummed. *Yes, yes, I can't wait. After she gets her fantasy, then I want a turn.*

We'll work on it, I promise. But we can't scare her.

His dragon grunted. *I would never hurt her.*

I know, dragon. I know. But remember, she's human and needs to learn to trust you.

Elliott's voice shouted from the kitchen, "Are you two coming? I'm starving."

Sarah shook her head and stepped away from him. He wanted to put his arm around her shoulders and hold her close as they made their way down the hall. However, he knew she wasn't quite ready for the highly affectionate and possessive displays dragon-shifters did on a regular basis.

All in good time.

He put out a hand. "Shall we?"

She gingerly put her hand in his, and he squeezed.

And as they walked toward dinner and a shadow of what their life was going to be, Hudson stood a little straighter and kept stealing glances at his human.

Because, yes, Sarah would be his the next day. And despite how he'd offered merely to protect her and had acknowledged an instant attraction to her two years ago, he wanted so much more now. He cared for Sarah, and maybe one day, they'd even love each other.

But he was getting ahead of himself. Tonight was all about winning over her boys and taking the first steps toward melding their blended family.

SARAH WATCHED from the doorway as Mark and Elliott yelled at each other and at the video game. It was some sort of race, and the shouting was merely about the competition. Seeing Mark relax and let his mask drop a fraction made her smile.

She often wondered if Mark had unknowingly learned how to hide his true feelings from observing her, when she pretended to be something other than what she truly felt inside.

Regardless, she needed to watch him carefully for the next few weeks. He'd done a few rash, impulsive acts in the past with sneaking out and running off with friends on Lochguard. She only hoped he wouldn't attempt that here and try to escape back to Lochguard on his own.

Warmth appeared at her back, and she resisted leaning into Hudson's broad, firm chest. Ever since he'd asked her to think of a fantasy, she'd had a hard time focusing on anything except for all the ways she wanted him to fuck her.

He murmured in her ear, and she couldn't resist shivering at the tickle of his breath. "They'll be fine for a bit if you want to escape to my home office and chat for a while."

Sarah kept her eyes fixed on the lads. "I don't know. Maybe I should stay here and watch them."

He placed a hand at her waist and lightly caressed her side. More supportive than sexual, although it still made heat rush throughout her body.

With Hudson, she really did act like a randy young lass with her first lad, despite her age and being the mother of two.

He whispered back, "Elliott and Mark are about the same age. At nearly nine, if we give them more than an hour to play the game, I'm sure they'll take it. Whilst not a good long-term strategy, I think a bit of spoiling in the early days might work to our advantage."

She turned her head a little to see his eyes. At the sight of his flashing pupils, her mouth went dry. Just what was his dragon asking for? Would it be more than talking?

Could she risk it without her sons coming to find her?

Yes, reverberated through her head.

Clearing her throat, Sarah finally found her voice. "Mark, Joey. You can play for the next two hours if you promise to stay in the house and hang out with Elliott. Can you do that?"

Joey waved a hand without taking his eyes from the screen. "Aye."

"Mark?"

He growled as Elliott cheered at something that had happened in the game. "Mum, you're distracting me."

"Will you promise to stay in the house?"

"Aye, aye, I'll be here. Now, please leave me alone. I need to concentrate."

As Mark leaned forward, clearly invested in whatever was going on in the race, Hudson spoke up from behind her. "Elliott, stay with them, okay? I need to talk to Sarah for a bit. We'll be in my office."

Elliott's tone was distracted as he replied, "Fine, Dad."

All three lads focused solely on the TV screen, and Sarah smiled. If nothing else, the three boys could bond a wee bit over video games.

Hudson whispered softly, "Come, Sarah."

She took one last look at the lads and allowed Hudson to lead her down the hallway and into what had to be his office. There was a wee sofa, a desk and chair, some bookcases, and an unlit fireplace that would make the room quite cozy in the winter.

Hudson shut the door, and she heard the click of a lock.

The fact she was alone with Hudson made her heart race in anticipation but also made her fidget with nerves. She lightly traced the surface of his big wooden desk, randomly touching objects along the way. "Do you often work at home?"

"Yes, for the most part. I teach the maths and computer science classes at the school, of course. But almost everything else I do here. The room is even soundproofed because of the delicate nature of some of my projects with the Protectors."

In other words, the lads wouldn't hear them, no matter what went on in here.

Sarah's heart thundered in her chest as she continued to look around the room, thinking of what to say to him without blurting out what was really on her mind—discussing his promise of fulfilling one of her fantasies.

She was torn between embarrassment and desire. Sarah was starting to realize that years of being neglected and sexually denied had taken their toll and had affected her on more levels than she cared to think about—self-confidence, worth, and boldness, to name a few.

And odd as it was, Hudson helping her to realize that fact had made her want to ask for things she never would've done with anyone else, not even in the early days of her first marriage.

Of what she truly desired with a man, something that her ex-husband would've abused. Hudson, however, might just be different.

Did she have the courage to find out?

The dragonman in question remained near the door, and his voice was gentle as he said, "There's no need to be nervous, Sarah. I'm not going to rip off your clothes and immediately bend you over the desk and take you."

She paused her hand on the row of books she'd been half-heartedly perusing and drew in a breath as wetness rushed between her legs at the image.

Hudson's voice was deeper and husky, and he growled, "Unless you want that."

Sarah bit her lip, trying to think of how to respond. Aye, she wanted that and so much more. But voicing it was still hard. Her ex-husband taking everything she wanted and rejecting it had made her hesitant to say anything for fear he'd use the knowledge to make her suffer or bend to his will.

Hudson took a step toward her. "Tell me what's wrong, Sarah. I can smell your arousal, so I know you're not repulsed by the idea. But something made you tense and keep your gaze averted."

Could she do it? Risk the truth and hope that the side of Hudson she'd seen was the true one?

Then she remembered him making her come with his mouth, his fingers, and all without belittling her or doing anything but making her feel desirable and even beautiful. He hadn't even tried to fuck her, despite his raging erections.

Maybe he did care about her needs.

She'd already decided to mate the dragonman. If she wanted more than merely his protection, she would have to gather her courage and be at least a little brave.

Although she couldn't make herself look at Hudson as she said softly, "Early in my marriage, before I knew all the horrid truths of Rob and his bargains, I tried to be bold. He'd ask me what I wanted in bed, I'd tell him, and then he'd deliberately deny me. It didn't take long for me to learn to keep my mouth closed, bear whatever he wanted, and try not to cry."

"Sarah…"

Tears prickled her eyes, but she pushed them away. "Trust isn't an easy thing for me to give, Hudson. Especially when it comes to sex."

She heard him move a little closer. "I can't change your past, no matter how much I wish I could. But I'm not your ex, Sarah. I've tried to prove that since the night we met right before the play. If you give me one chance to prove you can trust me with this, too, and tell me what you want, I promise I won't deny you." His voice was even closer when he added, "Look at me, Sarah. Please."

It was the please that did it, and she turned. She expected pity in his gaze but instead saw a mixture of honesty, desire, and concern.

And when his pupils flashed to slits and back, it only reminded her more of how different Hudson was from her ex-husband.

At that moment, she wanted to give him a chance. Because if she didn't take this leap now, she might never be able to do it.

Her voice was husky to her own ears as she finally said, "I don't know if I'm brave enough to say it. But maybe I could write it down."

Heat surged in his gaze, and Sarah's nipples tightened in response. "I like that idea."

He moved to his desk and rummaged around

until he found a notebook and a pen. Pulling out the chair at the desk, he gestured. "I'll sit on the sofa whilst you write, to give you some privacy."

After a second of hesitation, Sarah nodded and sat down. Once she did, he leaned down to her ear. "Ask for anything, Sarah, I mean it. You deserve it and so much more."

She bobbed her head, and Hudson moved across the room to sit on the sofa. She peeked at him and couldn't help staring at the muscled, sexy dragonman sprawled so easily on the cushions, uncaring that his erection clearly strained against his trousers for her to see.

Pressing her thighs together, she focused back on the notepad. It was time to be a wee bit bold and possibly risk everything.

Chapter Thirteen

As Hudson watched Sarah write in the notebook, his hard cock pressed against his trousers, and he did his best not to move since every little bit of friction made him want to groan.

And the pleasure was a good distraction from the anger he was doing his best to keep hidden.

Oh, he'd be dealing with that later. But Sarah had barely agreed to this, and he would focus on her and this moment alone. After all, if she did write down what she wanted from him and let him read it, then it would show an enormous amount of trust. He hoped she went through with it, too, because it boded well for a true future between them.

Someday, though, he was going to have to find a way to destroy Rob Carter without getting caught.

His dragon spoke up. *I'd better get a turn. You'd end up killing him.*

His beast sniffed. *You say that as it were a bad thing.*

Sarah bit her lip a second, garnering his full attention once more, and Hudson's cock throbbed a beat. How could anyone resist her, let alone deliberately neglect her?

Hudson pushed all his anger and thoughts of her ex-husband from his mind. He wanted the next little while to be solely about Sarah.

His dragon spoke up. *You'd better do what she asks and convince her how much we want to please her. She'll never give me a turn if you scare her.*

I have no intention of scaring her, dragon. I'm more curious about what she wants from me.

Me too. And if it takes her writing things down to ask for what she wants, give her a notebook to always write down her fantasies, no matter when they strike.

The image of a notebook filled with all of Sarah's desires made his balls tighten further.

Not wanting to work himself up to the point he'd come with a few strokes of his dick, Hudson did his best to count to a hundred and then contented himself with studying Sarah's dark hair, her full lips, her long eyelashes.

Anything but the memories of when she'd been naked and writhing on his tongue.

He barely resisted the urge to palm his cock. It was only when Sarah stood, held the notebook against her chest, and walked toward him that made him focus back on the present. She reached him, and he stood, waiting. After a few beats, she kept her gaze averted as she handed him the notebook. As he took it, he asked, "May I read it?"

She nodded and went to stand in front of the empty fireplace.

One day he hoped she wouldn't need such distance from him when unsure of his reaction, almost as if she were bracing for disappointment and hurt.

His dragon growled to hurry him up. Taking a deep breath, he opened it and read:

I WANT to feel your hands everywhere, fingers anywhere, you in complete control of what I do. Tease me with your hands, spank my arse, make me even wetter. I want to suck your cock before you make me beg for release and follow through, letting me come. Then bend me over and fuck me until I scream.

HUDSON NEARLY CAME JUST READING Sarah's words. Bloody hell, he wanted her even more now, if that were possible.

Needing to tame his dick and bollocks, he took a deep breath and closed the notebook. It was time to begin. "Come here."

She walked slowly, her gaze on the floor the entire way.

When she stopped in front of him, he held up the

notebook. "I just want to make sure one last time that this is what you want?" She nodded but still didn't look at him. "Right, then look at me, let me see your eyes, and then I'll give you everything you asked for."

She bit her lip a second before she finally met his gaze.

He saw heat mixed with shame and hesitancy. Bloody hell, just what had her husband said to make her think she should be ashamed of her desires?

His dragon growled, but Hudson said quickly, *Let me do this alone the first time so my focus is completely on her.*

His beast huffed but fell silent, knowing Hudson was right. If it went well this evening, then Sarah could get used to being the focus of both him and his dragon instead of just his human half.

Hudson tossed the notebook aside, raised his hand, and traced her cheek. Moving his head closer, he stated, "Kiss me."

She hesitated a second but then closed the distance between them. Hudson didn't wait to thrust his tongue into her mouth and pull her close, fondling her arse, her back, her hips, loving how she squirmed against him.

With herculean effort, he leaned back. He wanted to ensure he completed everything she'd asked for, and at this rate, he'd want to bend her over and fuck her too quickly. Cupping her cheek, he murmured, "Now let's truly get started."

After caressing her cheek one last time, Hudson

sat on the couch, sprawled his legs, and ordered, "Strip for me, quickly, and kneel between my thighs but don't touch me yet."

He half expected her to hesitate, but Sarah quickly shucked her clothes, revealing her hard nipples and lithe body. The scent of her arousal was stronger now, and he barely resisted licking his lips. He'd have his feast later. But first, Sarah would have hers.

She knelt, kept her eyes on the ground, and placed her hands on her thighs. Hudson asked, "Are you looking down because you feel ashamed or because you truly want to be submissive. Tell me, and I'll know better how to proceed with what you want."

Sarah swallowed. Her voice was barely more than a whisper. "More ashamed, although being told what to do when I'm naked makes me wet."

Considering how much she'd had to control her emotions, her husband's lies, and so many other things over the years, it made sense that handing over control could be freeing, even if only for a little while.

Hudson didn't yet know if she were a true submissive, but for this evening, she wanted his dominance, and he'd give it to her. She wasn't the first female who'd desired that from him. After all, Charlie had always wanted him in control for sex too.

No. This was all about Sarah and no one else. "I wish to give you everything you asked for, but only if you put any and all shame aside. You want this, I want this, and that's all that matters right now. Do you understand that?"

She finally met his gaze. "Aye."

He smiled. "Good. Now, take out my cock but don't do anything else yet."

As her fingers undid the fly of his trousers, they brushed against his pulsing dick, and he sucked in a breath. When her soft fingers finally took him out, he nearly begged for her to stroke him.

However, as she leaned back and let his hard cock strain into the air and finally settle against his belly, it brought him back to what Sarah wanted. "Without using anything but your tongue, tease my cock, lap my precum, and make me even harder for you."

Sarah's pupils dilated as she leaned up and lightly licked the slit at the crown of his dick before swirling the head and moving her tongue down to the base of his cock.

Hudson's eyes nearly rolled back into his head at her dainty motions. It was a good thing she wanted to suck him first so that he could last for her later when he finally fucked her.

She reversed back up his cock, this time with a trail of wet heat along the side. When she reached the tip again, she lightly scraped with her teeth.

As much as he wanted to groan at how he liked it a little rough, she hadn't obeyed him, which gave him a chance to do something else she'd asked for.

Somehow he fought through his lust-hazed brain and said, "I didn't tell you to use your teeth, did I?"

She shook her head.

"Then lay facedown over my lap so I can give you your punishment."

Her cheeks flushed, and he noticed the anticipation in her eyes.

Fucking hell, her fantasy was turning into one of his own.

Sarah managed to situate herself facedown on his legs, her belly on his thighs and her side pressing against his cock, displaying her soft, perfect arse for him. He took his time rubbing his hands over her arse cheeks, warming her skin, learning her slight curves by touch. "When you ask me to be in control, I take it seriously. And if you don't listen, then I'll have to do this."

He smacked his hand on one cheek and then the other, Sarah arching into the touch with a moan not of pain but of pleasure. After he repeated the action a few more times, until her skin turned slightly pink, he stopped and ran his hand down to her pussy. She was so wet that Sarah dripped onto his leg. Lightly fingering her entrance, he murmured, "Given how wet you are now, it wasn't much of a punishment, was it? I think I need to torture you in a few other ways."

Flicking her clit with his thumbnail, Sarah tried to move more into his touch. He shifted his hand away. "I didn't tell you to move." She laid still, and he rewarded her by plunging two of his fingers into her cunt and stroking her slowly. "I can't wait to fill this pussy and pound into you, until you can't think of anything but how much you need to come." Her breath hitched, and he smiled. "I know you want to suck my cock, but I'm going to play with you a little first. Don't move, but feel free to make as much noise as you want."

As he rubbed her arse with one hand, he continued to stroke her cunt with the other one. Every few beats, he touched her clit a second before pulling back. Sarah's little moans and groans were getting more frantic, and he could tell she was on the brink of coming.

He stilled a second, and she cried out in disappointment. He lightly smacked her arse. "Don't worry, my little human, you'll come in a second. I just need to make it even more intense for you." The hand on her arse moved between her cheeks. "When you said to touch you anywhere, I think you were trying to make sure I included here, weren't you?"

Hudson lightly rubbed his finger against the rosebud of her arse. Sarah's breath hitched. Hudson ordered, "Answer me."

"Aye."

He moved his fingers to her pussy, gathered some of her wetness, and went back to her tight hole. He took a second to massage it before pushing a finger inside her. At her tight grip, Hudson's cock turned even harder.

Fuck, maybe one day she'd let him take her there, too.

But not tonight. He moved his fingers in and out of both her pussy and her arse, which made Sarah begin to squirm a bit, trying not to arch into his touch because he'd told her not to.

He added a second finger to her arse at the same time he pressed his thumb against her clit, and she cried out as her orgasm crashed over her, milking his fingers both places, the spasms going on for more than a minute. When they finally ceased, Sarah's body relaxed over his legs.

Removing his hands, he tugged off his shirt, wiped off his fingers, and tossed it aside before smacking her arse. "Good girl. To reward you for listening, I'll give you more of what you asked for. Kneel before me and suck my cock with your mouth, tongue, and teeth while you fondle my balls with one hand and stroke my shaft with the other. Do whatever it takes to make me come in your mouth."

As Sarah knelt between his thighs, Hudson watched her and willed himself to last longer than thirty seconds.

SARAH STILL THROBBED from the most intense orgasm of her life as she knelt between Hudson's legs.

Once he'd agreed to do as she'd written, Sarah had worried Hudson would only half-heartedly try to give her what she wanted before thrusting his cock inside her to find his own release. However, he hadn't even come once yet, she had, and he'd already done so much of what she'd asked for in the notebook.

She'd always wanted to be smacked on the arse and played with there. If not for giving control to Hudson, she would've asked him to do it some more. But she was enjoying his deep, dominant voice too much to break with her request.

And at least so far he hadn't taken what she'd revealed and tried to use it against her. That fact caused a flutter of hope in her heart that maybe, just maybe, for the first time in her adult life, she'd found a man who might actually care for her and what she desired.

As she finally settled on her knees and reached for Hudson's cock, all other thoughts fled her mind except for the hard, sexy dragonman in front of her. She took hold of his dick and leaned forward to lick the slickness of precum off the tip, moaning at his salty taste. He'd made her come so hard she'd lost her mind, and now it was her turn to give him the same. Not because he felt owed and demanded it or that she felt it was a debt to reply. No, Sarah simply wanted to feel him inside her mouth and revel in his own type of trust, given by allowing his most vulnerable part into her care.

She licked and nibbled and finally sucked him deep in her mouth, as far as she could take him, caressing his cock with her tongue as she did so. When his fingers threaded in her hair and he ordered, "Deeper," she nearly squirmed and swallowed him back as far as she could.

Lightly squeezing his balls, Sarah began to move up and down his shaft, licking and sucking and becoming lost to everything but his taste, his hardness, and being surrounded by Hudson's musky male scent.

The hand in her hair tugged a bit, and she stopped. Hudson's voice was strained as he said, "I'm going to come in a second, and I want you to swallow every last drop of my cum."

She moaned at the image, and Hudson guided her head, increasing his pace, using her mouth a little roughly, and yet his actions only made her pussy slicker.

He finally roared, and she felt the first jet of heat. She swallowed as he came, loving the power she had in this position, where she could do anything if she chose to, and he'd be at her mercy.

But she wasn't about to abuse his vulnerability. And when he finally relaxed back against the sofa and pushed her head away, Sarah licked her lips, reveling in his lingering taste, and met his eyes.

His pupils flashed rapidly, but she could still see the approval and satisfaction there. He'd obviously liked what she'd done.

The sight made her throat choke up. It was as if the loneliness, and sadness, and desolation of the near-decade of her marriage crashed down upon her. Never once had her husband looked at her like that.

Hudson's brows came together before he leaned down, scooped her up, and settled her in his lap. As he brushed the tears from her cheeks, Sarah suddenly felt like a fool. He was giving her everything she'd asked for, and here she was, ruining it by crying.

Hudson took her cheeks between his hands and said softly, "Tell me what's wrong, Sarah. Did I push you too far or use you too roughly?"

Something about his focused gaze made it so she couldn't look away. It also made her want to tell him the truth. "No, you were wonderful, better than I ever imagined."

He searched her eyes. "Then tell me what's wrong? I'm not letting you go until you do."

She couldn't help but smile at the hint of order in his tone. When he raised his brows to emphasize the point, she sighed. "I'm sorry. It's just that a man has never looked at me that way before, like you were happy with me, and pleased, and not finding fault with everything I did. It-it brought back memories of my marriage and reminded me of yet another reason why I was so unhappy."

Anger flashed a second before it turned into something much fiercer. Hudson leaned closer, his voice intense as he replied, "Of course you pleased me, Sarah. You were bloody fantastic, almost like a fantasy come to life."

Her cheeks heated, and she finally broke her gaze to stare at Hudson's chest, lightly covered in hair. Free of his intense look released some of her tension, and the urge to tease him rose up in her. As she lightly ran her fingers through his chest hair, she murmured, "Just imagine if we actually had sex."

He groaned, and she felt his cock stir under her arse. "Don't tease me, my little human. As much as I want to keep you here in my office and at my mercy all night, it's probably nearly time to get the boys to bed. We have our mating ceremony tomorrow evening, after all."

She did meet his eyes again at that. Smiling, she said, "I guess that means we're going to be old-fashioned, saving sex for the wedding night."

Hudson laughed, the sound echoing in his chest, and suddenly Sarah's mixed emotions faded until she only felt a mixture of calm and happiness.

Her dragonman had a way of finding those little bits of herself she'd hidden for so long, brought them out, and made her believe they could have a future together.

If she wasn't careful, she'd fall in love with him.

Stop it, Sarah. They would be mates, and the sex

would be fantastic, but for all she knew, Hudson could still be in love with his late mate.

An unfamiliar surge of jealousy crashed through her, but she pushed it away, knowing it was incredibly selfish. The dragonwoman was the mother of his child and dead; Hudson was entitled to his memories and feelings of her.

Hudson leaned forward and kissed her gently, taking his time to caress her lips, lightly stroking her tongue with his own, and finally pulled back. "Tell me you aren't having second thoughts about becoming my mate."

She shook her head. "Of course not."

He stared at her as if waiting for more. But Sarah was already emotionally exhausted and unable to deal with admitting more than that, of voicing what she'd once yearned for before she'd become so cynical.

Needing distance before she started blubbering those thoughts, she kissed him once and slid off his lap. "You're right, it's getting late, and I need to get my lads home."

He watched as she dressed, his pupils flashing the whole time, reminding her she hadn't even experienced his dragon side yet. Not that she was afraid. Given what some of the humans on Lochguard had shared with her, it was an experience unlike any other.

When she deemed herself presentable, she went

to the door. However, Hudson reached her before she could touch the handle, pulled her close, and kissed her again. This time it was desperate and needy, and he dominated her mouth as if to remind her of all they still hadn't done.

Hudson finally pulled away and murmured, "I can't wait until tomorrow when I can finally claim you completely as mine, Sarah."

Wishing she had the courage to ask him exactly what he meant, Sarah merely bobbed her head. "Until tomorrow."

She then unlocked the door and exited. In short order, she rounded up Joey and Mark, and they headed back home.

And even once her sons were asleep, Sarah merely lay in bed, replaying everything that had happened with Hudson in his study, doing her best not to think of every reason why the dragonman wouldn't show up for the ceremony. Or how something else would go wrong since, in her experience, if something could turn to shite in her life, it inevitably did.

Chapter Fourteen

H udson placed the sandwich in front of his son and sat across from Elliott for their last lunch together before Hudson mated Sarah.

Elliott dug into his food while Hudson studied the boy, trying to ascertain if he was hiding something from him. The whole deal with Sarah and her sons had been quick. And while Elliott seemed fine, Hudson also knew that his son could hide his feelings if he thought it might upset him. He'd learned that the hard way shortly after Charlie's death.

Hudson cleared his throat. Elliott stopped midchew and looked up at him. Hudson finally spoke. "Whilst I wish I could take weeks or months for us both to better get to know Sarah, Joey, and Mark, I hope you understand why I can't."

Elliott swallowed. "I know, Dad."

"It'll be a big change, for sure. But no matter if

you're gaining both a stepmother and two stepbrothers, you'll always be my son, Elliott. And I hope you won't hesitate to talk to me about anything."

His boy shrugged. "I know. I like Sarah, and I like Joey. But…"

Elliott paused, and Hudson prodded, "But what?"

His boy looked down at his plate. "I think Mark hates me, and I'm not sure why. I tried being nice, and we had fun with the racing game. But as soon as we finished, he kept trying to start a row with me."

Hudson knew Sarah's eldest son was going to be the hardest to win over, and he'd address it. But if the boy was hurting Elliott, it would become his top priority. "Did he try to hit or fight you?"

"No, not hitting or anything. But he just went on about how he didn't want another brother, and his father wanted him, and you were going to keep him away."

Even though Hudson knew Rob Carter didn't want Mark for Mark—probably only for the money his parents would most likely offer if he could get the boy back—he wasn't about to share that information with his son.

So instead, he asked, "Did he say anything else?"

Elliott shook his head. "Not really. Although my mobile phone, the one I only use for emergencies, is missing."

Hudson didn't want to think the worst of Mark,

but he had a sinking suspicion the boy had stolen it. "Where was it last?"

Elliott shrugged. "The living room."

"And when did you notice it missing?"

"After the Carters went home."

Hudson resisted a sigh. As far as he knew, Mark didn't have a working mobile to contact anyone, which was probably Sarah's doing, to keep her ex-husband from reaching them without her knowledge.

But if Mark was really determined and now had a phone, it could be bad news.

He reached over and pushed Elliott's plate closer. "Don't worry about the phone, and finish your lunch, son. We have a lot to do before this evening."

Elliott didn't pick up his sandwich but merely stared at it. "Do you think Mark or Joey stole my phone?"

"It's possible, although I don't know for sure."

His son lifted his gaze. "But why would they do it?"

"That, my dear lad, is what I need to find out, if it's even true. As I said, I don't know for sure. But don't worry, I'll get it all sorted." He paused, searched Elliott's eyes, and asked, "Did anything else happen last night when I left you alone with Mark and Joey?"

"No, not really. It was fun until the very end, like I said. Joey is a lot of fun, and I think we'll be great friends, maybe even like brothers someday. I've always wanted a little brother."

Hudson smiled at his son, grateful that the change to their family wasn't going to be completely awful and difficult. He also suspected Joey would embrace him and Elliott with everything, no questions asked. "It'll be an adjustment, but always talk to me when you need it. I'm sure Sarah will gladly listen, too, although I'm not going to push or rush you to accept her before you're ready."

Elliott pushed around some crisps on his plate. "Do you think she'll see me as her son one day?"

Hudson's heart squeezed a fraction. He knew how much Elliott had wanted a mother over the years, especially as Elliott's memories faded of his own. He reached over and took Elliott's hand. He squeezed it as he said softly, "You'll be a brilliant stepson to her, I know it. If you can help her as much as possible and be your cheery self, there's no way she won't soon love you just as much as I do."

His son smiled at him. "Then I'll make sure to help her heaps, Dad."

Hudson matched his son's smile. "Good." He gestured toward Elliott's lunch. "Now, hurry up and eat. Your uncle Brooklyn will be here soon to collect you and get you ready for the mating ceremony."

And as they both went back to eating, Hudson's dragon spoke up. *If Mark does something rash, there may not be a mating ceremony.*

I'm aware of that, dragon.

But maybe if Hudson acted quickly enough, then

he could prevent Mark from doing anything stupid and causing his mother even more worry.

SARAH HAD BEEN so busy getting her lads ready, packing what little they'd brought from Lochguard to take to Hudson's place, and being visited by the various human mates of Stonefire—who all felt the need to give her advice about what it was like to be mated to a dragon-shifter—that by the time her brother, his mate, and their daughter arrived, she was ready for a nap.

Not that she'd be able to have one anytime soon, even if Dawn had taken Mark and Joey for a bit, to give her time to see her brother and make final preparations.

As she trudged toward the Protectors' main building, she took a deep breath and rolled her shoulders. The only good thing about being so busy was that she hadn't had a lot of time to think about Hudson, her emotional breakdown the night before, or what she'd say to him when she finally saw him again.

Part of her wanted to just let out all the pent-up anger, and frustration, and sadness she'd kept inside nearly all her life, hoping that by letting it all out, she could finally start to piece herself back together again. And yet, the cautious part of her was afraid of baring her soul and scaring Hudson away.

A small voice said to ask her brother how he'd done it. After all, Lachlan had hit rock bottom, clawed his way up, established himself a career, and won the heart of his dragon mate. If he could do it, then it should be possible for her too.

However, that would take far more courage than she could probably muster right now, especially given how strained things still were with her older brother.

As she reached the front door to Stonefire's main security building, she did her best to pack away all her complicated emotions and walked into the building. The person at the front desk instructed her to go to the main meeting room used for visitors, and Sarah stopped at the closed door. Taking a deep breath, she knocked and went inside.

Her brother stood holding his wee daughter in his arms as his mate, Cat, sat at the table and searched through a large nappy bag.

Despite everything going on, Sarah couldn't help but smile as her brother cooed at his daughter and gently rocked her. "Hello, Lachlan. Cat."

Cat grinned and was instantly at her side, pulling her into a hug and squeezing before releasing her. "There's so much I want to ask you, and yet I don't want to overwhelm you, aye? Come, come, sit down and chat for a wee bit. The head Protector said they'd be bringing tea and biscuits any moment. And

I'm starving, so I want some before we go anywhere else. Driving takes so much longer than flying. I'm not sure how you humans can stand to do it so much."

Her sister-in-law was always so cheerful and full of energy. Even after a year, Sarah sometimes still didn't know exactly how to respond to it. "Oh, aye, we have time for some tea and biscuits. Especially since I haven't eaten anything since this morning."

Her brother slowly came over and frowned down at her. "You look pale, Sarah. Are you sure this dragonman of yours will take care of you properly?"

Sarah knew her brother had tried more and more since their reunion a little over a year ago to fall back into the role he'd had when they were children. Back then, Lachlan had done his best to protect her and was the only one who had really ever taken care of her.

Years apart as adults had led them down very different lives, and eventually it had completely broken down their relationship. And maybe it was her exhaustion or how she was constantly teetering on further emotional breakdown since meeting Hudson, but her temper sparked. "I'm in my late twenties, Lachlan. I'm fully capable of making my own decisions."

His own temper flared in his eyes, but he kept his voice soft for the sake of his daughter. "I just don't want you to end up with another bastard like Rob."

She narrowed her eyes at him. "Hudson is *nothing* like Rob. Keep insulting him, and I'll leave. I'm tired and overwhelmed and don't want to put up with your older-brother shite on my mating day."

As Sarah exchanged glares with her brother, Cat cleared her throat, stood up, and gently took her daughter, Felicity, from her mate. "Lachlan, just stop, aye? You know Finn would never allow her to mate someone who would hurt her."

He grunted, and Sarah rubbed her forehead, trying to stop a headache from emerging. "Does no one think I can make a good decision anymore? I'm not the young, naïve fool I was as a girl."

Cat bit her bottom lip and looked contrite. "I'm sorry, Sarah. We just want what's best for you."

Sarah sighed. "Aye, I know, I really do. But you've both been doing this for a year now, and it's a wee bit insulting, aye?"

Cat exchanged a look with Lachlan and then met Sarah's gaze again. "Sorry, Sarah. But I will say that whoever this male is, he's been good for you already. You're expressing emotions more easily than before, that's for sure." She paused and asked softly, "But will Hudson make you happy?"

Happy. Such a simple word, but one she really hadn't understood in such a long time. "I don't know, Cat, but I hope so. It'd be easier if Mark wasn't so determined to go back to Lochguard or would stop accusing me of trying to make him forget his father."

The room fell silent, and Sarah knew it was because her brother was holding his tongue about what exactly he thought about Rob as a father.

As Felicity squirmed a bit and waved her arms, Sarah decided she desperately needed a distraction. She motioned toward her niece. "Can I hold her a while?"

"Aye, of course." Once Cat had situated the bairn in her arms, some of Sarah's combativeness melted away. It was hard to remain angry when her niece smiled so adorably. Sarah suspected Felicity would take more after her mum than dad, personality-wise.

Cat sat next to her mate and asked, "So what's going on with Mark? You still haven't told him the truth of why you finally decided to divorce Rob last year?"

She rolled her eyes. "Oh, aye, he'd love that. Hey Mark, your father was willing to let the dragon-shifters kill you rather than behave and try to be nice to them. I'm sure that'd go over well."

Finn and his clan had even locked up Rob to protect him from the clutches of violent moneylenders, until some secret operation had taken the crime syndicate down.

Not that Rob had been grateful. If he'd had the means, Sarah was sure he would've left Lochguard with guns blazing, destroying any dragon he could find rather than be nice to them. She still didn't fully understand his hatred of dragon-shifters, but then again, at this point, she no longer cared.

Lachlan's voice garnered her attention, and she looked up from her niece to her brother. He asked, "Is Rob out of jail yet?"

She bobbed her head. "Aye, although I don't know where he is right now. It's not as if his parents would tell me."

Lachlan grunted. "Aye, well, at least you'll be safe here. If he shows up, you'll have a dragon clan to protect you."

She sensed his words were a sort of peace offering to mitigate his earlier harsh ones. "Aye, and not only Hudson and his family will watch over me, but Dawn and Blake here are nice too. I don't know the clan leader all that well, but if Finn trusts him, then I'm going to try to do the same." She readjusted the blanket around her niece. "I'll be protected, Lachlan. Don't worry."

Even if she knew her brother would always worry these days, she didn't want to rehash that discussion. Sarah changed the subject and chatted a bit about her newfound friends and acquaintances. Everyone visibly relaxing as she did so. Maybe she and her brother being on different clans would be a good thing for their relationship. They could still keep in touch, but Sarah could have her own space, giving her a chance to try and discover a bit more of herself.

It wasn't long before Nikki knocked and entered, telling her it was time to get ready for the mating ceremony. While it was going to be a smaller, private affair—a larger clan-wide celebration would follow once Sarah and her lads were more situated—it would still be in front of roughly twenty people.

She'd had a small ceremony before, with her ex. But she hoped this time around it would be a much better experience, one where drunken fights didn't explode that would force her to deal with the venue and all the staff, making apologies.

If today was to be her new start, Sarah was going to try her hardest to make it at least a halfway decent one.

Chapter Fifteen

Hudson stood inside a small room in Stonefire's great hall, wearing his traditional dragon-shifter outfit of dark-red material gathering around his waist and a length tossed over his shoulder and did his best not to pace.

Judging by the time, the ceremony should've started fifteen minutes ago. Yet his brother Bronx hadn't come to fetch him yet or given him an update.

Maybe something had gone wrong, maybe even something to do with Mark. He should've told Sarah of the outburst with Elliott and the missing phone but hadn't had a chance.

His dragon spoke up. *The boy is with his uncle. I think you're nervous for another reason.*

Of course his beast was right. With anyone else, Hudson would deny it. But not with his other half.

The last time I did this, I mated Charlie and thought it was a new chapter in my life. But it ended far too soon.

And you're afraid it'll happen again.

This time it's more complicated. What if I can't protect Sarah? What if her ex or his parents find a way to take her sons and make her life miserable?

Stop fussing so much. Mating her is a huge first step toward protecting her. This situation is completely unlike what happened to Charlie. There was nothing you could've done then, unlike now.

His dragon was right, but it didn't mean he still didn't worry.

Protecting females had never ended well for him. Charlie had been the most recent, but he'd failed his mother on some level as well. When she'd asked him to go with her to stretch her wings and take a dip in the lake, he'd been at that teenager stage when he didn't want anything to do with his parents.

She'd ended up being injured by some human hunters, though, and had eventually died a slow, agonizing death.

No one had blamed him, and yet Hudson had always wondered if his presence could've saved her.

His dragon said softly, *Random circumstances will always happen. But Sarah is human, and so dragon hunters or regular humans afraid of dragon-shifters won't be a problem.*

So you say.

Are you going to wallow and back off? I thought you wanted to protect Sarah. Make a bloody decision.

At the thought of Sarah walking away forever, mating another dragonman, a growl escaped his lips. *She's mine, and I will find a way to protect her.*

Good, because I still haven't had a turn with her yet.

Before he could tell his dragon to be patient, there was a knock, and Bronx poked his dark-haired head in. "Are you ready, Hudson? Sarah's waiting."

He nodded and followed his brother down the hall to the small event room that would hold his mating ceremony.

It was time to make Sarah his mate and then prove he could protect her, any way possible.

SARAH STOOD in a dark-red mating dress on top of a small dais, her two lads sitting in the front row of chairs with Lachlan's family, and did her best not to frown or worry her bottom lip.

She'd taken a few extra minutes to compose herself before saying she was ready, but she was still nervous. Even though she knew Hudson was her best choice, not to mention just the thought of sharing his bed forever warmed her body, it was still all happening much faster than she would've liked.

At least Mark and Joey had put on the nice clothes Lachlan had brought with him from Lochguard. And while Mark had his arms crossed with a frown, Joey beamed up at her. Maybe one day

Mark would understand why she'd had to rush mating Hudson like this.

Although at that moment, Hudson walked out onto the wee dais and all other thoughts fled her mind. Most of his leanly muscled chest was visible, and the material swayed around his narrow hips as he walked. But it was his flashing eyes that made her take a deep breath. They were full of heat, and anticipation, and determination.

Hudson wanted her, apparently, and that helped to ease her own nervousness.

He stopped about a foot away and smiled down at her. Her own lips curved in response.

This day was nothing like her wedding day all those years ago, for so many reasons. The biggest one being Hudson was a far more honorable man than her ex would ever be.

He took her hand, squeezed her fingers, and calmness settled over her. Despite how rushed things had been, how much more there was still to learn about Hudson, at that moment, all she wanted was to claim him as her own.

Bram appeared on stage with a wooden box that he laid on a tall, narrow table right behind Hudson and Sarah and opened it to reveal two silver armbands. After clearing his throat, Bram said, "It's time to begin."

He walked off the dais and took a seat next to his mate. As everyone had explained it to her, a mating ceremony was between two people for dragon-shifters. Hudson had volunteered to go first earlier, to give her an idea of how it was done on his clan.

So he nodded, squeezed her fingers one last time, and said, "When I first met you two years ago, it was completely by chance. Your love for your son was paramount, and it called to me in a way that I didn't fully understand until Bram asked if I was interested in mating you. A resounding yes went through my mind, and over the last few days, I've realized that my instinct was right. Not only because you're beautiful, but you're kind, a caring mother, and whilst you rarely reveal it to others, you also have a wit and sense of humor that makes me laugh. I know blending our families will be a challenge, but with you at my side, I look forward to it." Hudson reached into the open box on the table, took the silver armband engraved in the old language, and continued, "I stake my claim on you right here and now, Sarah MacKintosh Carter. Do you accept?"

Afraid her voice might crack if she spoke, Sarah nodded. Hudson smiled gently at her and then slipped the cool silver around her upper bicep. He caressed where the metal met her skin, and she resisted a shiver.

As if sensing she needed the support, Hudson took her hand again and laced his fingers through hers. His solid, warm touch helped to calm her racing heart, and she cleared her throat. "I'm afraid I can't be as romantic about our first meeting. To be honest, I was rather rude and shouted at you. But despite that, you still offered me protection. I was unsure at first of what to expect, but there's just something about you that makes me feel safe and wanted, something I haven't experienced in a long time. I know there will be challenges raising all three lads together, but in the end, I think it will all be worth it. Together, our families will be stronger. And maybe with time, I'll finally learn to trust completely again." She bit her lip, afraid he would take that as an insult, but only understanding reflected in Hudson's eyes. The sight gave her the courage to continue the last bit. "In order to do that, I stake my claim on you, Hudson Wells. Do you accept it?"

He grinned and said, "As the Scots say, 'Aye.'"

She smiled at his words, reached for the slightly larger silver armband, and slid it onto the bicep without a tattoo. Once it was in place, she returned her gaze to his and couldn't look away.

It would be all too easy to become addicted to his possessive, heated look.

Bram stood and stated, "Right, then. Now you're mated, it's time to move to the next room to celebrate."

Cheers and clapping went up. Hudson pulled her close, kissed her lips softly, and murmured, "Your first dance is mine, Mrs. Carter-Wells."

Even though Sarah didn't like keeping her ex-husband's surname, she'd decided to hyphenate it for her sons' sake. "As long as you show me how."

He hauled her up against his front and whispered for her ears only, "Well, we know how you like taking orders. So just follow my lead, and you'll do fine."

Her nipples tightened at the memory of Hudson's strong, commanding voice telling her what to do the night before. "Just keep it decent, aye? Dragon-shifters might be comfortable with nudity and lots of public displays of affection, but us humans are a bit more modest."

He chuckled, moved her to his side, wrapped an arm around her waist, and guided her down the dais and across the floor to the adjoining room. "Even dragon-shifters don't break into sex or orgies in front of the children." He lightly pinched her bottom, and it sent a rush of heat through her body. "Although you can think of what you want to do later when we're alone in our bedroom. Either we can finish your first request, I can think of something, or you can tell me another. I want tonight to set the tone for our mating and future."

Her cheeks heated despite her best efforts. "I'll think on it, aye."

He grinned. "Good. Now, let's check on the boys, allow everyone to congratulate us, and then we'll dance. The sooner we go through all the motions, the sooner I can have you all to myself."

And as they did as Hudson had laid out, Sarah's

tension faded bit by bit. She was now mated to a dragon-shifter, so at least the DDA couldn't kick her off Stonefire.

Not only that, but her partner of choice wasn't a selfish, power-playing arsehole like her first marriage.

True, there would be plenty of challenges with Mark and becoming a family in general. But this evening and night were for Sarah and Hudson alone.

And she couldn't wait to be alone with Hudson, free of any interruptions, and see what happened with her new mate.

Chapter Sixteen

I n all the rush of the day, Hudson hadn't had a chance to talk with Lachlan MacKintosh alone.

But as he watched Sarah chat with her sister-in-law Cat and a few humans from Stonefire—Jane Hartley, Melanie Hall-MacLeod, and Ivy Kinsella—he noticed Lachlan stood on the opposite side of the room talking with Bram.

When Bram left Lachlan, Hudson decided to pounce on his chance. Murmuring he'd be back soon, he checked to ensure Sarah nodded and then went toward Lachlan.

His dragon sniffed. *I don't see why we should leave Sarah alone. Her brother will be here tomorrow and maybe a day or two past that.*

Between Cat and the Stonefire humans, Sarah couldn't be in safer hands. And whilst Sarah said her relationship with her

*brother was a bit strained, he's important to her. I need to talk
with him and determine if I can help them mend things or not.*

*If you say so. But do it as quickly as possible, like with
the rest of the celebration. I want Sarah naked and in
our bed.*

Me too, dragon. Me too. Now, hush.

Lachlan might be human, but as he sized Hudson
up as he approached, it was easy to see the human
male protecting his sister when they were younger.
There was a quiet strength to him.

Hudson put out his hand. "We finally get to
chat."

Lachlan shook it and then dropped it. "It
would've been nicer if you'd talked with me before
mating my sister."

He raised an eyebrow at the male's gruff tone.
"She's her own female. I didn't need to ask your
permission."

As soon as the words left this mouth, he nearly
cursed. The last thing he needed was to enter a dick-
swinging contest with Sarah's brother.

Lachlan crossed his arms over his chest and
stared a beat before replying, "No, but Sarah is my
only sister. I failed her for too many years, and I'm
trying to make up for it. She deserves happiness this
time around. Will you give it to her?"

He nearly blinked at Lachlan's easily admitted
shortcomings. In his experience, males didn't do that
to near strangers.

His beast sighed. *Their relationship is complicated, remember?*

Even though he didn't need to prove anything, Hudson still stood a bit taller and nodded. "I'm going to try my best." He lowered his voice for their ears only. "Although I promise you, I'm nothing like the arsehole she was married to before. If you ever need help hunting him down and teaching him a lesson, let me know."

Lachlan's shoulders eased a bit, and the corner of his mouth ticked up ever so slightly. "Aye, I will. The only reason I haven't tried to make his life hell is because of my nephews."

Hudson's glance went to the far corner, where all the older children were eating, drinking, and playing some sort of card game. Even Mark looked to be participating, although he still sat a bit away from everyone else.

Lachlan spoke again, and Hudson forced his gaze back to the human. "Maybe you can finally convince Sarah that her lads need to hear a bit of the truth about their father. I don't want to hurt them, but quite a few of us are worried that sheltering them will lead to Rob taking advantage."

He nodded, thinking about Mark's row with Elliott and how he might've also stolen the phone. "I agree, but right now, I'm just trying to get them to accept me. Joey is easy enough to win over, but Mark is harder. Do you have any advice?"

Lachlan's brows drew together. "He reminds me too much of myself when I was younger, which means he's going to keep everything to himself and be angry at the world. And if he doesn't find a way to let some of it go, he'll act out. Although I hope not the way I did."

Hudson knew Lachlan's past as an alcoholic. "I think he's a bit young yet to do that."

"True." Lachlan's blue eyes, so similar to Sarah's, stared at him a beat before he added, "Here's about all I can tell you—Mark desperately wanted attention from his father and almost never got it. I've helped when I could over the last year, trying to give him some male attention, but with my new bairn, it became harder. Spend time with him, Joey, and your son, and maybe you can bond a little that way. Anything to do with football will get him smiling."

"Yes, I'd already planned to talk with the Stonefire coach as soon as possible."

Lachlan smiled. "Good." He clamped a hand on Hudson's shoulder a second before dropping it. "Take good care of my sister, Hudson. Whilst I still haven't made up my mind about you completely, I hope both my gut instinct and my mate's dragon are right. I'll see you again before we leave Stonefire, aye? Maybe we can plan something all together."

Hudson nodded. "I'll talk with Sarah and be sure to set something up."

Lachlan caught someone's gaze across the room

and said, "I need to chat with Rafe about something. Until later?"

He grunted his confirmation, and with that, his new brother-in-law walked toward the only other adult human male in the room, Rafe Hartley.

Hudson's gaze moved back to Sarah, and he smiled as she laughed at something Cat said. While he'd originally offered to be her mate so he could help someone who needed it, he now hoped for more. Hudson wanted to be the one who made her smile, gave her strength, and made her scream his name in pleasure.

To achieve that, he'd need to win over more than just her, but her sons as well.

So he went over to where the children played their game and decided to check on Elliott and his two new stepsons.

WHAT HAD BEGUN as a stressful evening had turned into an enjoyable one for Sarah. Aye, the one glass of wine everyone had been allowed for the celebration —dragon-shifters and lots of alcohol didn't end well —had helped a wee bit.

But between Hudson's near-constant presence, her sister-in-law's ability to make people laugh, and even chatting with some of the other human women from Stonefire had all helped her relax and believe she could be happy here.

Oh, Lochguard had been nice, and she'd forever be grateful for Finn letting her stay there. But Sarah had always been the outsider, the special exception, only allowed to stay because of her brother.

However, now she was mated to a Stonefire dragonman, which brought a different sort of acceptance.

Such as now, when she was alone with Cat, Jane, Melanie, and Ivy, and the four women were about to offer her advice about how to handle Hudson's dragon.

Cat lowered her voice, and everyone in their little circle leaned in a wee bit closer to hear her. "Dragon halves like to be in control. It can be hard for some of us to give in to them sometimes, be it a matter of trust or dominance, but if you can trust the inner beast, all I can say for the partner is...oh my. Even though I'm female, she's still a lusty one. And quite enthusiastic."

Since Cat was mated to her brother, Sarah cleared her throat and looked to the other human women. "Maybe advice from someone not sleeping with my brother might be better."

Jane laughed before her somewhere-in-the-south-of-England accent filled the space. "Quite right. I wouldn't want to hear what Nikki did with mine. Although they've been caught having sex in the open before by my mate, Kai. Let's just hope I never stumble upon them myself, or I might have to wash my eyes out with soap." She shivered. "Probably for a month, or maybe two."

Jane and her brother had both mated dragon-shifters. Them both adjusting and still being close gave Sarah hope for her and Lachlan.

Melanie—a curvy, mahogany-colored-haired female with an American accent—jumped in with a sigh. "Tristan is too possessive to ever attempt anything like that on Stonefire itself. Only if we fly far away, where no one will see us, will he allow us to have sex outside."

Ivy's cheeks turned pink. Her accent also marked her as from somewhere down south. "Zain does it more subtlety. Try not crying out when your dragonman has his hand between your thighs, under the table, when you're trying to eat dinner with a group of people."

Jane's gaze turned soft. "Kai much prefers whisking me into a room, lifting me against the wall, and claiming me that way."

Sarah blinked. "You're all so open about this."

Cat grinned. "About sex? Aye, we are. I'm only holding back because I'm with your brother, and I know I wouldn't want to hear about what my own siblings were up to." She waggled her eyebrows. "Although Lachlan is a surprise in that department, I assure you."

She bit her lip, almost afraid to blurt out her questions. And yet, she didn't think these women would judge her.

Taking a deep breath, she asked the three humans, "How do you trust their dragon half not to hurt you?"

Jane answered, "It depends on the situation, I think. From what I've heard, a mate-claim frenzy can be intense."

They all glanced to Melanie, the only human of them to have had one, and she nodded. "It is, but mostly it's a blur, and you soon lose track of when the dragon half or the human half is in charge. By the end, you're mostly sore, starving, and exhausted."

Jane spoke again. "But I'm like you, Sarah, in that I'm not my dragonman's true mate and didn't have a mate-claim frenzy. And it comes down to trusting the dragonman in question. I know it's been a rushed sort of courtship, for lack of a better word, but have you shagged Hudson yet?"

Unused to such blunt speech, Sarah's cheeks heated. However, if she wanted to both learn to fit in as a dragon's mate and learn more about what to expect, she needed to get past her embarrassment. "Not the whole way yet, no."

Ivy asked, "But you were naked with him and enjoyed it?" She nodded. "Then that's a good first step. My path with Zain was, er, complicated. And slow. But if you feel comfortable naked with Hudson, don't fear his touch, and crave more, then you must trust him at least a little."

Sarah only knew the basics of Ivy's story—of how she'd once been a Dragon Knight, an enemy of dragon-shifters, and later had turned on them to help the dragons. And during the process, she'd fallen in love with a Stonefire dragon-shifter named Zain Kinsella.

But the woman's words made sense. At this point in her life, Sarah wouldn't shuck her clothes for just anyone, unlike when she'd been much younger. And never had a man's gaze on her naked body made her so hot and wet before. Only Hudson seemed to have that ability.

Melanie placed a hand on her arm, and she looked at the shorter woman. "I've known Hudson the longest out of all of us here, even before he lost his mate, Charlie. And not only is he a good dragonman, who helps anyone who asks, but in recent days, it's the most relaxed and happy I've seen him in years." She squeezed Sarah's arm. "Neither part of him would ever hurt you, Sarah. I promise you that. I think you both can be the second chance you each desperately need, if you just risk a little to seize it."

At the thought of actually being happy, her throat closed up. She glanced at Cat and saw understanding in her sister-in-law's eyes. Cat said softly, "Lachlan had trouble believing happiness was possible too,

Sarah." She took one of Sarah's hands in hers. "But this is nothing like with that bastard you were married to before. There's nothing I can really say to convince you to open up a little to your new mate, but I hope you know that if he ever hurts you, all of the MacAllisters, MacKenzies, and Stewarts will rain down hell on him."

She smiled at the image, although Jane spoke before Sarah could think of a reply. "All of Stonefire is at your back too, Sarah. You're one of us now."

Everyone nodded in agreement. And as Sarah looked at the four fierce, protective women around her, she did her best not to cry. This was what it was like to have friends and be accepted. It'd been so long since she'd experienced it, and Sarah couldn't think of what to say beyond, "Thank you."

Nikki's dark-haired head popped into their circle, a frown on her face. "Why the bloody hell does everyone look so serious? Aren't we supposed to be celebrating?"

Sarah smiled. "We were just chatting about mates, frenzies, and a few other things."

Nikki raised her brows. "Without me? My mate might be human, but he can stand up to any dragonman in that department." She lowered her voice. "And we know all the places on Stonefire where you can escape for a few private minutes, if you get my meaning."

Jane shuddered. "I don't need to think of my

brother like that or where you might've done it with him."

Nikki placed a hand over her lower belly. "Well, I'm still trying to decide where we conceived our second child. My bet is that it was against the wall on one of the landing areas. Rafe had wanted to teach me a lesson after I pretended to drop him, although I'm not exactly sure I really learned my lesson in the end…"

As everyone laughed, Sarah relaxed a fraction but couldn't help but notice a flash of sadness in Jane's gaze as she stared at Nikki's hand over her belly.

But it was gone as quickly as it'd shown up, and the tall woman threaded her arm through Sarah's. "Now, let's make sure you eat enough to keep up with your lusty dragonman all night long. And maybe for a bit of the morning too."

And so their group joined the other human women—Evie, Dawn, and Samira—at one of the tables, and they chatted even more about inner dragons and how to ensure they shared with the human halves. By the time Hudson collected her to leave, she wasn't as nervous about having sex with him and his inner dragon.

If anything, she was very much looking forward to it.

Chapter Seventeen

I t took far longer than Hudson had wanted to finally say goodbye to everyone who'd attended their mating ceremony, ensured their boys were safe with his and Sarah's siblings—her sons would stay with their uncle, and Elliott with Hudson's brother Brooklyn, giving them each something familiar—and whisk Sarah away to his home.

No, wait—their home.

Both man and beast hummed at that.

Sarah had asked to clean up before joining him in their new bedroom. As he waited for her, all he could think about was Sarah's eldest son. Indeed, the only dark spot from the evening was how Mark had refused to talk to Hudson, even when he'd taken the boy aside to ask him how he was doing.

His only replies had featured muttered words

about wanting to see his real father and that Hudson had stolen his mother away from his dad.

He and Sarah would need to sit down and discuss how to handle Mark, and soon. While Hudson understood her need to try and protect her sons, if Mark didn't learn at least some of the truth of Rob's actions, those secrets could come back to bite them all in the arse.

His dragon sighed. *Yes, yes, it's important. But surely we can focus solely on our mate for one night.*

His beast was right. Banishing all thoughts but Sarah naked and at his mercy, Hudson lazily stroked his already hardening dick. *One night. And remember, Sarah is open to you claiming her after I have her first. Just try not to scare her.*

His beast sniffed. *I know. I would never hurt her.*

Before he could reply, Sarah walked into the room wearing a sheer negligee that did nothing to hide her hard nipples or the dark hair between her thighs.

Hudson growled, taking his time to scan her body to let her know without words how fucking beautiful she was to him.

When he finally met her deep blue eyes, she bit her lip as she rubbed her hands down her sides. "Do you like it? It was a gift from Dawn and Nikki."

His first instinct was to rush over, pull Sarah close, and have his wicked way with her to show just how much he liked it.

But he'd promised to let her dictate their first time. Well, first time with actual cock-in-pussy sex, at any rate.

He stood and slowly walked over. Never breaking his gaze, he rubbed the material back and forth over one of her nipples, and Sarah sucked in a breath. "Whilst I prefer you completely naked, I also think you like the extra friction against your nipples." He rubbed some more, and the scent of Sarah's arousal grew stronger. "Am I right?"

"Aye."

He smiled, reached down to the hem, and slowly, ever so slowly, lifted the material up her thigh until he reached between her thighs and stopped just short of touching her cunt. "Tell me what you want, Sarah. Because all I can think of is finally sliding into that hot pussy, feeling you come around my dick, and making you mine."

Her cheeks flushed. "W-with no condom?"

He barely repressed a growl at the thought of Sarah round with his child. "Is that what you truly want?" She nodded, and he rewarded her with a light brush of her clit. She moaned, and it took everything he had not to toss her onto the bed, spread her thighs, and take her hard and fast until she screamed.

He murmured, "What else do you want? I want to prove to you that your needs are just as important as mine, Sarah."

She swallowed as her heart raced. She finally

replied, "Then take control again and tell me what to do."

Fisting his hand in her long hair, he tugged her head back gently and said, "Kiss me."

He crushed his lips down on hers, and Sarah moaned, her nails digging into his chest as their tongues battled and stroked, and Hudson owned every inch of Sarah's mouth. The ceremony had been a public way to claim her, but now he would do it privately with his tongue, cock, and fingers.

As he continued to kiss her, he moved a hand to her breast and pinched her nipple. Sarah moaned and arched her hips against his. Pulling away, he kept his grip on her hair. "I didn't tell you to grind against me."

Her breath hitched, and he quickly moved his hand to her pussy, wet and drenched for him. "I think the thought of another spanking has you dripping down my hand, doesn't it, love? Answer me."

"Aye."

"Good." He brushed her clit once and then released her. "Then undress, go on all fours on the bed, spread your legs wide, and wait for me."

As Sarah tugged off her negligee and moved to the bed, he watched her lovely arse sway. Even once she positioned her bum up and spread her legs so that her glistening pussy was on display for him, he could do nothing but stare a few beats. She was so bloody beautiful.

His beast growled. *And ours. Hurry up and fuck her. I want a turn. If she likes your dominant voice, she'll like mine even better.*

Not about to get into a pointless argument with his beast, Hudson went to a drawer in his dresser, removed a dark-red scarf, and moved to the foot of the bed. He lightly dangled the material over her arse and dragged it back and forth until Sarah finally moaned.

Removing the fabric, he went around to the side until he could take Sarah's mouth in a hard, quick kiss. Once he finished, he took her chin in his hands and said firmly, "Make as much noise as you like, but don't come until I say you can. Understood?"

"I'll try."

He lightly caressed her cheek with one finger. "Your trust is something I don't take lightly. If at any time you don't like what I'm doing, we'll have a word that'll make me instantly stop. No questions asked. I won't be angry or try to make you feel guilty. If you aren't enjoying it, then I'm not. Okay?" She nodded. "Then tell me what the word should be."

She bit her bottom lip and then replied, "Frozen."

He smiled. "So you can imagine dunking me in an icy river and shriveling my cock?"

She smiled, and the sight transformed her face from beautiful to gorgeous. "Maybe."

Playfully swatting her arse cheek, he chuckled.

"There's the side to my female that you show me and few others."

He rewarded her with another kiss and then lifted the scarf. "Now, let's get back to making you orgasm around my cock. I'm going to tie this around your eyes. But first, remember your safe word, Sarah. Say it now."

"Frozen."

"Good." He moved the material around her eyes, tied it behind her head, and waited.

But she didn't say a word and stayed where she was, her delectable body waiting for him.

Hudson stroked his cock a few times as he debated the best way to slowly torture his female and make her come harder than she ever had before, and then went to work.

SARAH HAD HESITATED a second when Hudson had asked for her to wear a blindfold. To be in darkness and give her trust to him wasn't an easy thing to do.

But at his gentle caresses and memories of everything he'd done with her, her sons, and even with his family at the dinner they'd attended together, she finally decided it was time to stop waiting for him to end up turning into another Rob.

So she'd let him blindfold her, and now she was

on all fours, in darkness, and her heart thudded as she waited to see what Hudson would do.

The longer he did nothing, the wetter she grew. If he didn't do something soon, she'd start trickling down her thighs.

Although a part of her wondered if Hudson would merely lick up her honey.

She shivered at the thought, and Hudson's voice finally caressed her ears. "I think it's time to warm you up a bit."

She felt his hands on her arse, and he caressed her in slow circles, which made her arch toward him. The light touch was nice, but after his rough kiss earlier, she wanted more than nice and gentle.

She truly wanted to feel claimed by a dragonman.

He smacked her arse hard, and she groaned as she arched her back and laid her head on the bed. It was amazing how quickly she was getting addicted to his firm touch.

As he smacked the other side, and it shot straight to her pussy, Sarah was glad she'd written that first fantasy for him, asking for what she truly wanted and finally getting it.

His hands soothed the slight sting with gentle caresses before one hand moved between her thighs. He lightly ran a finger through her folds and said, "Yes, you're nice and wet. But I think you could be wetter."

His touched vanished, and she cried out. Hudson's firm, soothing voice filled her ears as she heard a drawer open and close. "I won't stop until you orgasm, Sarah. I need you to trust me and have a little patience. The reward will be that much sweeter. I promise you."

Easy for him to say. Sarah had barely ever orgasmed in the last decade until Hudson had made her come, and it was as if her sex-starved body wanted it over and over again until she couldn't move from being overloaded with pleasure.

Hudson's hand returned to her arse, and he gently ran a finger between her cheeks. He massaged a cool, wet substance against her back entrance and murmured, "You liked me playing here last time. Do you want that again?"

"Aye."

Something small poked against her, and then she gasped at the slight burn before something not much bigger than a finger rested inside her arse, and Hudson removed his touch. "We'll start with that. Still, it should make you nice and full for me when I fuck you and make you come."

She wiggled and bit her lip at the pleasure that shot throughout her body. "Will I come soon?"

His hands went up her back and around to her breasts. He pinched both her nipples before lightly twisting them. Sarah cried out and leaned her head deeper into the mattress, afraid her knees might give out otherwise.

"I'll forgive your impatience this time as we're still learning each other. But some day, you'll know to beg when you want to orgasm."

She was about to do just that when she felt the hard, thick head of his cock rubbing against her clit. "For now, remember not to come until I say you can."

Between the blindfold heightening every sensation and the plug in her arse, it took every bit of control she possessed not to come at the friction against her bundle of nerves. When he slapped his cock against her clit a few times, she whimpered.

Hudson ran a hand down her back, stroking up and down, until she felt him take hold of her hair and tug lightly. "I think it's time to finally feel your hot, wet cunt around my cock. Now, spread your legs a little wider."

She did as he asked and held her breath as she felt him at her entrance. She waited for him to plunge deep and take what he wanted, but Hudson merely rocked gently, thrusting a little deeper each time until she relaxed. He murmured, "There we go. Now you can take me."

He finally rested inside her pussy to the hilt, and she sucked in a breath. Even though she'd had his cock in her mouth, it felt so thick, and long, and hard inside her, making her feel even fuller because of the plug in her arse.

She felt his lips behind her ear, on her neck, and then on each of her shoulders. He murmured closer to her ear, "Your pussy is fucking perfect, Sarah. I love the way you grip me, and I can't wait to fill you with my cum as you scream my name. Then you'll truly be mine."

His words, of course, made her skin even hotter. But more than that, she wholeheartedly believed he wanted her and would choose her over others.

She wasn't merely an orifice for his cock, or a way to receive monthly payments. No, despite all of her baggage and issues, he desired her, and he desperately wanted to claim *her*.

And at that moment, she fell a little bit in love with Hudson Wells.

Not that she had time to dwell on that as he released her hair, moved one hand to her hip to keep her in place, and the other to her clit. "You tensed a bit, which means I'm not doing my job right."

He pulled almost the whole way out and slammed back in. Sarah bit her lip to keep her hovering orgasm at bay.

But he didn't move again. Instead, he leaned down, maneuvered her back onto her hands, and turned her head. "Look at me, Sarah. See how much I want you and then kiss me to convince me you want this too. Only then will I let you come."

The blindfold fell away, and when she finally met his gaze again, his pupils flashed rapidly, but it didn't scare her. No, she was consumed by his heat, and tenderness, and almost possessiveness.

Then he kissed her, and she not only took everything he gave, but kissed him back, swirling her tongue, nipping his bottom lip, and even squeezing her inner muscles until Hudson groaned into her mouth.

He pulled away, and she whispered, "Did I convince you?"

The caress on her cheek was so gentle, so caring, Sarah's eyes heated with tears. "That you did. Let's get you squirming again, and then I'll let you come, Sarah."

He pushed her head back down, and she leaned forward into the mattress. As Hudson moved his hips, thrusting faster with each piston, he caressed her hip, her back, and eventually her breasts.

By the time his hand reached between her thighs and circled her clit, Sarah was breathing hard and doing everything she could to wait for his order.

Deep down, she knew he wouldn't ever truly punish or hurt her if she failed. But she wanted this, to please both herself and him.

Hudson's grunting grew more frantic, but his voice was calm and commanding when he said, "Now, Sarah. Let me feel you claim my cock."

He pressed hard against her clit, and she let go.

Wave after wave of pleasure crashed over her, making her scream out and lose all sense of herself for who knew how long. When she finally started to slump forward, her body shaking from the intensity of her orgasm, Hudson stilled and growled out her name as he filled her with his seed.

He slumped over her a second before rolling to his back. She nearly cried out at him leaving her body, but then he drew her to his side, cuddled her close, and pulled the blanket over them.

For what had to be minutes, they merely lay together, Hudson stroking her head, her neck, her shoulders, anywhere he could touch. Sarah snuggled against him, playing with the hair on his chest.

While he'd fulfilled her desire to be dominated, the aftermath, lying here with him in comfort and warmth, was even better. Something she'd dreamed of for years but had never had from her ex-husband.

Almost afraid Hudson would disappear, she hugged herself closer against his body and drew in a deep inhalation, memorizing his hard, hot body and unique musky scent that was purely Hudson.

His voice rumbled inside his chest, under her ear, as he said, "I'm not going anywhere, Sarah." He tilted her head up and kissed her softly. "Did I pass muster?" He waggled his eyebrows, and she laughed.

"Do you need a report card, Mr. Wells?"

"I just might. I think you screaming as you gripped my cock means good marks, but I need to be sure. I can't be disappointing my new, beautiful mate the first night. This has to set the tone for our future."

A future. Something she hadn't dared dream of before but started to think she might have, and a less lonely one at that.

Sarah couldn't stop smiling at her dragonman. "What if I said I needed a few more performances to truly judge you and give you honest marks?"

His pupils flashed, and she felt his cock hardening against her thigh over his body. "I think I might need to insist on it. Just to ensure you get the full range of my abilities." Hudson's hand moved to circle her arse slowly, his touch both calming and arousing at the same time. "Maybe even with my dragon in charge?"

Even though he said it casually, Sarah felt his body tense a wee bit.

He was afraid she didn't want to accept all of him.

A sudden boldness surged through her. Aye, she quite liked when Hudson took charge and gave orders in bed. But Sarah wanted to tease him a bit too.

She moved a hand to his cock, stroked him, and then moved to fondle his balls. Hudson sucked in a breath, and she finally answered him, "Aye, I'm curious about your dragon. Should I clean up for him first?"

His pupils flashed more rapidly. "As long as you're fine with it, he is. He wants as much cum inside you as possible." Hudson's hand moved to the butt plug and tapped it lightly. "And this, too, if you're not uncomfortable or too sore."

Her pussy was a tad sore, but she wouldn't mention that. She wanted Hudson—all of him—far too much. "Do you trust him?"

"With everything that I am."

There was nothing but truth in his voice. "Then I'll be at his mercy, willing to try anything."

With a growl, Hudson rolled her onto her back and took her lips in a rough, demanding kiss. Only when they both breathed heavily did he pull back. To her surprise, his pupils were mostly still round. "When will you dragon come out?"

"In a few seconds. But I just needed to taste you for myself, to claim that fucking beautiful mouth one more time, to hold me over until it's my turn again."

Never breaking her gaze, she remained a bit bolder than normal. "Maybe later I can claim you again. With your cock in my mouth."

Hudson groaned. "You're going to be the death of me, Sarah."

She smiled broadly, enjoying her newfound power with this dragonman. "I know you're nearly forty, but I didn't think you were quite such an old man yet."

"Old man, huh? Well, I'll let my dragon show you just how wrong you are. Ready?"

She nodded.

He traced her cheek. "My dragon also knows your safe word. If it's too much, use it."

After so many years of trying to close off her emotions, to pretend her former harsh reality hadn't bothered her, it was hard to feel so many things at once.

Safe. Cared for. Desired. Treasured.

But Sarah was determined not to cry tonight. Instead, she focused on how his hard cock lay against her belly, on his warmth, even the faint sheen of sweat on his back. Aye, it definitely didn't take much to stir her arousal with this dragonman. "Aye, I remember. Frozen." She lightly ran her nails down his back. "I'm ready."

Hudson's pupils changed to slits and remained that way. His voice was slightly deeper as he spoke. "Now you're mine. I've wanted to fuck you hard for days. My turn."

Hudson's dragon positioned his cock and thrust into Sarah. She moaned at the sudden fullness. No gentle caresses or foreplay with his beast half, it seemed.

But as he raised her legs and put them against his shoulders, opening her up further, she forgot about everything but the near-frantic pounding between her thighs, the growls, the murmurs of Sarah being his.

The pressure built, and she wondered if his dragon would care if she came or not. Then she felt the side of a hard talon pressed against her clit, and she came, arching as much as she could off the bed.

Hudson's dragon growled, leaned down, and nipped her breast. Hard. "My mark. You're mine."

And then he stilled and filled her pussy with hot jets of cum.

Dropping her legs to the side, Hudson's form mostly collapsed over her, but not quite enough to squash her. They both breathed heavily, and she waited. Hudson trusted his inner beast, and Sarah had begun to trust Hudson. Even if she had no idea what came next, she waited patiently.

A few seconds more, and Hudson rolled over her and took her hand with his. Bringing it to his lips, he kissed the back of it, and she noticed his pupils were round again. "Dragon halves are, well, a bit more determined to get to the point, if you could tell."

She moved to snuggled into his side, and Hudson pulled her close, just like before. "I wasn't sure what to do."

He stroked her lower back, and Sarah's eyelids grew heavy. Hudson's voice did nothing to wake her up, as it was soothing and made her feel warm and safe. "We'll work on it. He was as randy as a teenager, but next time he'll go a bit slower. Although later, I'll have to leave my own bite mark on your other breast. I can't have him outclaiming me."

She nuzzled his chest. "Maybe in a bit? I'm so tired right now."

He kissed the top of her head. "Sleep, my human. I can't promise you a whole night as I want you too much, but rest and recover a little because it's going to be a long night of me worshiping you until we both can't move from so much pleasure."

She smiled and closed her eyes. "Sounds lovely."

As Hudson continued to rub her back, Sarah soon fell asleep in the arms of a man she actually trusted. And maybe loved a wee bit. Not that she was anywhere near ready to admit that to anyone.

Chapter Eighteen

It was nearly noon the next day when Hudson stood in the kitchen, making sandwiches for him and Sarah.

He'd finally tired out his human to the point she needed more than an hour's sleep to recover. And so he was trying his best to resist her, letting her rest for as long as possible before they had to go and collect their children. While one night wasn't nearly enough and Hudson had barely whetted his appetite for his new mate, they'd both agreed that their sons needed them more. It would be a hard enough transition, and they needed to start work immediately on blending their families together.

His dragon grunted. *You had more time with her than I did.*

It's not my fault if you like to fuck quickly, and I take my time. Learn some patience, and you could have more time with Sarah.

His beast sniffed. *I like it hard and fast. Sarah seemed to enjoy it too.*

Memories of Sarah digging her nails into their back as his dragon made her come flashed into his mind. There were no doubt marks on his skin, and Hudson didn't care. *Regardless, stop blaming me for hogging her. At any rate, you'll probably sleep most of the day anyway as we deal with the boys.*

I'll nap a little. But I still need to learn about Mark and Joey. Until I can figure them out and notice their tricks or tells, they're a puzzle I want to crack.

His dragon enjoyed being able to read people. Children were sometimes harder, though, as they could more easily believe something wholeheartedly even if it was a lie, like Santa Claus or the Tooth Fairy. *I can use all the help I can get, so keep me updated.*

As it was, Hudson would have to find an opening with Sarah this morning to discuss childrearing and what they expected of each other.

Maybe not the most romantic or sexy of topics, but Sarah came with her sons, much like he did with Elliott, and Hudson wanted them to one day be a true family. One who loved each other, trusted each other, and would support each other, no matter what.

And that was going to take time and hard work. Hudson had learned with the death of his first mate not to take things for granted, and he wasn't going to put off to tomorrow what he could do today.

As he went through what he could say to Sarah about it, he lost track of time. Eventually he sensed her presence, turned around, and smiled at her rumpled appearance—a half-heartedly tied robe, mussed hair, and still swollen lips from his night of worshipping her mouth. "Good morning, my human. I must not have worn you out as much as I'd thought."

She smiled, walked toward him, and placed a hand on his T-shirt-covered chest. Even through the material, her touch sent a rush of heat and desire through his body. "I smelled coffee, and then my stomach rumbled, telling me to wake up. Some dragonman made me work up an appetite, it seems."

Hudson pulled her close and kept a hand on her lower back. "I probably should've fed you more last night, but I couldn't bring myself to leave you." He kissed her cheek, her nose, the side of her neck, loving the little noises she made when he did so. "Although in the future, I'll take better care of you."

She caressed his cheek, and he met her gaze again. "We should take care of each other."

And even though he wanted to keep talking about last night or how much he craved Sarah again, he knew this would be a good time to broach the important topic of their boys. "And what about the children? In the haste to mate, we haven't really discussed that."

She nodded. "True."

Her stomach rumbled, and both man and beast growled. He guided her to one of the chairs at the counter and then put a cup of coffee as well as a plate with a sandwich and crisps in front of her. "We can do this as we eat. I haven't had time to learn your favorites yet, but hopefully this is enough for now."

The corner of her mouth ticked up. One day, he'd barely notice it, but for now, it made his heart soar that she was so relaxed and at ease with him. "What if I said my favorites were Danish pastries? You'd make those for me?"

"Of course. They'd be a learning curve, but I'd try."

She searched his gaze. "Why would you do that? It's an awful lot of trouble."

He looked at her plate. "Eat something first."

Sarah didn't hesitate, and once she swallowed her first bite, he finally answered, "I like taking care of people. And even more so with you, when you give your body so freely and let me control you. It's part of my duty, as well as a joy to look after you." She blinked her eyes quickly, as if she was trying not to cry, and he frowned. "What's wrong? Do you want me to be a horrible cook so you can do it? I can easily burn toast and cook a fried egg until it's rubber. Just ask."

She shook her head and laughed. "No, no. I'm a passable cook, but that's about it. If you're better than me, then have at it." She bit her lip and then added, "I'm just having a hard time believing you're real. First a night of the best sex of my life, and now a man who wants to cook for me. It's like a dream."

He wanted to pull her into his lap but resisted, not wanting to risk distracting each other with kisses and touches. Instead, he sat next to her and pushed her plate a little closer toward her. Once she ate some more, he continued, "But surely you saw on Lochguard that dragon mates are a fairly protective, caring bunch. There are always exceptions, of course. But I hope to prove I'm not one of them."

She touched his hand and threaded her fingers through his. Once he squeezed hers, Sarah met his gaze again. "I saw it, aye, of course I did. But I was going through a divorce, trying to adjust to a new kind of life, and watching couples in love was a bit painful. To be honest, I hadn't thought of men or even sex most of the year I was there. My lads were everything and took my entire focus."

And since they'd come back to what he wished to discuss, Hudson decided to stay on topic. "I want to be a good stepfather, Sarah. But to do that, I need to know what you expect, what I expect, and hope we come up with a compromise for how to handle all three of the boys. There's not exactly a manual for this sort of thing."

"Not for human and dragon children moving in together, no, I don't think so." She sighed. "Mark will be the hardest one. Joey has always been the easy child, the one who rarely gets into trouble or fusses too much. Joey mentioned last night he can't wait to call you Dad."

He brought their entwined hands to his mouth and kissed the back of Sarah's. "I don't need Mark to ever call me that, if he's never ready. I just want to ensure he doesn't try to run away."

Sarah frowned. "Run away? Why would you say that?"

"Well, it's just some of the things he's said to me." As he explained about Mark accusing him of trying to force his dad away, of replacing him, and his words to Elliott the night they played video games, he noticed some of Sarah's tension returned by the tightness of her jaw and slight frown between her brows.

He finished with, "So while he hasn't issued a direct threat, if he somehow thinks his father is waiting to take him back and we're stopping him, it could end badly."

She bit her lower lip, and he hated that she was worried. Hudson put his arm around her shoulders. "We can do our best to make sure that never happens. But to do that, I think Mark will need to hear of what happened last year on Lochguard, when his father was imprisoned there. At least a little bit of it, at any rate."

She leaned into his side, avoiding his gaze. "It might seem silly or selfish to others, but I know what it's like to have parents who don't really care about you or even despise you. It's the worst feeling in the world, and I'd hoped to spare my lads that."

He only knew the basics of Sarah's upbringing. Maybe learning more would help him understand her a little better. "What happened when you were a child, Sarah?"

For a few beats, she remained silent, and his beast grumbled. But Hudson had loads of patience, and he was finally rewarded when Sarah sighed. "My father never wanted a daughter. To him, females were weak and were only good for one thing—fucking. But he had no desire to do that to a child or his own offspring, thankfully. But he ignored me until I was old enough to start asking questions. That's when he first hit me and knocked me unconscious. Or so Lachlan tells me since I can't remember it."

Hudson laid his cheek against the top of her head, wishing he could find the bastard and kill him. Too bad he was already dead.

Sarah continued, barely noticing him, lost to her memories. "My mother didn't care and was too busy trying to please him and get whatever scraps of attention he'd throw at her. Lachlan was the one to teach me how to be small and quiet and how not to draw our father's attention. My brother also tried his best to always be with me when my father was drunk and shouting around the house, looking for his next punching bag, and would step between me and our father whenever he could.

"Lachlan did his best to protect me, and I always felt safe with him. And it was me and him against the world. His love meant everything. But then eventually, maybe inevitably, he abandoned me too."

IT'D BEEN SO many years, and yet the memories of when Lachlan had started drinking, never keeping his promises, and eventually reaching rock bottom to the point he'd nearly hit Sarah were as fresh as if they'd happened yesterday.

Lachlan had apologized so many times over the last year, but they had never really sat down and talked in any depth about the events leading to the destruction of their formerly close relationship, the tipping point that had led to Lachlan seeking help for his disease.

A gentle squeeze brought her out of her mind, and she was back in the kitchen, surrounded by Hudson's strong, warm body, and she noticed how he was stroking her hair, her arms, her back, murmuring soothing words she really couldn't hear.

Eventually he asked clearly, "What happened,

Sarah? It sounds like you and your brother were close growing up. What made him abandon you?"

She could brush it off, pretend it didn't mean anything.

And yet, that's exactly what she'd been doing with her brother over the last year, and it hadn't eased her hurt or mended their relationship at all.

Maybe talking with Hudson would help her get the courage to do the same with her brother.

Still, she was overly aware of the tall, muscled dragonman at her side, the one who could shift into a rather large dragon. So she first asked, "Will you promise to listen and not then rush off to kill or hurt Lachlan?"

Hudson frowned. "That tells me I'm not going to like what I hear."

"Probably not. But if I'm ever to work things out with my brother, I need him alive."

Her dragonman's pupils flashed before he grunted. "Fine. I won't hurt him, although I won't promise not to talk to him about this, male to male, at some point in the near future."

Unable to keep looking Hudson in the eye, she focused at a point on the far side of the kitchen, not really seeing anything. "Aye, well, let me tell you what happened. Even though Lachlan had been slipping away for a couple years, he was the only one I wanted at my wedding to Rob. To be honest, me hastily believing Rob's false words and marrying him so quickly stemmed from my brother's abandonment of me too. I think marrying Rob was my way of trying to prove to myself that I was lovable to someone."

Although she could scoff at it now in retrospect, back then she'd been so desperate for affection, it hadn't taken much to convince her Rob had cared for her. A few loving words, some chocolates, a few gifts.

"Sarah…"

Not wanting Hudson to say she was lovable when he didn't really mean he loved her, she hurriedly added, "Regardless of naivety and craving affection, I still wanted my brother there. In my heart, he had always been my only family. But he never showed up to the engagement party, and the night before my wedding, I still hadn't heard from him about attending.

"I knew some of the places he'd gone and where he lived. I finally located him and confronted him. Things devolved, and he raised his hand as if to strike me." She felt Hudson tense at her side, but she continued on before he could do anything. "Then I must've made a sound, and a look of horror dawned on Lachlan's face. He quickly turned toward the wall and asked for forgiveness. I asked one last time for him to get help to stop drinking, and he agreed. We lost touch for years after that. He eventually came to see my lads once in a while, but never for long, and we never really talked about anything of consequence during his visits."

"Until last year, when you moved to Lochguard."

She nodded. "He's truly changed, especially since mating Cat and having Felicity. He's become the loving brother from my childhood again, at least with his new family. However, he and I still haven't found that same camaraderie and caring and connection we had growing up." Her throat closed up, and her voice cracked as she whispered, "And I'm afraid we might never have that again." She finally met Hudson's eyes again. "All of this has weighed on me for years, most of it from my very first memories, and I had vowed never to allow my children to feel unwanted or unloved. Maybe it was naïve—and probably a wee bit stupid—to hide Rob's true character from my lads, but I just wanted to give them what I never had —a family that wanted them."

"I know, love. And if there was a way to spare your boys, I would. But if Mark runs off to find his father and his parents use that as proof that the boys should be with them instead of you, that would be so much worse. Not only would it tear your heart out, they'd soon learn the true extent of what their father can be like and then they'd probably feel something like what you did, maybe even worse if they truly believed a rosy view of their dad. A little anger now might be worth it in the long run. It may take time, but I want us to all be a family, to be close, to care for one another. But we can't start doing that until we know no one will try to run off at the first opportunity."

She searched his gaze, knowing he spoke the truth. And yet it went against everything Sarah was to say yes and that aye, she needed to pain her sons in the short term to save them in the long run.

Hudson pushed a section of hair off her face. "It doesn't have to be today, and maybe you won't have to reveal the full truth. But maybe you and Mark could spend some time alone today, feel out what he needs, and make a decision from there?"

Aye, talking a little she could do. She nodded. "I'll do that. Just talking with him alone might help me see just how exactly he views his father, and I can form a plan from there." She bit her lip and then said softly, "Or we can form a plan, if you want to help."

Hudson nodded without hesitation. "Of course. I don't want to take over, but I will always be here to help you, Sarah. Always."

There was nothing but honesty and earnestness in Hudson's gaze. It was hard to believe she could have this dragonman at her side in the future, always having her back.

But maybe, just maybe, the coming months and years could be so much better than anything she'd had in the past. "Thank you."

He caressed her cheek and then tilted his head a

fraction. "Do you think Lachlan and his family can stay a few more days?"

She studied Hudson's face closely, but she couldn't read him any longer. "Why? You aren't going to 'teach him a lesson' when I'm busy, are you?"

He shrugged. "I was thinking maybe me and Cat could watch all the children whilst you two spent some time together. Although I might have to give a few warnings to your brother, just so he knows I'll protect my mate from anyone who tries to hurt her, even if it's him."

Maybe she should feel irritated at his overprotectiveness, and yet it felt...nice. Almost like he cared for her.

As if one day he could love her.

Stop it, Sarah. She had enough to worry about for now, figuring out if he was the one to finally love her and mean it was not on her shortlist.

At that moment her stomach rumbled, and Hudson frowned as he released her and turned her back toward her plate. "First things first, eat some more. Then we'll get ready and see the boys."

Even a week ago, Sarah would never have been so bold. But desperate to feel her new connection to Hudson again before facing the world, she murmured, "I've always wanted to fuck in a shower. We'll still be getting ready but could release some tension at the same time."

His pupils flashed and he smiled slowly. "I think

that can be arranged. After you eat enough to keep up with your lusty dragon mate."

She laughed, and then they both ate probably quicker than they should've.

But later, as Hudson made her come under the hot spray of water, his heated gaze on hers, she didn't care.

Chapter Nineteen

It was late afternoon by the time Sarah walked with Hudson to collect her boys from the guest cottage where Lachlan and Cat were staying on Stonefire. Even though she wasn't about to have it all out with her brother quite yet, she was still a wee bit nervous.

Would her brother be able to tell she had something on her mind? Would he decline to stay longer on Stonefire when she asked him to? Would they never address the past head-on and become the dear older brother she'd missed for so long? What if he didn't have time for her but only wanted to focus on his new family?

Her stomach churned at all the what-ifs. Taking a deep breath, she told herself, *Stop it, Sarah.* The possibility of making up with her brother made her anxious, but worrying wasn't going to change the outcome. Lachlan was sober, as well as a husband and father now, and he would never physically hurt her. She just had to wait and see if he'd ever be more than a polite stranger to her ever again.

Hudson squeezed her waist and whispered, "It'll be all right, Sarah. Even if he can't stay longer, I'm sure he'll come back when you ask. After all, he and his mate rushed here for your mating ceremony, no questions asked."

She glanced up at her mate and tried her best to smile. "I didn't think you'd be so nice when it came to my brother."

He grunted. "Just because I don't like what he did to you doesn't mean I don't want you to reconcile. Trust me, when you say something you don't mean and never get the chance to take it back, it's far worse and will eat away at you forever."

She frowned, sensing there was something important behind his words. "What are you talking about?"

"Later, love. Let's deal with your elder son and your brother first."

Sarah wondered if his words about regret had to do with his late mate. Since the afternoon he'd talked about Charlie's death, he'd only mentioned a few happy things with Elliott but never alone with her.

The fact she didn't know more caused a wave of guilt to crash over her. Hudson had patiently listened to and supported her through all her confessions and baggage, and she hadn't tried to do the same for him.

And she wanted to. Once she was sure her lads were safe and she tried to set things in motion to reconcile with Lachlan, she was going to find out more about her supportive, sexy dragon mate. She might not be able to do anything to change the past, but if she wanted a true partner in life, Sarah needed to reach out to Hudson as much as he reached out to her.

They reached the front door, and Hudson knocked. A beat later, Cat answered the door with Felicity in her arms. "Hello, you two. You're earlier than I thought you'd be, aye? Didn't you see my text about not coming until dinner?"

Sarah smiled and touched her niece's chubby cheek before answering Cat, "Aye, but I need to talk to Mark and Joey a bit. I don't want them to feel abandoned."

Cat motioned inside the cottage, and they entered, going to the living room. "Well, they aren't back yet, but you're more than welcome to wait with us."

Her heart skipped a beat. "Not back?"

"Aye. Even if they haven't formally enrolled in the school here yet, last night, one of the Stonefire teachers, Tristan MacLeod, mentioned a field trip to the sea for today, and the lads asked if they could go.

You and Hudson had left by then, so Lachlan gave his permission. I hope that's okay."

It's only a field trip. "I'm sure there are plenty of chaperones, aye?"

Hudson grunted. "In the rush to mate, I'd forgotten about the trip to the sea. But yes, there should be. Dragon parents, like most dragon mates, are fairly protective."

Cat bobbed her head. "Not to mention Blake and Dawn were going along with the teachers, plus a few of the Protectors." She looked between her and Hudson. "Is something wrong?"

She sighed. "I just worry about Rob and his parents, aye?"

Cat sat down in the chair and motioned for Hudson and Sarah to sit on the sofa. "You're mated to a dragon-shifter now, not to mention there's another human child living on Stonefire, so it should be harder for them to win custody by saying it's not done. Especially since Rob only recently was released from jail, so he's not exactly a paragon of fatherhood." She paused a beat and then added softly, "You know Lachlan and I will do whatever you need, aye? You just have to ask."

She shifted in her seat, but Hudson took her hand and squeezed. His warm touch helped to steady her. "About that…would you and Lachlan be willing to stay a few more days? I understand if you're busy, of course."

Cat smiled. "Aye, of course we'll stay. We'd planned to stay a week, at least. Trust me, I don't want to drive straight back with my wee daughter just yet. It must be the dragon in her, but she doesn't like cars and basically never sleeps." Cat readjusted her hold on her daughter and smiled down at her. "One day you'll fly, my little one, and then you won't have to worry about cramped cars for most of your life."

As she watched her sister-in-law coo over her daughter, Sarah remembered when her own lads were young. It'd been hard, especially with no help from Rob, but it had been some of the best days of her life, having someone to love and love her, no questions asked.

And even though she'd asked Hudson not to use a condom, her small yearning for another child turned into a rush of wanting. Not just because a wee bairn would truly meld her and Hudson's family together, but because she wanted to experience parenthood with a partner who cared.

Hudson squeezed her hand again, and she met his gaze. He smiled warmly at her, as if he could read her thoughts, and she knew he would be a wonderful father.

Cat cleared her throat. "Do I need to leave you two alone for a bit?"

Sarah's cheeks flushed. Thankfully Hudson spoke so she could tamp down her embarrassment at being caught mooning over her new dragon mate. "When will Lachlan be back? I need to speak with him alone."

Sarah wasn't the only one that caught the dominance in his voice, and Cat raised an eyebrow. "Should I be worried?"

He grunted. "I won't hurt him. But he and I need to talk."

Sarah whispered, "Hudson."

"What? Talking is allowed, right?"

Cat jumped in. "You should just let them talk sooner rather than later, Sarah. Maybe they'll even have a boxing or wrestling match, or some such shite. My brothers did that with Lachlan, and afterward they became friends." She shook her head. "I truly don't understand males sometimes."

Sarah hadn't heard that story before, and her mouth dropped open. "I don't want Lachlan and Hudson to fight."

Hudson placed a hand on her knee. "I doubt it'll come to that. Although if he wants a friendly sparring match, I won't say no. You can learn a lot about a male that way."

"But you're a dragon-shifter and he's human. He'll lose."

Pain flashed in Hudson's eyes but vanished before she could blink. "I would never hurt you or your family, Sarah. I wish there was some way I could make you believe that."

Brilliant, Sarah. Push him away at the first opportunity.

She had to fix this. "It's just my first instinct that someone wants to hurt another. But I'm trying to change that. I have been for the last year. Just...be patient with me. Please."

His gaze softened, and he brought her hand to his lips and kissed the back of it. "I know, love." He leaned down and whispered for her ears only, "I've earned your trust one way. I'll work harder to do it with your clothes on."

Her cheeks burned. "Hudson."

She darted a glance at Cat, but the dragonwoman was chatting nonsense to her daughter, trying to give them privacy.

Sarah really did love her sister-in-law.

As she tried to think of how to steer the conversation to more benign and less emotional topics, the front door opened and shut. A beat later, Lachlan entered the room.

But he wasn't alone. No, Stonefire's tall, blond-haired head Protector, Kai Sutherland, was right behind him.

And judging by Lachlan's frown, something was wrong.

Cat was the first to ask, "What is it?"

Her brother blurted, "Joey is missing."

Sarah's heart stopped beating a second as she stood, barely noting Hudson did as well. "Joey's missing? What happened?"

Kai stepped forward. "He and another child ran

off to watch the birds on the cliffs. Both of the children are now missing."

Joey was missing. Not Mark, but Joey. Why? Had Rob gotten to him?

Not that she was in the right frame of mind to think of the reasons or ask Kai questions. Her baby boy could be hurt, or kidnapped, or who knew what.

He could even be dead.

She sucked in a breath as her knees weakened, and Hudson hauled her against his side, supporting her. His solid presence helped the spots at the edge of her vision disappear. Sarah needed to stay conscious, to find out what she could about her youngest. Joey needed her now more than ever. She had to be strong, no matter what happened.

She stood a bit taller, and Hudson squeezed her side in comfort as he asked, "Who's the other missing child?"

Kai answered, "Bram's niece, Ava. More Protectors have been sent to search the area, and Rafe has contacted some human law enforcement near them as a precaution. Bram wants Sarah and Hudson to come to the Protector building to offer any information that could help."

Hudson's deep voice seemed far away when he said, "Do you need me to carry you?"

Taking a deep breath, Sarah did her best to regain her strength further. Her son needed her.

Panic and worry would have to be put aside until later.

Right now she needed to fight for her wee son. "I can walk."

And as they made their way toward the Protector building, Sarah focused on putting one step in front of the other. Joey had been lost once before, and Hudson had found him. She had to put faith in the dragon-shifters yet again, hoping they could bring her son back to her once more.

Chapter Twenty

Bronx Wells ignored the phantom pain of his missing lower leg and tried to focus on the maps in front of him.

He'd once been in charge of Stonefire's search and rescue team. Losing his leg on Lochguard about a year ago had changed all that, of course. He could barely get into the air to fly unassisted, let alone swoop in to save someone.

But he knew the reasons behind why someone became lost, strategies on how to find them, and more about the lay of the land in the North of England than anyone else on Stonefire.

And right now, his brother's new stepson and his clan leader's niece needed all the help they could get, even if he couldn't search for them himself.

His inner dragon sighed. *Just because we can no longer head a wing formation doesn't mean we're useless.*

Hush, dragon. I need to concentrate.

According to Nikki and Sebastian, the two Protectors who'd gone with the children for the field trip, Joey and Ava had asked to look closer at a bird's nest near the cliffs. Since there was high, sturdy fencing to keep them from falling or climbing over, they'd been given permission.

But a commotion with Mark trying to run off had taken everyone's focus, especially once Rob Carter had been found nearby, waiting for his eldest son.

By the time Carter had been detained for questioning and Mark had been given into the close-eyed care of Tristan MacLeod, Joey and Ava had been nowhere to be seen.

Not over the cliffs on the beach below, not further down the pathway, not even near the vans that had taken them seaside.

Carter wasn't talking, and so far they hadn't found anyone lurking about who didn't live in the nearby town—none of the residents had created any red flags during the preliminary background checks done so far.

And the tire tracks and dragon footprints in the mud and sand might be related, but it hadn't rained in a couple days, so they could be from anyone.

Which lead Bronx to two possibilities: the children had fallen off the cliff and had been washed out to sea; or, they had been taken away by someone either on dragonwing or by a car or van.

Neither outcome was a happy one, but a kidnapping would give the children a greater chance of still being alive.

He'd just noted all the roads leading from where the kids had been last spotted and where else the dragons flying on patrol should look when one of Stonefire's Protectors, Zain Kinsella, waltzed into the room. Bronx asked, "Have Lucien and Nate finished their search for the latest dragon hunter news on the dark web?"

While no one wanted the dragon hunters to be responsible for taking two of Stonefire's children, it was one of the more likely scenarios. Any and all information could help Bronx pinpoint the search further.

Zain shook his head. "Not yet."

Bronx grunted his disappointment. But before he could ask anything else, the voice of his younger brother, Hudson, filled the room. "I can help them with their search and speed up the process."

He turned and saw Hudson was with his new mate, Sarah. It took everything Bronx had not to show emotion at how his brother's new mate looked about ready to fall over. The female hadn't had an easy time in life, and this event wasn't any better.

His dragon said, *We'll find them. She's part of our*

family now, and no matter what it takes, we'll find Joey and Ava.

Buoyed by his dragon's determination, Bronx replied, "They could really use your help, especially since you have the right type of clearance. They're in the main Protector IT room. I can stay here with Sarah to ask her some questions and answer hers whilst you're gone."

Hudson looked down at his mate as he asked if it was okay to go. The tender expression on Hudson's face told Bronx that his brother truly cared for the human.

And as she looked at him, touching his cheek as she answered of course, Bronx ignored the wave of jealousy that flooded his body. He'd had that sort of closeness and connection once.

Until he'd killed his mate.

His dragon growled at the thought, but he wasn't about to have that argument again about how they weren't to blame. So he tossed his beast into a mental maze, needing the quiet.

Hudson looked at him as he guided Sarah over. "Watch over her, Bronx. And fetch me without hesitation, if needed."

He nodded, ensured Sarah sat down, and said, "Of course. Now, go. I need to know if the dragon hunters have become more active again anywhere in the North of England now that the Dragon Knights are disbanded."

His brother nodded and left the room. Bronx slowly sat down, somewhat awkwardly because of his prosthetic lower leg, and spoke gently to Sarah. "I need you to tell me everything you can about Joey when it comes to curiosity, interests, and taking risks. Can you do that?"

Sarah nodded. "I'll try."

He took his sister-in-law's hand and made his voice as kind as possible. "Bram has told me what he can about his niece since her father is back in Ireland, dealing with the recent death of his mate and taking care of her family. If you tell me what you can about Joey, it'll give me the full picture. That way, I can try to think like they do." He squeezed her hand. "So tell me what you can about your youngest son."

And as Sarah did her best to describe Joey's interests in fauna, his tendency to follow animals without thinking of the consequence, and his overly trusting nature, Bronx took mental notes.

He only hoped it would give him the last missing pieces of the puzzle about why the pair would leave the group. Or even worse, prove how they'd been taken by force.

Chapter Twenty-One

Hours later, Sarah sat next to the bed inside Stonefire's surgery and gently stroked Mark's forehead as he slept.

The doctors had finally been forced to give him a sedative to keep him from trying to break free and run again.

It devastated Sarah that her eldest had tried so hard to get away from her to be with his father, a father who didn't really want him beyond what money he could bring in.

And in huge part, it was her fault for coddling her lads all those years and perpetuating the fantasy about how their father truly wanted to be with them when he'd been absent for months at a time. She'd always told them how he had to work away from home to ensure they had a roof over their head.

Even now, she still didn't know how she could've

shared more about Rob's debts and affairs with other women or how he'd only return when his parents had threatened yet again to cut him off.

Without the promise of money, Rob would've left them long before Sarah had divorced him.

Someone entered the room, but she didn't turn around. Since Hudson and his brother were still working to find Joey, she assumed it was Dr. Sid or Dr. Innes come to check on Mark again. Or maybe even Cat trying to get her to eat something, not that she had any sort of appetite right now.

However, it was her brother's Scottish voice that filled the room. "You need to rest, Sarah."

She didn't take her gaze from Mark's sleeping face as she asked softly, "Would you be able to sleep if Felicity were missing?"

Lachlan pulled up a chair next to Sarah and sat down. "Probably not. But I recall a certain lass making me eat whilst waiting to see if Cat would pull through."

Last year, an explosion inside a warehouse on Lochguard had caused many people to be hurt, including Cat. For a short while, no one knew if the dragonwoman would survive the encounter. And even if she did, the doctors had worried about a miscarriage.

Sarah had taken charge for a bit to ensure Lachlan kept up his strength. And of course he'd use that now to try and get her to listen. "At least you knew where Cat was. I don't even know where the bloody hell Joey is, let alone if he's still alive." A sob choked her throat, but she did her best to push past it. "He's just a child, Lachlan. And too trusting and sweet. Someone could so easily use that against him."

Her brother placed a hand on her shoulder and squeezed. "He's also with Ava Moore-Llewellyn, who's a few years older and by all accounts, extremely clever for her age."

She shook her head. "I know you're trying to comfort me, but the lass just lost her mother a few months ago. She's not going to have such a clear head."

"Sarah."

At his firm tone, she finally met her brother's eyes. Fire and determination flashed there, along with love. "All of Stonefire is looking for them, not to mention the other dragon clans in the UK are helping as much as they can from a distance. They'll find them one way or another."

No matter what had happened was left unsaid.

"And say for once in my life things go well, and Joey is brought back to me." She lowered her voice for Lachlan's ears only. "Mark was so determined to get away from me that they had to drug him unconscious. I-I don't know what to do anymore. It's like if I find even a wee bit of happiness, the universe finds a way to tear me down. And I'm so incredibly tired of it all."

Tears trailed down her cheeks, and her brother brought her into a hug. She held him close, his arms reminding her of how safe she'd always felt when they'd been growing up.

His voice was low as he replied, "I don't know about the universe, but it can right itself. I have to believe you will find happiness as well, little sister. You deserve it more than anyone I know."

She paused, wishing she could believe the words as strongly as her brother.

And yet, as she turned her head to look at her eldest son again, tears pricked her eyes. "Nothing will be right until Mark stops hating me."

Lachlan squeezed her tight a second before replying, "I know you wanted to protect your lads from their father, but I think the time is past for that, Sarah. You're going to have to show Mark a bit of the truth, I think. No matter how painful it is."

She sighed. "Hudson had suggested the same thing before Joey went missing."

Lachlan leaned back so he could look into her eyes. "I know mating him started out for protection, but he cares for you, Sarah. It's plain for all to see, and he only wants what's best for you and the lads."

"I know." She looked away from his eyes. "But you, of all people, know how difficult it is to trust someone so completely."

His voice was so quiet she almost didn't hear it. "Aye, and part of your deep distrust is my fault."

She leaned back until Lachlan dropped his arms. "We don't have to do this now, Lachlan."

His face turned grim, and he motioned toward the sofa on the far side of the room. "I think we do. It's better than sitting and fretting. I'd rather you be angry at me, and release some of your tension that way, then close in and find new ways to blame yourself."

He studied her, no doubt thinking of other ways to convince her, and Sarah knew her brother wouldn't just walk away because she asked it. After what seemed hours, she murmured, "Aye, a distraction would be nice, I suppose."

Her brother rose. After looking at Mark's sleeping form one last time, Sarah stood and stumbled, surprised at how her legs didn't want to work. Lachlan supported her until they both sat on the sofa.

Lachlan frowned at her. "I'd rather you rest, but somehow I don't think that'll happen."

She shook her head. "I wouldn't be able to sleep if I wanted to." She searched Lachlan's eyes. "So say what you need to say. I know you're eager to go back to Cat and Felicity."

Her brother's brows drew together. "We'll start right there. Aye, I love my mate and daughter. But I also love you, Sarah. It doesn't have to be either or."

"You've had a hard life, too, Lachlan." She bit her lip, gathering the courage to say what she'd avoided for the past year. "I was a big enough burden for you as a child. I don't want to also be one in the present."

Something fierce flashed in Lachlan's eyes. "I can't even imagine what your worthless ex-arsehole said to you during your marriage, but you're not a burden. You're my sister, the only MacKintosh blood family I want anything to do with." She opened her mouth, but Lachlan continued before she could say a word. "I know I didn't act that way when Rob dated and married you, and I'm sorry for it. Mum not wanting to leave our abusive father when we were old enough to offer her help, aye, well, it snapped something inside me. That's why I started drinking. It was selfish and destructive, and it hurt more than me —it also hurt you. I will regret that for the rest of my days. But know that I'm here for you now, Sarah. Always." He took her hand and squeezed. "And I think honesty is the only way to repair any sort of damage. So rail at me if you need to. Shout, cry, whatever you need to do, so I know how deeply I hurt you. Maybe after that we can finally try building a new bridge together, one where our fucking awful parents don't matter as we create our own loving families."

The sincerity of his words, combined with the regret in his eyes, caused her eyes to fill with tears. But she cleared her throat, pushing them away. She'd cried so much today already, and she didn't need more tears. They would solve nothing.

Right now, she needed words. She might not be able to do anything to find Joey or have Mark instantly accept her and his new stepfather, but she could at least settle things a bit with Lachlan. Maybe that would help her stay strong for all the rest of it.

Taking a deep breath, she tried to be as honest as she could with her big brother. "Aye, you hurt me when you all but disappeared. But it would be selfish for me to place all the blame of marrying Rob on your shoulders. It was mostly me." Lachlan frowned, but she pushed on. "I-I desperately wanted to be loved, Lachlan. To find someone who wanted me for me, who would give me something different from what our parents had. So much so, it made me naïve and a fair bit blind. I was also young and starved for affection, which made me an easy mark for Rob."

"To get his bloody money."

That much she had revealed to Lachlan over the past year. "Aye. I can admit that if I'd had you in my life at the time, maybe you would've seen Rob's ulterior motives. But then again, maybe not. One thing Hudson has taught me is that we can fight and overcome the horrible aspects of our past to make the most of the present and the future. It's not easy, and it still makes my relationship with him difficult as I truly learn to trust him, but bit by bit he's showing me that not all men are selfish arseholes, that men can truly love their children, and if you care about someone, you do your best to make them happy, not feeling guilty or worthless.

"And I think we need to do something similar for us, Lachlan. We need to stop feeling guilty or letting the past dictate every possible happiness for the future. All I ask is that you be honest with me, share your life with me, and love your new family with all you have. If you can do that, and I do the same, I have hope that I can finally get my big brother back."

Lachlan's voice was rough as he said, "I'm always here, Sarah bear. But no more guilt and secrets going forward. Aye, I can do that."

She smiled at the use of her childhood nickname. "I think having some secrets is healthy. I have no desire to know what Cat's dragon does to you when you're alone."

He grinned, and the sight made her so happy. "Aye, I think we can avoid that. Especially since I have no desire to know what Hudson does with you."

He shivered dramatically in revulsion, and Sarah laughed. And as they smiled at one another, Sarah felt a burden slip from her shoulders.

There was still a massive, steaming pile of shite blocking her road to true happiness, but it was a little smaller now.

Mark's weak voice instantly garnered her attention. "Mum?"

At his voice, Sarah jumped up, raced to her son's

side, and brushed some hair off his forehead. "I'm right here, Mark."

His gaze was a bit unfocused, and Sarah tried not to hold her breath as she waited for him to rail out at her.

He'd already been unconscious by the time he'd been brought back to Stonefire. But by all accounts, he'd been shouting and blaming her for everything before then.

Mark finally averted his gaze and mumbled, "I want Uncle Lachlan."

As Sarah's heart shattered a bit, Lachlan was at her side. He gently touched her arm in comfort before saying, "I'm here, lad."

Mark kept his head turned, and Sarah had a feeling he wanted her to leave.

But she wasn't going to. It would almost be admitting defeat, and she refused to give up on her son, be he troubled or not. "Tell your uncle whatever you wish, but I'm staying right here until you can share if you know what happened to Joey."

At his brother's name, Mark frowned and looked back at her. "What about Joey?"

Lachlan answered, "He and the dragon girl named Ava are missing, Mark. If you know anything, anything at all that can help us find them, you need to tell us."

Mark's face turned pale. "No, it shouldn't have

been Joey. Dad said they'd take two dragon kids as a distraction, so I could get away."

Sarah's fear ratcheted up another notch. "Who was supposed to take them?" Mark stayed silent, and Sarah leaned forward a bit. "Who was supposed to take them, Mark?"

"I don't know. Friends of Dad, someone who owed him a favor. But they weren't supposed to take Joey." A wildness entered Mark's eyes for the first time. "Is he really gone?"

Lachlan nodded. "Aye, he's missing. No one has been able to find him or the dragon-shifter child."

For the first time in months, Mark looked like a wee, scared child again, one that realized he might've fucked up big time.

It worried her that he didn't seem to care if two dragon children had been kidnapped. But right here, right now, she needed to focus on keeping Mark talking more than anything else. So she gently touched his cheek in reassurance and asked softly, "Is there anything else you can tell us to help find Joey?"

Mark shook his head. "Not really. Dad would know. Where is he?"

Oh, how she wanted to start telling the full-blown truth to Mark right here and now. But while Sarah knew she would have a lot to say to Mark, and they needed to have a lengthy, long-overdue discussion— she might even need to get professional counseling for her son—she had to share the latest information she'd learned right away with the Protectors. So she replied, "Your father is with some of the dragon-shifters."

He frowned. "How? He said he'd kill them before letting them capture him again."

Sarah had to trust the Protectors knew what they were doing, and Rob wouldn't be a threat, at least not under their watch. Instead, she asked a difficult question, "Do you think he should do that? Kill them?"

Mark shook his head. "No. I don't like it here, but I don't want to kill anyone."

He just, apparently, condoned kidnapping.

There was so much to say, but she needed to share the latest details with the Protectors ASAP. Finding Joey was her top priority for now. She'd focus on Mark as much as she needed once both of her lads were safe. She nearly reached out to brush his hair back, but Mark looked away from her again before she could touch him. Resisting a sigh, she somehow made her voice strong as she said, "I'm going to leave you here with your uncle whilst I talk with those in charge of the search party. Promise me you'll stay put, aye?"

Mark hesitated a second but then nodded. "Aye, I'll stay. I want them to find Joey. He might be annoying, but he's still my little brother."

At his wavering voice, she dared to lean over and

kiss his forehead. Since Mark didn't flinch or back away, she counted it a small victory.

Sarah straightened up and glanced at Lachlan. "Will you stay with him until I get back?"

He nodded. "Aye, of course. Go, Sarah. They'll need to ask Rob some more questions now."

She steeled her jaw. "No, this time I'm the one who needs to talk to him."

With that, she stormed out of the room and ran as fast as she could toward the Protector building. She didn't know how much longer Rob would be held there since the DDA was sending someone to collect him.

She pushed her legs even harder, needing to reach him before that happened. Rob had threatened her children for the last time. And one way or the other, she was going to get the information from him she needed, even if she had to beg every dragon-shifter on Stonefire to help her.

Chapter Twenty-Two

Hudson rubbed his bleary eyes as he made his way toward Kai's office inside the Protector building. He'd helped Nate and Lucien gather data for hours now, and they'd ordered him to take a break to check on his family.

But just as he'd been about to leave, Zain had told him to go see Kai in his office without providing a reason. With everything going on, he knew the head Protector would only require his presence for something important, so Hudson had run. He stood there now, knocked, and the door opened revealing Kai, Bram, Nikki, and Sarah.

The fear mixed with anger in his mate's eyes made him instantly alert. Hudson went to her and took her hands. "What's wrong?"

Sarah explained how Rob had arranged for some children to be taken as a distraction, giving him time to try and take Mark away, and how Joey hadn't meant to be one of the targets. She finished with, "And now I need to talk with Rob. He won't speak to anyone else, and the DDA will be coming soon to collect him. I'm the best chance at trying to get information out of him since he and I are both human, and the DDA can't punish me if I accidentally slap him."

Even as his dragon nodded his approval of Sarah hurting the male, Hudson ignored his inner beast and growled. "There's no fucking way I'm allowing you to go in there alone."

She shook her head. "But I won't truly be alone. You and the others will be watching through the observation glass, ready to help me if I need it. Not to mention he's tied up too." She bit her lip a second before she said, "More than that, I need to try on my own at first, Hudson. Between my rage at what he was willing to do—sacrifice innocent children for his scheme—and knowing you will have my back if I need it, I want this chance to face him."

Hudson didn't care who was watching, he cupped her cheek. "Of course I'll always have your back, love. Although I hope I don't have to murder the bastard as I'd rather not go to jail and abandon you."

She smiled slightly. "It won't come to that."

Part of Hudson wanted to say no. He was going into the room with her no matter what.

And yet, he knew how much Sarah needed this.

Not only to help find her son but also to face the male who had made her life a living hell for so long, to finally have the chance to say what she should have done for so many years.

His dragon murmured, *She is stronger now than before, and we'll be watching the whole thing. It's different from Charlie—we're not entirely helpless this time. We won't let the situation get out of control.*

He knew his beast was right. They'd only be in the next room, not waiting on Stonefire while Sarah was who the bloody hell knew where. However, it still wasn't easy to ignore his protectiveness when it came to his new mate. He wanted to ensure they had a future together.

Sarah stroked his jaw and whispered, "I'll be okay, aye? You've helped me find myself a bit, Hudson. And the latest version of Sarah Carter-Wells can handle this, I promise you."

Seeing how far Sarah had come made Hudson want to pull her close, kiss her, and tell her how he felt. Because even if it had been a short time, he loved his mate.

Although he knew love also meant trust, and he would have to trust Sarah in this. He nodded. "I know. But I'll be watching, and if he so much as looks at you in a way I don't like, I'm barging into the room."

She smiled and patted her hand against his chest. "Give me at least a few minutes, Hudson. Once I'm done, you can say whatever you like. Although I'll have to be the one watching you then, to ensure my mate stays free for many years to come and doesn't end up in some DDA jail cell."

Kai finally grunted nearby and spoke up. "I'll be watching everyone with you, Sarah. I won't have Bram going to jail either."

Stonefire's clan leader growled, "Carter's lucky my mate convinced me to hand him over to the DDA. But if anything has happened to my niece, I will find a way to destroy him."

Hudson blinked at Bram. It'd been a long time since he'd seen the male so angry.

But before anyone could think of how to respond to Bram's words, there was another knock on the door. Bronx walked into the room and met first Bram's and then Sarah's eyes. "Everything's ready for you, Sarah. I also have my core team in the observation room so we can start planning a possible extraction immediately with Kai and Nikki."

Sarah nodded but leaned a bit more against Hudson. He rubbed her back as she replied, "Aye, well, then let's get started, shall we?"

As Hudson led his mate out of the room and followed his brother down the hall and then another, he murmured to Sarah, "Once you get the information you need about Joey and Ava, don't forget to tell him to go fuck himself."

Despite everything, she smiled at him. "Oh, aye, I plan to."

He grinned back at her as Bronx stopped in front of a door. His brother said, "He's in here, Sarah. Wait a minute before entering so we can all settle inside the observation room. Don't hesitate a second about calling out for help if you need it."

Once Sarah nodded, the rest of the group left them alone in the hallway, and Hudson kissed her lips gently. "I believe in you, Sarah. Now go face that bastard and find out what you can so we can bring Joey and Ava home."

She squeezed his hand in hers. "Aye, I will. But I might have to play up my old self a wee bit at first to lower his guard. So don't be alarmed if I seem afraid or start stuttering or some such thing. Rob loves to talk about himself and prove how much more clever he thinks he is."

He grunted. "I won't like it, but as long as it'll only be an act, I won't crash into the room and defend you."

She nodded. "A certain dragonman helped me build confidence in myself. And I don't think I could completely go back to the person I was when I was married to Rob."

"Good." He kissed her one last time and wanted to tell her he loved her but knew it wasn't the right time. Instead, he added, "I very much can't wait until our family is whole once more, and then I can have the new Sarah all to myself again for a few hours."

With that, he finally released her, and it took everything he had to leave her and enter the observation room. As Hudson stood in front of the two-way glass and crossed his arms over his chest, he glared at the piece of shite sitting in the other room and almost willed for the human to give him a reason to pummel him.

His dragon sighed. *I would like that, but we can't risk our mate and new family.*

I know, dragon. But there's nothing wrong with a bit of fantasy.

Then Sarah entered the room, and Hudson pushed aside everything to watch how his mate handled her ex.

SARAH TOOK one last deep breath, willed her face free of emotion, and then entered the room.

The dark-blond, brown-eyed form of Rob sat handcuffed to a chair across the room. As soon as he noted it was her, he laughed. "If they think sending you in here is some sort of enticement, then they're in for a bloody big surprise. If anything, your presence makes me sick. If what Mark said is true, you're fucking a dragon now, disgusting little bitch you are."

At one point, the words would've made Sarah look down at the ground, say nothing, and take his vitriol.

But now, Sarah wanted to stand tall and tell him to sod off. However, she had to play up the old role Rob was used to, so she quickly glanced downward and tried to slump her posture a bit.

And even though they couldn't see through the glass on the far side of the room, she swore she could feel Hudson's gaze on her.

Rob's voice garnered her attention again. "That's right, you've realized your mistake now, you whore. But I won't take you back. The lads will be mine, though, after I tell the DDA how your bloody dragonman abused them."

Sarah couldn't stop herself from looking up at Rob and blurting, "That's not true."

Rob smiled cruelly. "Aye, maybe. But Mark said he'll say whatever I want, as long as he can stay with me."

For a beat, betrayal and pain crushed her heart at just how far Mark was willing to go to get away from her.

But then she reminded herself that Mark only knew the fairy-tale version of his father. She had to hold onto hope that once some of Rob's true nature was revealed, her son might change his mind. Especially since Joey had been taken, which had obviously frightened Mark.

It wasn't only Mark she had to think of at the moment, though. A group of people were watching and no doubt recording this entire conversation. Rob had already admitted to one falsehood, so she needed to get him talking more to both hang himself and to help them find Joey.

"And what of Joey? They took him. And if he's dead, you won't get your bloody money from your parents. You should at least care about that."

Rob shrugged. "They won't kill Joey. They wanted live dragon brats to study, experiment on, and use as broodmares to make more bastards to harvest for dragon's blood. Once they realize Joey is human, they'll give him back to me."

The thought of any child, but especially her youngest son, being poked, prodded, and who the bloody hell knew what with made her stomach churn. But the other missing child, Ava, would be treated far worse because she was a dragon-shifter.

More than that, Sarah had met the lass during the play, and Ava was almost old enough to be used as a broodmare.

At that thought, Sarah's anger intensified. She needed to save Ava *and* Joey. Both of them. And to do that, she needed to find out more without making Rob overly suspicious.

But how?

Then she remembered something from the year before, about why Lochguard had kept Rob locked up on their clan—his outrageous debts. "Are you sure they'll give him back to you? If you owe them money, they might just sell him instead."

Rob shook his head. "No, the hunters just want to test new weapons, or something like that, on dragons and create their own dragon's blood farms with slaves. My old cell mate owes me, and he'll give Joey back to me. Especially if we can use him as bait to catch some more dragon brats."

Hunters probably meant dragon hunters, and there couldn't have been too many men who'd shared a jail cell with Rob.

It might be enough for the dragons to find the children, but Sarah wanted to see if she could get more. The less time Joey and Ava had to spend in the hands of the kidnappers, the better.

She stood a wee bit taller and shed some of her old habits to state firmly, "You think you're so clever, Rob, but the DDA won't just let you walk free."

He grinned in the way that meant he was a step ahead of her. "So says the daft bitch. I have my ways. I'll walk free, I promise you."

She barely resisted a gasp as his meaning sank in —he knew someone inside the DDA, some person who would look the other way.

Triumph flared in Rob's eyes. "Oh, aye, I know people. And soon enough, you'll have no chance in hell of ever keeping the lads. And once all the dragons are either enslaved or killed off, and Britain controls them, you'll be homeless, penniless, and have to sell your body just to eat. Oh, wait, no, that won't work." He gave her a derisive look. "No bloke would want to fuck that."

With a growl, Sarah walked over and leaned down toward Rob and spat out, "Your words no longer have power over me, Rob Carter. And you're the one who's going to end up at rock bottom, you fucking arsehole."

He blinked, unsure of what to say when she actually stood up for herself.

Not wanting to be near him any longer, she turned and left the room. As she leaned back against the closed door, she willed her heart to slow down.

Before she could think of how she'd might've just screwed up finding Joey, Hudson was at her side. He pulled her into a hug, and she laid her head on his chest. "I'm sorry. I lost my head at the end."

He tilted her face upward until she could meet his flashing eyes. "Don't fucking apologize. I would've ripped his head off far sooner and then stomped on his dead corpse for good measure."

"It's a bit violent and yet oddly still romantic."

He snorted and then cupped her cheek. "You did brilliantly, Sarah."

She searched his gaze. "Did I? I should've tried pushing him for more before exploding."

He shook his head. "No, you did great. Kai and Bronx said it might be enough, especially if they tap into all the contacts the dragon-shifters in the UK have across the island. And Bram's mate, Evie, is going to ensure someone she trusts from the DDA deals with Rob before she puts out feelers to find the traitor within their ranks." He stroked her cheek, and some of her tension faded. "Not to mention I'm bloody proud of you for telling him off."

"It did feel good." As the adrenaline faded from her body, she leaned more heavily against Hudson. "I want to hear what Bronx and Kai have to say and then go back to Mark."

"Did you want me to go with you?"

She hated the slight hesitation in Hudson's voice. He was a caring, patient, protective dragonman, but hearing how her son would've leveled abuse allegations against him was going a step too far. "I-I don't know. I think I need to deal with Mark on my own." She bit her lip and then whispered, "We can live apart until he's more accepting, if that's what you want. I know hearing what he would've done for his father can't be easy for you."

He growled. "Don't even bloody think it. I can't say I'm happy about what Mark was going to do, but I know his father was behind the idea, not him. We'll make this work, Sarah. I lo— er, care for you and your boys. We'll focus on finding Joey first and then figure it out from there."

She stared at Hudson a beat, trying to process his

near slip. It couldn't be right—he couldn't love her. She'd brought nothing but trouble to his life.

But she didn't get to respond because Kai appeared in the hallway, along with Bronx. "Come on, Sarah. We have a few more questions, and then we need to adjust our plans. After that, you can go back to your eldest son and wait for updates."

She looked up at Hudson, and he nodded. "Go, love. I need to check on Elliott and give him some reassurance about all this. I'll be home whenever you need me."

He kissed her gently and slipped away.

Sarah wanted to shout for him to come back, but didn't. They both had to take care of their children, the threats, and only then could they figure out a path together.

So Sarah went with Kai and Bronx, answered their questions, and went back to the surgery. Since Mark was asleep again—naturally and not via drugs, Lachlan shared—she curled up on the sofa in the room, and exhaustion took over. She fell asleep, hoping things would be better when she woke up.

Chapter Twenty-Three

Persephone "Percy" Smith had always been alone.

Abandoned by a human mother who didn't want her half-dragon child, she'd grown up in the only orphanage in England, Wales, and Scotland dedicated to dragon offspring. None of the other children had wanted anything to do with the freak who had a large birthmark covering her neck, shoulder, upper chest, and bicep, and so she'd learned to be her own friend, enjoy her own company—her inner dragon had been silenced early on—and had constantly dreamed of the day someone would adopt her. About how someone would finally see past her freakish exterior and truly want to love her as their own.

But the years had ticked by, her dream never

happening. And then shortly after her thirteenth birthday, after her first period, Percy had learned a fucking hard lesson about life and that dreams and happiness were steaming piles of bullshit.

Sold to a fringe group of dragon hunters, she'd been kept a prisoner inside this old, crumbling mansion for the last seven years. She'd been raped repeatedly, beaten for fun, and studied like some sort of a lab rat in a maze or inside a cage.

She'd dreamed of escape, wanting to be free so she could get her inner dragon back and finally embrace who she was—a dragon-shifter. She'd never even learned to fly before her captivity, and it was the one wish and dream she hadn't quite gotten the strength to toss aside—to shift into her dragon form for the first time and finally feel the wind under her wings.

But even if Percy could escape, she had no one to run to for help. Fleeing her prison would've meant starving or freezing to death in the wilderness. What she knew of dragon clans wasn't good, and no one wanted half-human bastards like her. Both the orphanage and her captors had made that abundantly clear.

However, after seven years of hell with no real plan of how to escape, she finally had the possibility of leaving this fucking place, one she hoped she could take and use to gain her freedom.

Because Dr. Giles Stanton's team—he was the

human in charge of this dragon baby-farm-slash-research-lab—was bringing her the two children they'd recently snatched and had ordered her to take care of them. Stanton had said it would make her useful as they waited to see if she was finally pregnant or not.

Given it'd been seven years of males fucking her with no baby, Percy doubted it.

And yet, they'd keep trying, using her for their twisted research purposes.

Some might've shivered at the thought of how her captors would try to force her to have sex again with the catatonic dragonman, but emotions were deadly inside Stanton's compound. Percy wasn't even sure she could feel anything anymore, apart from distrust or cynicism.

But if she could run, could finally give a double-finger salute to all the arseholes working in the compound, she'd take it. The only thing she wanted to do before she died was to embrace her dragon again, shift, and be able to fly in the sky. What happened to her after that, well, that didn't really matter.

Voices grew closer outside in the hallway, and she pushed every thought, wish, or plan out of her mind. Some of the males here were extremely good at reading people, and she couldn't risk them sensing her newfound determination.

A key turned in the lock to her small set of

rooms, and the door opened. Her least favorite guard, Denny Browne, gave her a once over with heat in his cruel blue eyes. Ever since Stanton had forbidden the guards from touching her last year—to test out her fertility with half and pure dragon-shifters—Denny had been looking for a way to defy the order.

Ignoring the bastard, she instead focused on the two children in front of him, both of them bound and gagged, dirty, and clearly rumpled. The girl was probably ten or eleven, and the boy was several years younger. Both had fear in their eyes, but only the girl's pupils flashed to slits and back.

It'd been so long since Percy had seen her own eyes do the same, but she ignored the longing in her heart; she refused to give Denny the satisfaction. Instead, she kept her voice cold and addressed the guard, "What do you want me to do with them?"

Denny shrugged. "You're a woman. Mother them. And teach them to obey, or all three of you will suffer." He leered at the little girl. "She can be my new pet."

The boy and girl cried out behind their gags, but Percy managed to ignore their distress and Denny's veiled threat for now. Once she was alone, she'd talk to the children and maybe soothe them a bit, but not before.

And if she had her way, it would be a cold day in

hell before Denny ever touched the girl. "I'll need extra rations, bedding, and clothes for them."

"You'll get whatever Dr. Stanton sends you."

She knew that to be true, and Percy wouldn't hold her breath.

After a few moments of staring the guard down, he finally pushed the children toward her, gave her another lewd stare, and locked her inside the room.

Without hesitation, she marched the two children to the bathroom, turned on the fan and the shower, and squatted down to their eye level. Keeping her voice as low as she could and still be audible, she said, "This is the only way we can talk without them hearing us. I need to be quick. So if I take off your restraints, will you remain quiet?" The two children looked at each other, but Percy growled at the hesitation. "We don't have time for this. I understand you're scared, but I'm your best hope at getting out of here, as long as you have someone missing and looking for you. Do you?" They both nodded. "Good. Then stay quiet as I take these off, and I'll explain."

As she removed the restraints first—Percy had long ago learned every weakness when it came to keeping her locked up in this bloody place—she continued talking. "My name is Percy. I want to leave here just as much as you. But tell me this—do you have a phone number memorized to call someone you care for?"

Percy took off their gags and waited to see if they'd scream. Not that anyone in this fucking place would care, but it would make things more difficult for her to convince them she was on their side, at least for the moment.

Finally, the girl said, "Yes, I can call my uncle. If he knows where I am, he'll come and get me. I know it."

The boy spoke up. "My mum and uncle and stepdad will come too."

Ah, to be a child who was wanted. Percy had no bloody idea what that felt like.

But it was an essential tool for her plan, so she nodded. "Good." She motioned toward the boy. "We're going to turn our backs, and you get undressed and into the shower. If you aren't clean when they come back, they'll be suspicious." She turned her and the girl around without asking and whispered into the dragon girl's ear. "Now, I have a mobile phone in here, and I can tell you exactly where you are. But only if your uncle will give me a place to stay for a few weeks, free of charge. Will he do that?"

The girl's pupils flashed before she answered, "Are you a dragon-shifter? I don't see a tattoo, but my dragon says she thinks you are one."

"I was born one, yes."

No point in revealing how her dragon hadn't

talked to her in a long, long time or that she hadn't really ever been taught to be a proper dragon-shifter, even before she'd been sold to Stanton. The orphanage had wanted them to act more human than dragon, no matter if it slowly destroyed their souls in the process.

The girl bit her lip and then said, "My uncle should help another dragon-shifter, especially if you get us back home."

Not exactly an ironclad promise, but it'd have to do. She leaned a fraction closer. "I have no reason to hurt you." The girl looked extremely skeptical for a child, so Percy added, "I understand you're scared. But no matter what the others say, I won't hurt you, little girl. I was brought here when I wasn't much older than you, and trust me, you don't want the same fate I had." Curiosity sparked in the girl's eyes, but Percy ignored it. She wasn't going to share her nightmare of a past with her. "What's your name?"

"Ava."

"Well, Ava, we don't have much longer before I have to turn the shower off." Percy moved to the wall, removed one of the tiles she'd worked loose years ago to hide items, and took out the mobile phone she'd stolen recently from one of the guards. She made it a habit to routinely steal and return them, to always have a fresh battery, just in case.

After taking it out of the plastic bag, she turned it

on and waited for it to load. "Once we make the call, you need to still act scared and not let the guards know help might be coming. Can you do that?"

Ava stood a little taller. "My uncle will come." Percy raised an eyebrow. "He will. But yes, I can. Joey might be harder, though. He's still a bit young."

She leaned closer to the girl's ear. "Then we'll have to tell him our plan didn't work."

The girl frowned. "You want me to lie to Joey?"

Percy wanted to laugh at this dragon girl's innocence, but didn't. "Yes. No one can know we called your uncle."

After Ava's eyes flashed a few times, she nodded. "I can do that."

"Good." She handed the phone to Ava. "Now, here's what you need to tell your uncle."

She gave the easiest directions she could to the old mansion and watched the girl dial. Almost instantly Ava cried out, "Uncle Bram!"

Percy hissed. "Quietly."

Ava nodded and cupped her hand over her mouth and bottom of the phone and talked for about two minutes. She lowered the phone, but instead of ending the call, she offered it to Percy. "He wants to talk to you."

"We don't have time for that."

"If you want his help, talk to him."

The girl was fairly cheeky for her age. But Percy

grabbed the phone and copied Ava's gestures so her voice wouldn't carry. "Hello?"

A male's voice, in a Northern English accent, came over the line. "Who the fuck are you?"

"The person trying to help your bloody niece." She pushed Ava away, toward the far wall, so she wouldn't hear her. "I suggest you come to save us, or she'll be raped within the week. These fuckers are twisted. But lucky for you, not heavily armed."

There was silence for a beat, and then the male replied, "How do I know this isn't a trap?"

"You don't. But will you risk it?"

He grunted. "No. But if you harm my niece, I'll fucking have your head."

"Stop with your threats and send someone here. Quickly. I can only keep them safe for so long. Find out where they keep Percy Smith, and you'll find us."

She hung up and turned off the phone, stashed everything back behind the tile, and turned around.

The boy had wet hair and a towel around his shoulders. He whispered, "Is help coming?"

Without missing a beat, Percy shook her head. "No. But I'll watch over you."

The boy's expression fell, but Percy ignored it and looked to Ava. "Your turn. I'll take him to get dressed as you shower." She whispered, "Quickly."

Ava nodded, and Percy guided Joey out of the room. "Come on. The sooner you're dressed, the sooner I can feed you."

And so Percy acted as if she reluctantly took care of them, waiting to see if her gamble had paid off.

She didn't dare hope for a bloody thing. But maybe, just maybe, someone cared enough about the children to actually save them.

All they could do was wait and see.

Chapter Twenty-Four

Someone poked her shoulder, and Sarah jolted upright, blinking. For a second, she wondered where she was, but then she saw Mark standing over her. He still wore his hospital gown, but his gaze was uncertain.

Without preamble, he blurted, "Did they find Joey yet? Can you check?"

For the first time in a long time, Mark looked lost and young and merely like a lad who needed his mother.

So Sarah opened her arms and motioned for him to hug her. For a beat, he did nothing. Then he sat next to her and wrapped his arms around her. "I'm so sorry, Mum. I didn't know they'd take Joey."

Stroking Mark's hair with one hand, she squeezed him close with her other arm. "All of the dragon clans are looking for him. And if there's a way, they'll rescue him. Not to mention Joey's stronger than most people think."

He nodded, and Sarah simply held Mark for a few minutes, both embracing in silence, as she tried to figure out what to say next. She wished she could continue to shelter Mark, make him believe his life never had any worries, but knew they couldn't keep going on like that. Joey had been kidnapped as a result, and she couldn't risk someone else getting hurt in the future.

With a sigh, she finally leaned back until she could look Mark in the eyes. She stilled her hand in his hair and cupped the side of his face. "Joey being taken wasn't your fault. It was your father's. He admitted as much to me and the others."

Mark frowned. "Why would Dad want Joey kidnapped?"

"He wanted a distraction and didn't care that some friend of his would kidnap children to do it. Although, I'm curious—how did he even know you would be there?"

Mark looked down. "I called him and let him know. He said he wanted to see me and take me away."

She softened her voice. "Why did you want to leave so badly, Mark? You must've known he wouldn't have taken you back to Lochguard, like you wanted.

He hates dragon-shifters. That's why he left us last year."

"H-he said the dragons would want to hurt me or force me away because I'm human."

"But certainly you can't believe that? You loved being on Lochguard and saw firsthand how almost everyone welcomed you."

He shrugged one shoulder. "That was Lochguard, and Dad said he knew Stonefire's reputation, and it was heaps worse."

Sarah wished she'd done more than tell Rob off. No, she should've slapped him for using their son and manipulating him. "Stonefire is a lot like Lochguard. If you'd talk more with Daisy, or the other humans living here, you'd find that out."

He frowned, and his voice turned angry, but he kept his gaze downward. "It's more than Stonefire, though. I miss my friends in Glasgow. And then we moved to Lochguard. I'd just made friends again, and you said we had to move here. And now you want to replace my dad." He finally looked at her, tears in his eyes. "Why can't we go back home to Glasgow and live like before? Dad wasn't home much, aye, but that was okay. Because I had school, and football, and friends. And, and…"

She stroked his cheek. "And what, Mark?"

"And you didn't want to replace me with a new brother, a new dad, and probably even a new bairn sometime. They're all so much nicer than me and make you smile. I always make you frown or angry. You'll not want me soon. I thought maybe if I threatened to go to Dad, you'd try harder to keep me."

Her heart squeezed at Mark's words. "Come here." She hugged him tightly again. "I'm your mum, Mark. I'll always want you."

His voice was muffled against her shoulder. "Not true. My mate Jimmy back in Glasgow got a new stepdad, and soon his mum only ever shouted at him. Told him he was trouble and that she'd send him off to his grandparents if he didn't start behaving better."

"I don't know the circumstances about Jimmy, only about us." She leaned back to look into Mark's eyes once more. "Do you know the full reason why I wanted to mate a dragon-shifter so quickly?" Mark shook his head, and she continued, "It was because I got a letter saying your Carter grandparents wanted to take you away from me, especially if we moved back to Glasgow."

Mark frowned. "Why? They only ever talk about sending me and Joey away to a fancy school."

"Because to them, you are like a football— something they want to possess for a short while before kicking away. And they've never liked me and would love to take away my lads to make me sad. So

I did what I needed to do to stay with a dragon clan, where we could all protect you."

"But I saw you and Hudson kissing at the mating party. So you must fancy him, and soon you'll probably have another child."

Fancy wasn't a strong enough word for what Sarah felt, but she wasn't about to delve into her feelings with Mark before she'd fully examined them herself. "I do like Hudson quite a bit. He makes me smile and laugh. That's good, aye?"

"I suppose," Mark begrudgingly muttered.

She squeezed his shoulder and pushed on. "As for your fears, just know that Hudson never wants to replace your father, only be there when you need him. And Elliott is lovely, but he can never replace my two dear lads, aye? Never." She smoothed some hair off his face. "Do you think you could at least give him and Elliott a chance and see if you get on?"

Mark's voice was so faint she could barely hear it when he asked, "So you're not going to send me away for what happened to Joey?"

"If you promise to talk to me, tell me your fears and what worries you instead of sneaking behind my back, then I think we can start over, all of us—me, you, Joey, Hudson, and Elliott."

Or so she desperately hoped. It would be a hell of a lot harder if anything happened to Joey, but Sarah wasn't about to forsake her son when it was clearly Rob's fault for what had happened. Mark was only a child.

He nodded, but before Mark could answer, Hudson burst into the room and said, "They've had a call from Ava and think they know where Joey is too. They should be arriving there soon. Come. We can wait at the Protector building and hear the news in real time."

The fact at least Ava was alive right now gave Sarah hope. She stood, bringing Mark with her, and she looked at her eldest. "Do you want to come with us?"

Mark bobbed his head and went for his pile of clothes on a chair.

Hudson took her hand and squeezed. He whispered into her ear, "Better?"

"A wee bit. If they find Joey, then there's hope for us all."

He looked like he wanted to kiss her, but then he glanced at Mark and stepped back.

Rather than focus on the sting of his actions, Sarah helped get Mark ready and followed Hudson to the main Stonefire security building. All that mattered right now was finding out what happened to Joey. After that, she'd find a way to mend her new family, no matter what it took.

Hours later, Hudson sat next to Sarah on a sofa, her son Mark sitting on her other side—dozing against his mother—and debated if he should get them all something to eat.

He'd expected they would learn more about what had happened with the rescue attempt, but the Protectors and rescue teams were being fairly quiet about the details. Not even Bram, who sat on another sofa opposite with his mate, Evie, knew exactly what was happening minute-by-minute.

They'd been told how they were too close to the situation and the Protectors needed to free up any and all resources to bring home the two children, without interference, especially from Bram.

Glancing at his clan leader, Hudson could imagine how tough this had to be for Bram right now. Or even Sarah, for that matter.

After all, Hudson knew what it was like to wait to hear word about someone they loved being in danger. He desperately hoped it turned out better this time than it had in his past, both with Charlie and his mother.

Needing the reassurance of his mate's presence as much as she probably did his, he squeezed Sarah's hand in his gently. She looked at him and managed a watery smile.

Fuck. The sight shot straight to his heart. Hudson wished he could go and find Joey right here and now.

His dragon spoke up. *We did what we could, and Sarah needs us here. Especially if something goes wrong.*

No, I refuse to think of that right now.

I know, but it's a possibility. We need to be prepared if she receives the worst news imaginable, like we did years ago. If not for our brothers, who knows how we would've pulled through.

True, Bronx and Brooklyn had stepped up and helped with both him and Elliott. If, and it was only if as he refused to believe otherwise, the worst news came down, he'd do everything he could for Sarah. *But I still have faith in the Protectors. Joey and Ava were alive not long ago, and I believe they'll come home.*

His dragon's voice softened. *I hope so too.*

As he focused on Sarah's delicate hand in his, a sense of peace came over him. Maybe why memories of waiting for Charlie hadn't crashed over him was because he had a purpose again, to look after his new mate. He knew Charlie would've wanted Hudson to be happy again, and that happiness needed Sarah, which meant taking care of her always.

True, there were a shit-ton of problems to sort through still, but he loved his human, and he'd do anything for her. Even if it meant retreating for a bit so her eldest son could come to accept them.

His dragon growled. *I don't want to do that.*

Neither do I, but if keeping distance for a short while results in a healed whole family, I'll do it.

Before his dragon could argue some more, there

was a knock on the door. It opened, and Joey and Ava ran inside. Sarah rushed to her son at the same time Bram went to his niece. As they both hugged and kissed the children, Hudson's eyes teared up a bit. The children had made it home, and at least for now, Stonefire wouldn't have to endure more tragedy.

He could only hope this was a sign things would be better going forward, for them all.

Clearing his throat, he pushed the burst of emotion aside. This time the news was good, the best kind, and that was all that mattered.

Sarah finally released Joey enough to lean back, and she asked, "Are you okay? Did they hurt you?"

Joey shook his head. "Not much. The handcuff things hurt a wee bit, but then that nice dragon lady helped us. She told the bad guys off and cooked us dinner."

Hudson had noticed that Kai and Quinn Summers—another Protector—stood in the doorway. So he moved closer to them and asked, "Who is he talking about?"

Kai raised his voice so the humans in the room could also hear him, so he wouldn't have to repeat himself. "The dragonwoman who helped them is named Percy Smith. She was a prisoner, too, but helped us get the children away, as well as told us where to find most of the other captives in the same building." He glanced at Bram. "We brought them here, for now, to let you decide what to do with them for the long-term."

Bram nodded, standing but still keeping his niece nearby. "Of course. Once I get Ava settled with Evie, I'll come talk more about them. But where is this dragonwoman who helped the children?"

Kai shrugged. "She's with Bronx and Zain right now whilst the others we rescued are with Sid and Gregor in the surgery."

Hudson knew Kai well enough to read between the lines—the Percy woman was being interviewed and assessed. Zain was one of the best interrogators, but Bronx was the best at feeling out those who were victims or traumatized. Ever since Bronx had lost his leg, he'd focused more and more on assisting those who needed his help after some major rescue or traumatic event.

Kai motioned his head toward Ava and Joey. "Dr. Sid already checked them out. They're a little tired but physically fine."

Left unsaid was that they didn't know what sort of psychological effects the kidnapping would have on them. Since Hudson knew how things like this could bring nightmares—Elliott's had been pretty bad right after his mother's death—he'd keep a close watch over the lad, if he could.

Hudson watched as Mark went over to Joey. He tapped his brother's shoulder and whispered, "I'm sorry, Joey."

Joey frowned up at his brother. "Why?"

"It's my fault you were taken."

Sarah shook her head. "We can talk more about that later. Right now, let's just celebrate Joey coming home safe." She stood and placed an arm around each boy's shoulders. "Come, I'm taking you two home."

She met Hudson's eyes, and he was about to ask which home. But Joey spoke up. "Aye, I want to go home. Elliott will be worried too. Maybe he and Mark and me can all play some video games together? And maybe get some scones or cake? Scones and cake always make things better."

Hudson resisted smiling at Joey's words. He knew the lad and his mother both enjoyed them, and no doubt Joey wanted to cheer up his mum.

However, as Sarah glanced down at Mark, Hudson listened intently as she asked softly, "Will that be okay…for Hudson and Elliott to celebrate with us?"

Hudson held his breath a beat, waiting to see what the boy said.

When Mark bobbed his head, Hudson's entire body relaxed a fraction. Mark replied, "Aye, I need a rematch with Elliott anyway."

Mark looked at him a second before glancing back to the floor. He sensed the boy's answer was an apology of sorts, as well as a reluctant acceptance of Hudson mating his mother. Well, at least for now.

They had a long way to go, but Hudson would take it.

Sarah pulled both of her sons closer against her. "Aye, then a night of cake, and scones, and video games all together sounds perfect." She looked back at Hudson. "Right?"

He smiled, trying to convey how relieved he was at Mark's temporary acceptance. "Add in some sausage rolls, and it'll be perfect. Elliott will be thrilled, I know it."

He moved a little closer to his new family, and Joey took his hand. Hudson smiled down at the boy. "All right?"

Joey nodded. "Aye. Let's go home."

Home. He desperately wanted that, but time would tell how soon he could always be home with his new family.

His dragon huffed. *One thing at a time. Treasure tonight, and we'll figure out the rest tomorrow.*

Since he knew how precious the present could be, Hudson wholeheartedly agreed with his dragon.

Sarah smiled at him over her lads before looking at Kai. "Thank you, to all of you."

Kai merely nodded. "No worries. Go home and enjoy time with your family. I can answer more of your questions tomorrow."

Sarah led the way out of the room, and Hudson nodded to Kai, Quinn, and Bram before following his mate and stepsons out.

As Joey chatted about the dragonwoman who'd helped him, Hudson kept glancing at Sarah, her sons, and back again. They had a long way to go as a family, but at least they would be together tonight. More than ever, he was determined to ensure they remained a family in the future too.

Chapter Twenty-Five

S arah had hovered over her lads all evening, but she couldn't help it. She'd been afraid she'd wake up and find it had all been a dream, and instead, her life had turned into a nightmare.

But no, it was real. Joey was safe, Mark was at least trying to be less gruff with Hudson, and Rob had been carted away by someone Bram's mate trusted at the DDA.

Given her track record in life, it meant something was bound to go very, very wrong.

Stop it, Sarah. She didn't want to think like that any longer. Besides, as she stared at all three lads sleeping on the floor of Elliott's room under a makeshift tent of sorts, she held on to hope that everything would work out.

She felt Hudson's heat behind her, and he

whispered into her ear. "Come. They're asleep, and we should talk."

She slowly closed the door until it was only open a fraction—just in case Joey ended up with nightmares from his kidnapping and she wanted to be able to hear—and allowed Hudson to guide them down the hall to their room.

Once inside, he shut the door. She opened her mouth to protest, and he said, "Don't worry, I'll open it as soon as we're done. But I don't want to wake them. And if Joey has a nightmare, Elliott will come get us. I promise you."

She nodded and simply stared at Hudson. He'd been so supportive throughout everything, but she knew that not only had Mark's actions stung him, waiting for word of Joey must've reminded Hudson of when his late mate had been in danger and died.

Since her sons were asleep and taken care of, she decided to finally broach that topic. She closed the distance between them and laid a hand on his chest. "Are you okay? Waiting with me and Mark couldn't have been easy."

He brushed a strand of hair off her cheek and then traced her jaw. "It ended happily today, and that's all that matters."

"Is it?" She cupped his cheek with her free hand. "You've been so strong for me, listening when I need it. I want to do the same for you."

He shook his head. "You're the one who went through hell today, Sarah. You should let me take care of you."

As his fingers moved to trace her lips, she lost her train of thought for a second. But she quickly pushed it away. "Stop trying to change the subject."

After searching her eyes, he sighed. "No, it wasn't easy. But unlike with Charlie, I was able to help this time."

"More than help. Aye, you did the data gathering, and that's brilliant. But you also were there for me, and Joey, and even Mark, despite what he did or would've done."

She looked away from him and tried not to cry. If Rob had managed to go through with his plan, and if Mark had accused Hudson of abuse, she didn't know if she would've been strong enough to survive that.

What she went through with Rob had been hell, but she hadn't ever really loved him. Oh, aye, she'd been infatuated at first. But nothing she'd ever felt for Rob compared to what Hudson meant to her. Despite it being such a short time, she couldn't imagine her life without him.

He was her rock, the man who'd made her believe in trust, one who wanted to try so hard with her son, and on top of all that, understood her so well both in and out of the bedroom.

Hudson gently forced her head back to meet his

gaze. His pupils flashed rapidly, but his voice was soft as he replied, "I love you, Sarah. And that means I'll do whatever it takes to try to win over your sons because I know what becoming a family means to you."

She blinked, unsure if she heard him properly. "Pardon?"

He smiled slowly. "Maybe I should've waited to tell you, but I learned a long time ago not to hold back and wait for tomorrow. Both with my late mate and my mother. They were taken suddenly, and I left so much unsaid. I don't ever want to do that with you." He threaded his fingers through her hair and leaned a fraction closer. "So yes, I love you, Sarah Carter-Wells, and I'll spend every day trying to convince you that it's true."

Sarah vaguely knew of his mother's death, and she really should ask more about it. But as he gazed down at her, his eyes full of love, she couldn't find her voice.

He kissed her gently and murmured, "Will you let me take care of you now, Sarah? After today, you deserve all the pleasure in the world."

Even though her body instantly reacted to his words, she finally found her voice. "Aye, but let me say something first." He tilted his head in question. She took a deep breath and found the courage to push on. "You're such a good man, Hudson Wells. One I can hardly believe is real. You're kind and clever and a devoted father. You offer help to strangers and do everything in your power to help those you care for.

"I didn't think I'd ever find a man to trust, let alone love. And yet somehow you've convinced me, without a shadow of a doubt, that aye, I love you. You're bloody wonderful, too good to be true, and yet I won't push you aside. I want you to claim me, to make me yours for all your days. Because even if the road ahead will be a bit rough, and messy, and not perfect, I won't care as long as I have you." She leaned her forehead against his. "I love you, Hudson. And I desperately want you to show me you love me too, without words."

His pupils flashed, and he growled before taking her lips in a rough, demanding kiss. Each stroke, and flick, and swipe was a claim on her. Not just of her mouth or her body, but her heart as well.

When he finally pulled back, his hot breath danced across her lips as he said, "I love you, Sarah. You're my second chance, and I'll spend the rest of my life showing you how much I love you." He moved to her ear, nibbled her earlobe a beat, and then said, "Tell me your fantasy, love. And I'll give it to you."

Her heart thumped hard in her chest as wetness rushed between her thighs at his promise. It took her a second to blurt, "Take control, and because it's you, everything will be my fantasy."

He groaned. "I love you so bloody much, woman." He kissed her quickly before stepping back. His tone had that irresistible, firm hint of dominance as he ordered, "Now, strip and sit in the chair with your legs hooked over the arms, and then wait silently for me. With that sweet pussy of yours on display, I can learn all the ways to make you scream."

She shivered as she stripped and walked to the chair. After she managed to get her legs over the arms, she waited.

Hudson stared and stared some more. Each second made her lower lips throb and for wetness to rush between her thighs in anticipation of when he'd finally act.

And because it was Hudson, she knew he wasn't doing it to be cruel, stir her up, and walk away. No, he was going to make her orgasm mind-blowing by the end, even if he took his time. Aye, she trusted him to do that without any doubt.

He tugged off his top, and she took in his muscled chest, the hair dusting across it, leading down to his visibly hard cock inside his trousers. Licking her lips, she couldn't decide if she wanted him in her mouth or her cunt more.

Hudson's eyes flashed as he watched her mouth, so she licked her lips again. With a growl, Hudson shucked his trousers in record time and pumped his dick as he finally walked over to her. He lightly tweaked one nipple, and Sarah bit her lip to keep from moaning.

Hudson smiled. "That's right, focus only on the sensations, Sarah. When I lift your silence, you'll scream that much louder." He lightly traced her jaw, her cheek, her lips. "Put your hands on your thighs and keep yourself wide for me."

She did as he asked, and he rewarded her by leaning down to run his fingers through her slit, making her arch her hips a fraction. Back and forth he went, never quite touching her clit, until he plunged two fingers inside her, and Sarah gritted her teeth to not cry out.

But just as quickly, his fingers were gone, and she raised her hips, wanting his touch again.

Hudson shook his head. "Not quite yet, my love." He took his wet fingers and rubbed them along his cock. "First, you're going to suck my cock. And as you swallow me deep, knowing your taste is blending with mine, it'll make me so fucking hard, love. And you wet, I think."

Sarah squirmed as she stared at his cock. The things this man did to her.

Hudson chuckled, leaned down, and kissed her. "That's right. Pleasing me should please you, although I plan to make you come hard later, love. So hard that you'll never forget that you're mine and only mine."

Her heart thumped as she watched the tip of his

dick grow wet. Desperate to lick him, taste him, but not wanting to break his command, she opened her mouth. To please him, aye, but it would also show how he trusted her enough to place his cock in her mouth and know she wouldn't hurt him but only pleasure him.

Hudson threaded his fingers through her hair with one hand and ran the head of his cock along her lips with the other.

His precum glided over her skin, and she darted a tongue out to taste it.

Hudson's pupils flashed rapidly. "Eager to taste me, I see. Well, I can't keep my mate waiting. Take me as deep as you can and let me fuck your mouth."

Somehow Sarah kept her hands where he'd ordered them when all she wanted to do was touch him.

But as soon as he thrust his cock in her mouth, she moaned. His saltiness and her earthiness blended, doing exactly what he'd said—reminding her he was hers as much as she was his.

Hudson began thrusting slowly. "Use your tongue and suck me deep into that lovely tight throat of yours. Make me come so hard I can't remember my bloody name."

She moaned, and she tasted more of his essence on his tongue. She mewled again as she licked, and sucked, and tried to swallow him as deep as she could go.

Hudson's pace picked up, and as he thrust more wildly, she reveled in his loss of control, wanting to feel him let go completely, to claim him for the first time in the night.

"Fuck, Sarah. Your mouth is perfect. You're perfect."

His words made her suck harder, moaning to force vibrations on his cock.

He finally stilled and released in her mouth as he shouted her name, his hot jets of semen leaving salt and musk and pure Hudson in her mouth as she swallowed it all down.

He finally pulled out her mouth, wiped the spit from her face, and kissed her gently. His hand moved between her thighs and he groaned. "You're dripping for me, Sarah."

She smiled smugly as his cock stirred to life again a little. All because of her.

However, she didn't get to think of how far she'd come in terms of confidence and realizing her own sexual power and desirability because Hudson kneeled between her thighs and blew across her core.

It took every bit of restraint she possessed not to cry out and keep quiet. He murmured, "Soon, my love. Soon I'll let you scream. And then you can let go as loud as you want since the room is mostly soundproofed." He ran a finger through her center, and she pressed her legs even wider. Hudson chuckled. "I think it's time to reward you and that fabulous mouth of yours."

He licked her pussy slowly from one end to the other, careful to circle around her clit once but never quite touching it.

He whispered, "Close your eyes and simply feel the moment and revel in the sensations."

She did. And when Hudson finally lapped at her pussy again, she arched her back, each stroke seeming to be even more intense, more forceful, making her squirm.

When his fingers entered her, she leaned her head back, wanting to moan so badly. And yet keeping it in, with her eyes closed, made everything feel more intense. The pumping of his fingers hitting a spot deep inside her that heated her body. The swirl of his tongue around and around her clit. The gentle push of a thumb into her arse.

The sensation was almost too much, as if it would cross the line from pleasure into pain.

Then he took her clit between his lips and suckled, caressing the bud with his tongue, and her orgasm crashed over her. Wave after wave of pleasure rushed through her body, Hudson never ceasing his sweet torture of her pussy, arse, and clit, to the point she thought she might go mad from the never-ending intensity.

When she finally slumped into the chair, Sarah

almost missed Hudson's command. "Open your eyes, love, and look at me."

Her eyelids felt heavy, and it took far too much work to do as he bid. When she eventually managed it, Hudson cupped her head between his hands and kissed her, soft and gentle, a reminder he was there but knowing she needed a little more time to come down from her high. "Come here."

He scooped her into his arms and carried her to the bed. Once he lay next to her and spooned around her, his arm around her waist and one hand lightly stroking the pulse of her neck, he murmured, "I want you again, this time slow and gentle. I want your moans and sighs and to hear your lovely voice as you come." His hand ran down her front, lightly rubbing her still sensitive clit. "Tell me yes."

"Aye."

"Good."

He lifted one of her legs and wrapped it back around his hip. In the next second, his hard cock slid in from behind, and Sarah moaned. She felt so much fuller in this position.

Hudson kissed her neck, her shoulder, her cheek as he thrust slowly, each movement deliberate, as if indeed reminding her of his claim. And despite how wrung out she was from her first orgasm, the heat began to build again.

She was vaguely aware of Hudson caressing her

breasts, circling her nipples, and running his hand down her side.

But it all blurred together, especially once his fingers found her clit again.

Soon she cried out as she arched back against him. Hudson tightened his hold on her, stilled, and she felt his hot release inside her.

Breathing hard, Hudson notched his chin over her shoulder and held her tight. She reveled in his heat, his solid presence, and his scent.

After what must've been minutes, he finally kissed her cheek. "I love you, Sarah."

She wiggled back against him. "And I love you." She bit her lip, wanting to ask him something but unsure of ruining the moment.

Hudson gently squeezed her waist. "You're thinking and biting your lip, which means you're wondering if you should say something. Don't hold back with me, love. Ask or say anything to me."

Turning her in his arms, he moved her until Sarah lay on her side facing him. Gazing into his eyes, she took a deep breath and blurted, "Earlier you mentioned having regrets with your mother and your late mate. You told me about Charlie, but not really about your mum. What happened?"

He gently traced her cheek and studied her. But Sarah kept quiet, hoping her silence would prod him into answering. There was so much still to learn about her mate, but she sensed this was important to him.

HUDSON HADN'T EXPECTED Sarah to remember his mention of his mother. Maybe he hadn't pleasured her enough, given she still had her wits about her.

His dragon sighed. *She just wants to know you, us, more. Talk to her so maybe I can have a turn before she goes to sleep.*

She opened her mouth, probably to say not to worry, and that did it. Hudson replied before she could say anything, "I was fifteen. My brothers are older by three and six years, and even though those years mean nothing now, they were a big deal back then. They teased me about being the baby and how they didn't want to be seen with me, all the usual teenager and young adult crap you spout when trying to fit in.

"At any rate, from when I first learned to fly until the day she died, I usually accompanied my mother on flights to the lake or nearby mountains. She loved to talk about the flora and fauna, hoping one of her children would show interest. She would've loved Joey."

Sarah smiled at him and merely nodded, almost as if she was afraid to talk and break his spell.

His dragon growled. *Get on with it. I want her.*

Ignoring his beast, he did continue. "But as my brothers teased me about being a baby, and me wanting to prove I wasn't, the next time she asked me to go with her, I scoffed and said it was embarrassing to be flying out with my mum." He swallowed, the words still able to send regret flooding his body. "So she went by herself. She wasn't supposed to, of course, as back then, the DDA wasn't really that vigilant about the law or cared too much about the dragon-shifters, apart from the early stages of the sacrifice program.

"But mum didn't like to stay cooped up on the clan and went. And she never came home."

Sarah stroked his chest and asked softly, "What happened?"

He sucked in a breath and let it out. "Some humans in the area had created a contest to try and hunt a dragon without getting caught. They weren't like the dragon hunters or former Dragon Knights; they were just men trying to prove their dick sizes by hunting dragons. Mum wasn't a Protector, or anything like that, and far too trusting of humans. When she was sunning by the water, they mortally wounded her, and she died alone by the lake."

"And you blame yourself."

He nodded. "If I'd gone, I don't think they would've tried approaching two dragons. My mum died because I was trying to prove how manly I was. And in the end, I was a fucking idiot, one who let his pride and ego get in the way and hurt one of the people I loved."

For a few beats, Sarah did nothing but stroke his chest. Hudson finally looked down into her gaze, but instead of disappointment, or anger, or any other emotion he thought he deserved for all but sentencing his mother to death, all he saw was sadness. "Oh, Hudson. I, more than most, know what it's like to live with regrets. I married a man who used me, belittled me, and did everything in his power to make me feel worthless. But a certain dragonman taught me to believe in myself, and it made me finally accept that the past is that—the past. Maybe if you'd gone with her, it would've ended differently. Or maybe they would've gone after you too. More than that, you were still a child." She moved her hand to his cheek, and he leaned into her touch. "It's time to forgive yourself for being an immature child and focus on the future. If your mum loved you as much as I love my lads, I know that's what she'd want."

The only other person he'd shared this much with had been Charlie. And even then, his late mate had merely said she was strong enough to defend herself, and he should forgive and move on.

And then she'd died.

But Sarah's words, about experiencing hell and moving past it, seemed to stir something inside himself, something that resembled true forgiveness. If his little human could go through so much for so long and still have hope for love and the future, then he could do it too.

His dragon whispered, *About time.*

He cupped Sarah's cheek, brushed his lips against hers, and murmured, "I'm going to try, love."

"Maybe one of the first steps is sharing some of her favorite places with the lads. I'm sure they'd like that."

He nodded. "I think so. Well, at least Elliott and Joey."

She stroked his cheek. "I have hope for Mark. The way he hovered around Joey and later promised his brother he'd watch over him as he slept tells me Mark is starting to grow up. He also told me he'd look after Joey all the time to make sure no one hurts his brother. So I don't think he's going to try to run again, especially since Joey would never do that and Mark won't leave Joey behind."

It was a start, for sure. "Will you tell him more about his father's true self?"

Sarah grimaced. "A bit, aye. But I don't look forward to it. However, even if Rob gets thrown into a DDA prison, I'll still worry about his parents and what they'll try next."

"Don't worry about them. No matter what it takes, I'll keep this family together, love. I vow it."

She smiled, and Hudson couldn't get over just

how bloody beautiful Sarah was when she truly smiled.

She replied, "We'll do that together, aye?"

He nuzzled her cheek. "Always together." His hand stroked down her body until he could cup her arse cheek. As he lightly slapped her, he murmured, "Although I'd like to be together privately at least one more time tonight."

She laughed, and his beast stood tall. *My turn. Tell her.*

Just a second. Let me woo her a bit.

Hurry.

Sarah's soft fingers wrapped around his cock, and Hudson sucked in a breath as she lightly squeezed him. "I think I'd like that. Otherwise, I'll never get this constant need for you out of my system."

He rolled them until she was on her back with her hands pinned above her head. "I'm going to make sure you never tire of me, love. Never." She smiled at him, and he added, "Or my dragon. He wants a turn now. Ready for him?"

She arched against him and rubbed her hot, wet pussy against his cock. "Aye, I could do with a bit of hard and rough."

His dragon roared. *Yes, yes, I'll give it to her.*

Hudson nodded, kissed Sarah one last time, and then let his beast take control.

And after his dragon claimed their mate just as she'd asked—plenty hard and rough—Hudson held

Sarah in his arms. As they drifted off to sleep, Hudson squeezed his human a little closer. She was more than just his second chance at love. She was his future. And as long as they worked and fought for a happy ending together, he'd have everything he wanted and would hopefully never feel helpless again.

Epilogue

Many Months Later

S arah tried to ignore the bairn doing summersaults inside her belly as Hudson finally parked the car and turned off the engine. As Hudson always did when they came here, to the secret spot they'd found together for their family in the months after Joey's kidnapping, he looked around the side of his seat to the three boys in the back of the vehicle. "Remember, we're to all stay together. No wandering, Joey, not even if you see a baby dragon waddling off somewhere."

Elliott shook his head. "Babies don't shift."

Joey sat up taller. "You're wrong. There's one on Lochguard. Freya's a bairn and she shifts."

Sarah smiled. "I somehow don't think Freya is going to show up here, in the Lake District, so far from her home. And she's the only one we know of. But that doesn't matter—no wandering. Aye?"

Joey sighed. "Aye, I know."

Mark undid his seat belt and opened the door. "Can we get going? I have football practice later today, and I don't want to miss it."

Hudson nodded, and the boys climbed out.

Mark hadn't accepted Hudson as fully as Joey—who had taken to calling him Dad—but Sarah's eldest had been honestly trying to get along with his stepdad ever since Joey's return.

It helped that after many a conversation with her about some of Rob's true colors, not to mention telling him the truth about Rob now being in jail, he'd stopped talking about his dad, full stop. She'd worried at first, but the clan psychologist, Dr. Rossi, had assured her that if there was anything to truly worry about, she'd alert Sarah.

Her door opened, and Hudson put out a hand. "Let me help you."

She glared half-heartedly at her belly. "I'm the size of a whale, so be careful not to pull a muscle."

He snorted. "You're still small and perfect to me." He helped her up and kissed her gently as he placed a hand over her protruded belly. "How's the little one doing? More acrobatics?"

"I swear I've never had such an active child before."

He grinned and winked. "Blame the dragon half."

She smiled back at him. "I do. And you, when I feel like vomiting."

His gaze instantly turned concerned. "I thought that mostly went away."

"It has. Except for fish." She shivered. "Even just the smell of fish and chips will set me off."

He put a hand around her waist, and they started walking to keep up with their sons. "Since it's become a weekend tradition with the boys, I'll take them out and make sure we all brush our teeth before seeing you again."

Not for the first time, Sarah still wondered how she'd landed such a wonderful mate. "Thank you. It'll also mean I'll feel better when we're alone."

Unlike with her first two children, Sarah seemed to constantly be randy in the evenings with this pregnancy. Hudson didn't seem to mind and teased that she was becoming part dragon-shifter.

He waggled his eyebrows. "Then I'll brush them twice, just to make sure."

She laughed and leaned against his side as they caught up to the boys, who lingered near the lakeside. "It's too bad your brothers and their mates couldn't come today."

It had become a tradition of sorts, that once a

month all the Wells family would come here to laugh, and picnic, and just have fun.

While it meant a lot to Sarah, she knew it meant even more to Bronx's mate, Percy, given her past.

Hudson sighed. "Jayden got himself in a bit of trouble, sneaking off the clan's land with that human girl, Emily, and Brooklyn had to stay to deal with that. And you know Bronx won't take Percy far from Stonefire whilst she's pregnant, not until she's delivered safely, no matter how many months away it is."

Given her brother-in-law's past and the death of his first mate in childbirth, she understood. "I'm still unsure how long that rule will last. Percy hates being confined."

"I know, but he must've found a way to distract her today."

She smiled, knowing exactly how dragonmen distracted their mates best. "Aye, well, I guess, in a way it worked out as this might be the last time we can come here together as a family for a few months." She rubbed her belly. "This wee one's due soon."

They reached the boys, and Hudson murmured for her ears only, "Which is why I have a special surprise for everyone."

She raised her brows in question, but Elliott's hearing, keen as ever, had picked up Hudson's words. "Surprise? What surprise?"

Mark and Joey also gave Hudson their full attention, and her dragonman laughed. "Well, since we've been working to ensure Mark and Joey are now strong swimmers, I thought maybe you two would like a ride on my belly as I float in the lake in my dragon form. Elliott could float along with us in his dragon form too."

Joey's eyes widened like huge saucers, and even Mark smiled. Joey was the first to look at Sarah and ask, "Can we, Mum? Pretty please. I know how to swim now, and Dad would never let us drown."

She playfully tapped her chin. "I don't know. Maybe you need a few more lessons."

Joey grabbed her hand. "You could come with us too and watch us to make sure we're extra safe. Pretty please?"

Mark nodded. "You always say we need to do more things as a family, and this would be a brilliant way to do it."

As her two lads made puppy dog eyes at her, Sarah laughed. "Aye, aye, we can do it. But we come back to shore when I say, okay?" They nodded, and she looked to Elliott. "Do you want to float or join us?"

Elliott had only recently learned how to fully shift into a dragon, and he stood tall, clearly proud of that fact. "I want to shift and float. I've never swum as a dragon before."

She smiled at her stepson. "Then how about you

and your father shift, take a few practice laps, and then we'll join you?"

Hudson placed a hand on Elliott's shoulder and squeezed. "Sounds perfect. Now, let's shift."

Her lads turned their back, still unused to watching naked people change into dragons. But Sarah had at least grown accustomed to her mate and her stepson.

She couldn't help but smile as they shucked their clothes, and Hudson murmured a few words of encouragement. Elliott shifted first, his small body growing and expanding, wings sprouting from his back, his face elongating into a snout, and his limbs morphing into fore and hindlegs.

He stood in his small—at least compared to an adult—green dragon form. After he beat his wings a few times, he moved to the water's edge. Hudson said something else she couldn't hear and then closed his eyes. Sarah watched as the lovely, muscled form of her mate slowly changed into the tall, black iridescent scaled form of his dragon.

She always thought him pretty as a dragon, although Hudson always huffed that dragons were fierce and majestic, not pretty.

Still, she itched to touch his scales and couldn't wait until they could climb on his belly and move through the water.

As Hudson helped his son get his bearings in the

water—floating on his back using his wings and tail to move along—she said, "They've shifted."

Her sons turned around, and Joey blurted, "Will he ever take us into the sky?"

Sarah glanced down at Joey. "I don't know. But I'm looking forward to floating on a dragon. I'm fairly sure that's a treat for humans, aye?"

Mark bobbed his head. "Anytime we get to play with the human football teams, they're always jealous of my dragon stories. I've never heard of one of them floating on a dragon before."

The dragon coaches on Stonefire and Lochguard had devised a way for the children to interact better with each other—human and dragon—and regularly held games with each other. Mark had been so much happier ever since, having craved interactions with other human children. "Well, ask Hudson if you can tell them about today or not." She frowned. "I'm not sure if the DDA allows humans to float on dragons."

Mark replied, "I'll ask him. But if the DDA says we can't even float on a dragon, then they're stupid."

She bit her lip to keep from laughing. "Aye, I agree."

Hudson and Elliott had both made their way back and stood by the shore, gesturing for them to join them.

Joey and Mark dashed as Sarah waddled. As she reached Hudson, she sighed. "I never really asked how I was going to get on your belly, did I? I'm not very agile at the moment."

Hudson gave her a toothy dragon grin, meaning he had a plan.

He lay in the water several feet back, and she watched as Elliott carried first Joey and then Mark and set them down on Hudson's giant dragon stomach.

Sarah moved to the edge, but Hudson's tail gently came around her upper body, under her arms, and lifted. She barely shrieked and clung to him before he set her down next to her sons. She half-heartedly glared at him. "You could've warned me."

He gave another toothy grin, and she couldn't help but laugh. "But I'm fine, aye? So let's go. I'm curious to see if you're just like a boat."

Elliott went first, splashing a bit as he tried to move his wings to glide through the water, using his tail to steer. Although glide might be too nice of a word, given the splashes.

Still, she shouted, "Brilliant, Elliott. Keep going!"

He redoubled his efforts, and then Hudson followed. She watched as his wings slowly moved beneath the water, stroking and sailing them through with minimal splashing.

Aye, Hudson could glide through water.

And as she watched Joey and Mark cheer him and Elliott on, Sarah merely sat on her mate's dragon belly, her hand over her active wee one in her stomach, and couldn't stop smiling. Somehow, someway, she'd end up with a happy ending she never could've dreamed of. And she looked forward to a future of love and laughter with the sexiest, most caring dragonman ever and their blended brood of children who would always know just how much they were wanted and loved.

Author's Note

I think we can all agree that's Sarah's ex-husband was rotten and she truly deserved to find her happy ending. I don't think she could find a better match than Hudson Wells.

To be honest, when I made Hudson a widower early in the series, I had thought his second chance was going to be with someone else. For years and years, I thought so. But then Sarah made her appearance in *The Dragon Collective* and I knew she was exactly what he needed—someone he could truly protect this time and help bloom into a new, stronger version of herself.

Sarah's character is dear to me for many reasons, but least of which is that I also suffered verbal abuse for years and years (from my mother, not a husband) and if you think she took too long to find herself, then let me assure you it takes years to overcome being told how worthless, ugly, fat, stupid, etc. you are. I rushed it a bit for Sarah (it took me nearly a decade to find my confidence and truly believe in myself) but it's still a process. However, rest assured that Hudson will take excellent care of her for the rest of their days. :)

And yes, I let it slip that Bronx and Percy mate eventually in the epilogue. I'm actually really excited about their story for so many reasons. Percy is going to learn how to become a dragon-shifter, Bronx is going to heal from the death of his late mate, and his daughter Violet (who isn't much younger than Percy) is going to bring some much needed levity and bluntness to them both. Not only that, their story is yet another small step toward the end of the series due to secrets revealed from Percy's former prison. I promise I am getting toward a conclusion for the series, but to make it believable, it takes baby steps!

As always, I have a few people to thank with regards to getting this book out to my readers:

- My editor, Becky Johnson, and her entire team at Hot Tree Editing really make my stories shine.
- My three beta readers—Sabrina D., Iliana G., and Sandy H.—are amazing women who volunteer their time to read, comment, and find the minor inconsistencies and/or typos for me. I

truly value and appreciate their hard
work.

The next dragon-shifter story in the overall dragon-shifter timeline is Logan Lamont and Emma MacAllister's book (*The Dragon's Memory*, LHD #10), out May 5, 2022. The next Stonefire Dragons book, *Taught by the Dragon*, is Bronx Wells and Persephone Smith's story. Also, if you want to stay up-to-date with release information and news, then make sure to subscribe to my newsletter on my website, www.JessieDonovan.com

As always, a huge thanks to my readers for their support. Without you, I wouldn't be able to write these wonderful stories and revisit characters that have become like family to me. Thank you!

Also by Jessie Donovan

Asylums for Magical Threats

Blaze of Secrets (AMT #1)

Frozen Desires (AMT #2)

Shadow of Temptation (AMT #3)

Flare of Promise (AMT #4)

Cascade Shifters

Convincing the Cougar (CS #0.5)

Reclaiming the Wolf (CS #1)

Cougar's First Christmas (CS #2)

Resisting the Cougar (CS #3)

Dark Lords of London

Vampire's Modern Bride (DLL #1 / Summer 2022)

Dragon Clan Gatherings

Summer at Lochguard (DCG #1)

Winter at Stonefire (DCG #2 / TBD)

Kelderan Runic Warriors

The Conquest (KRW #1)

The Barren (KRW #2)

The Heir (KRW #3)

The Forbidden (KRW #4)

The Hidden (KRW #5)

The Survivor (KRW #6)

Lochguard Highland Dragons

The Dragon's Dilemma (LHD #1)

The Dragon Guardian (LHD #2)

The Dragon's Heart (LHD #3)

The Dragon Warrior (LHD #4)

The Dragon Family (LHD #5)

The Dragon's Discovery (LHD #6)

The Dragon's Pursuit (LHD #7)

The Dragon Collective (LHD #8)

The Dragon's Chance (LHD # 9)

The Dragon's Memory / Emma & Logan (LHD #10 / May 5, 2022)

Love in Scotland

Crazy Scottish Love (LiS #1)

Chaotic Scottish Wedding (LiS #2)

Stonefire Dragons

Sacrificed to the Dragon (SD #1)

Seducing the Dragon (SD #2)

The Dragon's Need (TDM #2)

The Dragon's Bidder (TDM #3)

The Dragon's Charge (TDM #4)

The Dragon's Weakness (TDM #5)

The Dragon's Rival (TDM #6, TBD)

WRITING AS LIZZIE ENGLAND

<u>Her Fantasy</u>

Holt: The CEO

Callan: The Highlander

Adam: The Duke

Gabe: The Rock Star

About the Author

Jessie Donovan has sold over half a million books, has given away hundreds of thousands more to readers for free, and has even hit the *NY Times* and *USA Today* bestseller lists. She is best known for her dragon-shifter series, but also writes about vampires, magic users, aliens, and even has a crazy romantic comedy series set in Scotland. When not reading a book, attempting to tame her yard, or traipsing around some foreign country on a shoestring, she can often be found interacting with her readers on Facebook. She lives near Seattle, where, yes, it rains a lot but it also makes everything green.

Visit her website at: www.JessieDonovan.com

Printed in Great Britain
by Amazon

76312917R00222